"WHAT'S HAPPENED?
WHO'S MISSING?"

"This truck arrived a short time ago," the Locrian on duty responded to Hugh's questions. "It was obviously on automatic control as it approached, which is not surprising, but it parked itself, which, as you know, is less usual. We waited for a minute or more. There was no communication from within, and no one emerged. We examined it closely and there is no living being aboard. I therefore reported missing personnel to the Safety Watch."

"Is there a robot?" Hugh asked.

"No, just the automatic controller."

"But you know that someone has been there." Hugh made it a statement; after all, the missing-person alarm *had* gone out.

"Yes. There are food containers which have been recently used. There are two sleeping units which appear to have been used and not repacked. The food remnants indicate a Crotonite, but the control station is configured for Erthumoi hands, body shape, and size. And there is one other disturbing thing on board—the frozen body of a native Habranha

FOSSIL

ISAAC'S UNIVERSE

HAL CLEMENT

D A W B O O K S , I N C .
DONALD A. WOLLHEIM, FOUNDER
375 Hudson Street. New York. NY 10014

ELIZABETH R. WOLLHEIM
SHEILA E. GILBERT
PUBLISHERS

First Printing, November 1993

2   3   4   5   6   7   8   9

DAW TRADEMARK REGISTERED
U.S. PAT. OFF. AND FOREIGN COUNTRIES
MARCA REGISTRADA
HECHO EN U.S.A.

Printed in Canada

To Isaac, of course

CONTENTS

1

HERE JUMPERS SUFFER MORE FROM WIND THAN WEIGHT

The slope was long and steep, and the lights her husband had installed made it stand out sharply against the scattered illumination of Pitville and the much dimmer background hills of the Solid Ocean. Janice Cedar knew that she should have been frightened. In theory, height should scare anyone except, of course, a Crotonite; in practice, after a Common Year under Habranha's gravity, she could lean over the edge of a hundred-meter ice ridge without a qualm. She just wasn't being pulled *hard* enough downward to affect her emotions. Her husband and the few other Erthumoi on the little world had the same trouble.

It took a lot of the fun out of skiing. Even armor full of diving fluid, which made most amusements either less fun or practically impossible, merely increased her inertia enough to make the wind less challenging.

She was able to push off and start accelerating, if one could really call it that, down the ramp without feeling her heart speed up at all. What little thrill the sport could furnish on this world would come a little later.

Her husband Hugh and their supervisor Ged Barrar stood watching her and waiting for their turns; Janice had wished briefly, before pushing off, that she had the Naxian ability to read emotion. The Assistant Director was a Samian, probably no more objective than the average Erthumoi, and she felt quite mystified why someone with no real body of his own, by her standards, should be interested in an Erthumoi sport. His stated reason might be true, but it had left her unconvinced. Barrar had admitted that the Cedars presumably knew what they were doing when they slid around on narrow boards in search of "fun," and that this might well be worth doing for morale, but that he couldn't really *feel* the point. He insisted that Hugh's status as the person in charge of safety required that this human amusement be studied in more detail. Someone in the administrative office, Hugh suspected, doubted that Erthumoi, or at least the particular Erthuma named Hugh Rock Cedar, really grasped the concept of *risk* at all. There were, he thought, reservations in high quarters about the wisdom of using him as Safety Director.

He hadn't worried at first; like his wife, he was kept by the low gravity from feeling any real fear of falling, and didn't consider skiing dangerous here. He assumed that Samians would be even less concerned, since most of their planets were high weight and their physiques certainly less prone to injury. The few members of the species on Habranha were mostly researchers, Diplomacy Guild representatives, or, nowadays, individuals from one or another of the Six Races who felt an interest in the hypothesis that the intelligent Habranhans might actually be a remnant of the Seventh Race, known so far only from archaeological data. None of the Samians were settlers; there was no room for settlers.

Hugh's first sight of Barrar "dressed" for skiing had caused him some other doubts, though. Instead of the six-limbed horizontally arranged sensibly stable walker which he usually employed, the administrator had appeared on something vaguely resembling a headless human skeleton made of some highly resistant—Hugh hoped—black and apparently resilient composition. The reddish-brown limbless, eyeless, and generally featureless slab of leathery-looking meat which was the Samian him-

self rode inside the rib cage, the fine wires which
connected it with the various effectors and sensors
of the "body" just barely visible from two meters
away. Ordinary skis were mounted on framework
feet which had been designed to fit them.

Even Janice, not usually a worrier, had tactfully
suggested on their way to the jump area that famil-
iarizing himself with a new mechanical body and a
new method of locomotion at the same time might
not be a fair trial of either, but Barrar had assured
her there would be no problem. New bodies were an
everyday affair to him. He had, indeed, managed to
ski with no obvious problems from the residence
area along the snowy, and often icy, streets of
Pitville and even to herringbone up the slope to the
top of the jumping ramp. He had still been standing
completely at ease when she started her run. Now, as
she approached its lowest part, she had to focus all
her attention on her own technique and forget the
Samian. Her husband would have to provide any
help his boss might need.

The jump ramp itself was of packed snow, some
of it natural and some the pulverized ice excavated
from the two shafts which gave Pitville its name.
They were only about a hundred and fifty kilometers
from sunlight, so the general temperature, while extremely variable like all of Habranha's weather, was
usually high enough to let a reasonably strong
Erthuma make snowballs out of water ice powder by
squeezing. The ramp was therefore fairly hard and
even moderately slippery, though its skiing surface
was constantly changing as the natural precipitation
which tried to cover it competed with the equally
variable winds which strove to sweep it clear.

The falloff at either side was stabilized by native
vegetation, carefully selected for deep roots and lack
of explosive quality. There were two basically different types of life on Habranha; one had a biochem-
istry enough like that of the Erthumoi to use ATP as

its "battery." The other and more common employed azide ion for the same general purposes, so that much of the world's vegetation and some of its animal life was either explosive or electrically hazardous or both. The winged natives belonged to the first category, lending strength to the mounting belief among the Six Races that they had not actually evolved on Habranha.

At the lowest point of the run, where the curve flung skiers upward again, the surface was hardest to predict or even to analyze by sight. Hugh had had the area lighted as well as possible, but no lighting would let human eyes determine how well the deposit was packed at any given moment. This was where the sport grew interesting. . . .

Janice kept her feet. She was traveling fast enough now to guarantee serious damage to her armor if she hit anything solid, explosive or not, and she was crouched to give the wind as little handle as possible.

For a brief moment she felt almost normal weight as she reached the bottom arc and caromed upward. Then she was off the snow beyond the first lighted area, with a fifty-meter gulf below her, and orbiting more or less toward a second and larger hill which started two hundred meters away. The target area was also well lighted, but for these few seconds she herself must be nearly invisible to Hugh. She had no idea of how, or how well, the Samian could perceive her.

She was busy with her poles, which looked more like broad-bladed oars; a skier's problem of staying upright either on or off the ground, in Habranha's feeble gravity and dense air, was much worse than on any Erthumoi-normal world. Strong wrists meant quite as much as good ankles in this kind of "jumping." She made a technically poor but not catastrophic landing on her right ski, which she had managed to keep aligned with her direction of flight, brought the other down, slowed aerodynamically for a few seconds with her poles held across her body, and finally felt sure enough of her traction to bring herself to a stop in normal ski fashion.

"All right. Who's next?"

She didn't ask vocally. Her armor and body cavities were filled with diving fluid, since her job often took her to the bottom of the Pits. Vocal cords evolved for gas don't work in liquid, and her armor carried a code transmitter whose output, while far more sophisticated than the short-and-long combinations of the original Erthumoi telegraph, was still much slower and clumsier than ordinary speech. It was loud enough to be heard for several hundred meters if the wind were not too strong.

"I'm coming. Be ready to pick up the pieces!" This was vocal language, through Barrar's speaker and the woman's translator, though originating in a device fully as artificial as Janice's coder. The Samian had no more voice than he had arms, legs, or eyes; how his species had come to evolve intelligence was a favorite challenge to science from the mystics who still rejected evolution as well as among the biologists themselves.

Husband and wife watched tensely as the plastic skeleton poled itself to the head of the ramp and paused for a moment while its driver presumably made a final evaluation of his problems. Both Erthumoi had time to wonder whether his feelings were normal enough, by their standards, for their own to qualify as sympathy. Then Barrar thrust himself forward and downward.

The mechanical body's acceleration was rather greater than the woman's; the framework must have set up more turbulence in the dense air but certainly had less total drag than her armored figure. Steering in the swirling air currents with the oarlike poles could have been a straightforward matter of logic, but for a living nervous system reason takes significantly longer than reflexes. Janice and her husband had the reflexes—had acquired them, in fact, under some five times Habranha's gravity; Ged Barrar did not.

The ramp was five meters wide, which was ordinarily plenty even in fairly high winds. By the time he was fifty meters down its slope, however, the Samian's overcorrected turns were bringing him almost to the edge, first on one side and then on the other. Janice could do nothing from the low end of the run; Hugh was tempted to lauch himself after the swerving figure in spite of the obvious fact that there was no way he could catch it in time to keep the plastic framework out of the bushes. Fortunately, he didn't have to.

"Relax, Hugh." The voice was not recognizable through the translation system, but the tone was that used by the equipment to identify male native Habras. Simultaneously three figures resembling dragonflies with three pairs each of, to Erthumoi, unbelievably short wings swooped into the lighted area above the ramp, diving toward the skier. They were flying almost in line, twenty-five or thirty meters apart.

The first missed; reflexes able to deal easily with Habranha's chaotic air turbulence were defeated by Barrar's inadequate attempts to steer himself.

"Ged! Just go straight! They'll pick you up!" Hugh keyed out before realizing how silly he was being. If the Samian had been able to go straight, there would have been no problem. It was too bad Janice had heard—but she'd never remind him unless he asked for it.

The next native had an additional second or two to allow for the extra variables, and neatly inserted four sets of handling appendages among the upper bars of Ged Barrar's pseudobody. This was light, far lighter than an armored Erthuma, and, with no obvious effort, the Habra lifted it clear of the ramp and around to the right of its upcurved end. Seconds later he set his burden down beside Janice, swooped gracefully up and around, and landed in front of them with his fellows.

"I'm coming," keyed Hugh. "I can't guarantee just where I'll land; you fellows should be ready for a quick lift."

"We know, Boss," came the translated reply. "We've seen you often enough. Come on down. We're ready."

Hugh came. By some combination of luck and personal skill he held a relatively straight course both on the slopes and in the air, and landed on both skis at once, fifty meters or so to one side of, and seventy short of, the waiting group. He slid to a halt beside them, spraying snow.

"Sorry. Didn't mean to bury anyone. Many thanks for the help—" he hesitated briefly as he glanced at body patterns—"Ted. Did you just happen by, or were you on duty?" He added for Barrar's information, "Ted's one of my safety people."

"On duty," replied the Habra. "We always have one flyer—one of us or a Crotonite—here when someone's using the jump. Today it seemed wise to have more."

"Not the most tactful of remarks, if my presence is the reason you intimate," interjected Barrar.

"The Crotonites keep telling us sad stories of what happens when crawlers try to imitate flyers. We recognize their tendency to make a good story better, especially at the expense of nonflyers, but we also know how long it takes to develop really good reflexes for flight or—is orbiting the appropriate word here? Children are children for a long time." The Samian shifted slightly, and Hugh quieted him with a gesture; such a phrase, he knew, carried no belittling implication to the natives. "We hadn't seen any of your people trying this before, Administrator, and felt that our responsibility involved safety more than tact."

"Quite right," keyed Hugh. "Thanks again."

"Yes." Barrar caught on quickly; he himself had a tact-demanding job. "I hadn't realized what my efforts would do to the air as well as to my own motion. I should have been more prepared for feedback. Your help was very much in order, Ted. I must go back and try again immediately; I should have learned *something* from this set of mistakes. Will your people stand by again?"

"Of course. As long as you care to keep practicing."

"I'll have time for only one, or at most two, more tries before work calls. I believe the Cedars can stay longer, but they probably don't need you so badly."

"We cover while anyone is using the slope," the native replied. "Even a minor fall can damage armor, and the temperature is low even away from the Pits."

"You don't seem to need protection from the cold," Hugh keyed. "It's a good thirty Kelvins lower here than at Pwanpwan. Far below water-freeze. I had the idea you were comfortable at two seventy or eighty."

"That's about right," Ted agreed. The Samian was making his way back to the starting point of the jump, but none of the natives had bothered to follow him yet. "It's not very obvious, but do we have protection. It seems to be—what do the Naxians call him?—the 'Muscle' who doesn't need it. This is poor light even for us, so you'll have to look closely to see ours."

At the implied invitation, the Erthumoi approached the nearest of the Habras. Like the other two, he was wearing male ornaments, not very noticeable even in good light at more than a few meters; but over this, held a few millimeters away from the body plates by what looked like little wads of sponge a few centimeters apart, was an extremely thin, transparent film. The light of Fafnir, as

Erthumoi called the small companion to Habranha's own sun, was not bright enough to reveal color; the supporting pads looked dark gray and the body plates rather lighter, but both Erthumoi knew that the latter were patterned randomly in shades of red.

The covering did not seem to include the three stubby pairs of wings, more reminiscent of fins to Erthumoi, currently folded back against their owners' bodies.

Hugh and Janice judged that the film was simply insulation. Even on Habranha, a flying creature of roughly human mass would need an active metabolism and should generate plenty of its own body heat. There was certainly no sign of an artificial heater that either could see, though admittedly the light was poor.

"I'm coming!" Barrar's voice interrupted the examination. The Habras took to the air at once, without apology. The Samian, either sensibly or tactfully, waited until he saw them swoop through the lighted region shortly below the starting point before he pushed off once more. This time no help was needed until he was off the end of the jump; he did what to Hugh, at least, was a surprisingly good job of holding his direction down the slope. Experience did seem to have helped.

The third dimension was another matter, however. No one afterward tried to judge how much of the Samian's subsequent contortions should be attributed to random Habranha wind and how much to Barrar's own unskilled efforts at control. A being may know perfectly well what feedback is, and even such physical laws as Conservation of Angular Momentum, but reasoning takes time; flying and jumping take reflexes. He was upside down before reaching the peak of his trajectory. His poles waved frantically; one was knocked from his grip as it struck the wing of the first native to attempt a rescue pass.

He was out of the lighted region now, and neither

of the Erthumoi could really see what was going on.
They might have made some gasp or other anxiety-
driven sound, but with no voices could only watch,
worry, and feel the discomfort as diving liquid was
driven slowly through their windpipes by the reflexes which would normally have made them cry
out. Barrar, as far as they could tell, was equally silent; whatever panic reflexes he might have been in-
dulging did not involve his artificial voice. The
translators should have been crackling with orders or
signals among the natives, Hugh thought briefly, but
even the radio spectrum seemed to be silent. The reflexes of the flyers were all aimed at flying, not
communicating.

A second Habra, barely missing the one whose
wing had knocked Barrar's pole away, secured a grip
on the Samian's skeletal leg—the skier was still upside
down—and for the moment seemed to end the danger
since the burden was so light. The limb, however,
had not been designed with enough foresight, and
proved unable under tension to support the weight of
the rest of the structure even in Habranha's gravity. It
came away at what the Erthumoi considered the knee,
and Barrar was falling again with less control than
ever, while Ted found himself holding a left shin, foot,
and ski. The translators started buzzing and crackling,
but emitted no comprehensible words; several of the
Habras were speaking at once. This lasted only a few
seconds before silence, except for the endless variable
fluting of the wind, returned.

Ted swung far to one side and tossed leg and ski
clear, while one of his companions made another attempt to intercept the falling Samian. The task
proved easier this time; Barrar had stopped trying to
do anything for himself, and the aerodynamic problems were accordingly less complex. The native secured a grip on the skeleton's shoulders while he
himself was nearly inverted, and without apparent
difficulty brought the rotation of the Habra-Samian

system to a halt with the remaining leg and ski underneath. Half a minute later Barrar was lowered beside the Erthumoi, and Ted was asking rather diffidently whether there would have been serious damage if they had let him fall head downward.

The Samian seemed amused.

"This walker shouldn't have been hurt. *I* certainly wouldn't have been, since there isn't any head on this machine."

"But your own body is fairly close to the top. If that had collapsed at the impact, wouldn't you have been injured or killed?"

"In theory, the frame should be able to protect me. I designed it to. Of course, I also designed these legs—it's hard to say just what might have happened. I am most grateful to you that I did not learn—what is that cynical Erthumoi term?—'the hard way.' I suppose my dignity would have taken some damage, at least. It probably should anyway, but as long as no Crotonites are on hand I can stand that."

The Habras seemed somewhat surprised.

"Why should it be any worse for Crotonites to see you? I've met some who react very badly to ridicule, even from their own kind and especially from what they call slugs or crawlers, but I don't see why being laughed at *by* a Crotonite is any worse than by anyone else."

"It's not completely sensible, I admit. I'm not an administrator by choice or taste, and maybe I'm too self-conscious. This is just a task until I can write something that will earn me scholarly status; in the meantime, I worry whenever I do something silly. Crotonites are very good at pointing out the silly doings of us crawlers."

"What's wrong with administration?" asked Hugh. "It's not my regular field, but I'm in it myself at the moment—organizing plans and people so as to minimize personal risks and take care of injuries when they do occur."

"But that's a sideline with you. You're basically an explorer and observer—a researcher. I can't do that because I didn't start in time to learn enough, but I can still get into analysis and theoretical work. This telling whom what to do and when is trivial. Administrators are—" the translator emitted the no-equivalent-symbol sound, leaving Hugh and his wife uncertain just what the speaker thought of administration, though the context had provided some clue.

"It involves everyone here and everything we're doing," Hugh pointed out firmly though not quite indignantly. "No one at Pitville, not even the Habras, is in a normal environment; everyone outdoors has to have some sort of protection, whether working or—"

"True. But Spreadsheet-Thinker and I find questions of competence much less confusing than ones of motivation, even among members of her species and mine; and it seems to be what people want to do rather than what they do best that we have to consider most deeply. Neither of us understands that. A nice scientific paper would be a relief, for me. at least."

"You have Naxians in your office."

"Knowing that someone is happy or unhappy about some part of what's going on doesn't by itself tell us *what* part. You use Naxians on general safety watch, I know, and still need to get more details when they report trouble. If that weren't true you'd use *only* Naxians."

"If I could get that many—and didn't need flyers, too. But you're right, in a way. What's your main trouble? Or would you rather not say?"

"Personalities. Spreadsheet-Thinker has earned her name, and can deal better with such complexities, but I'm more of a scholar—a scientist, even—at heart, if that figure of speech means what I think it does. It's *so* nice to be able to deal with variables one at a time. That's—I'll admit it to you, friend, but would rather you didn't tell any Crotonites—why I was trying this 'ski' activity just now. I must admit I was cheating. I have automatic controls in this body; our nervous impulses and reactions are far too slow for this sort of thing, even in this gravity. After the first failure I was able to reset my autodriver to handle the situation on the slope, but I would have had to find an excuse for not making the second run if you and your friends had not been here, Ted."

"What if you had made it to the jump-off point and they hadn't been here?" asked Janice.

"I prefer not to think about that."

"You realize now that engineering design, as well as administration, involves considering many factors at once, I hope," Hugh keyed. He knew the remark was less than tactful, but could see no way of squaring silence on the subject with his safety officer's conscience.

"I do indeed."

The Erthumoi smiled at each other, a gesture made meaningful by the transparent face shields of their armor.

"I hope, when your chance comes, you don't find scientific reality too much of a shock, too," Janice keyed, with some relief; had she been speaking, tact would have driven her to some effort to keep the laughter out of her voice.

"But I'll just need to center on something that needs to be proved, like this question of whether the Habras really originated on Habranha. Just concentrating on that one thing! I hope that's not a question you feel strongly about personally, Ted; I wouldn't want to make you uncomfortable. I've met people who consider origins a solved problem and for some reason resent the suggestion of alternative solutions."

"I think you miss the main point of science," Hugh cut in.

"But isn't science *trying* to prove something?" asked Ted. Janice wondered if he were evading the administrator's implied question; this didn't occur to her husband. If it did to the Samian, he let the point lie.

"Ideally, no, though things are seldom ideal," answered Barrar, rather to the Erthumoi's surprise. "If you have a preference, something you really want to prove, there's a tendency to notice and remember the data supporting that preference—I've worked with every one of the Six Races, and that's true of all of us. If it doesn't apply to your own kind, Ted, you have the potential of becoming the most objective scientists in the Galaxy."

Not even the Erthumoi had the open-mindedness or the courtesy to add, "if you aren't already," to the Samian's statement.

"What do *you* prefer?" asked another of the Habras.

"I'm lucky. Right now I simply want a nice, definite, unambiguous answer to the Pit project, so my administrative work here will count as successful." Hugh wondered fleetingly if Barrar might not be happier in the long run if he kept his illusions and hopes by remaining an administrator, but said nothing as the Samian went on. "Even that has its risks; if no firm answer is possible from the data we find, I could catch myself giving extra weight to some items to make their meaning more definite than it should be. That's why I'm trying to keep track of all the other work of this sort being done on Habranha."

"Didn't know there was any," remarked Hugh.

"Oh, yes. I'll summarize it for you if we both ever have time.

"Look, I'm sorry. I shouldn't be lecturing. You've asked, I've answered. The live problem is the

Spreadsheet-Thinker's and mine and our staff's. I must get back to work. I—well—"

"One of us will carry you," Ted hastily put in. "I assume you have other bodies at the quarters."

"Yes, of course. This one was merely improvised to let me try out this Erthumoi amusement for official and, er, other reasons. I fear I have not yet learned all I should about it. I will repair the structure and try again. I think I can travel on the three remaining appendages, if one of you will have the kindness to bring the lost one back to the Residence. I will want to examine it to learn why it proved defective. Go on skiing, Hugh and Janice, and see if you can invent some reasonably risky game for the Habras, too. It *does* take the mind off one's regular troubles, I find. You shouldn't have to be working to protect Erthumoi skeletons, even artificial ones like this, all the time, Ted. How about something like Cephallonian netball—in the liquid air of the Pits?" Barrar began to hobble away, Erthumoi and Habras watching silently. Hugh thought he could see why no major tripodal life-form was known.

The Samian was almost out of sight when one of the natives spoke.

"There are some bad plants along his way. I'd better watch."

"All right, Walt," agreed Hugh. "He may want help in his job, but we still have ours. Jan, we have time for another couple of jumps. Ted and Jimbo, are both staying, or is one enough?"

"Both. One might have to go for additional help while the first patches armor. I don't think it's very likely; you're both pretty good—"

"It's likelier now. I never knew—we never knew you were on watch here. Now we're more apt to get careless or take chances."

"Shouldn't we have told you? Or should we have told you at the beginning? We thought you might have resented it. The Crotonites said you would."

"Technically, you should have, since I'm your boss. Actually, I like your taking responsibility yourselves. I suppose that makes me a bad administrator, too. The only one really likely to be bothered is Spreadsheet-Thinker. She'd probably resent not knowing what's going on at any level of the operation. Let's stop talking for a while; my hand's getting cramped. C'mon, Jan. You first."

Actually, the jumps were delayed for a few minutes by a passing snow squall, and the couple was able to take only one more each. There was further talk with the Habras while they waited, Janice this time doing most of the code work. By common consent Barrar's problems were avoided; most of the debate was about finding better plants to stabilize the partly artificial hill on which the ski jump had been built. None of the natives was a botanist, but all Habras Hugh and Janice had met so far were imaginative and widely informed. This, of course, could have been observational selection, considering the sort of work the Erthumoi were doing on the little world; both were too experienced to assume that all members of any species were alike enough to be predictable.

All examined the slopes and agreed that something with still longer and stronger roots would help if it could be found. The winds, while chaotic in detail even here on the dark side, had a general trend toward the sunward hemisphere near the ground. The snow hills behaved enough like sand dunes to travel slowly in the same general direction. Temperature was sometimes so low that even considerable pressure failed to weld water-ice crystals together, though sometimes the welding did occur and dunes graduated to the status of hills. The fact that a rink was very hard to keep free of drifts was only one reason why skiing was more practical than skating on Habranha's Solid Ocean. Water is inherently a most peculiar substance; Janice and her husband had always known this after a fashion, but Habranha had really driven the fact home to them.

The natives mentioned that many plants could be identified by smell as well as appearance. The Erthumoi would have liked to check this, if their armor had not been full of diving fluid; a brief exposure to the local atmosphere was harmless, as they had long ago found. Its total surface pressure was nearly four times their normal, but it was relatively chemically safe. The oxygen partial pressure was only about a third of a bar, and the ammonia and hydrogen cyanide were significant only in Habranha's warmer regions where the gases were less soluble in water. They were already living at local pressure, since flexible environment armor was fairly comfortable and actually resisting the pressure to be expected when the Pit project was farther along would be impractical. Their use of diving fluid had been a concession to this fact from the beginning.

"I guess we'll go in now, Ted," keyed Janice as her husband came to a halt beside her. "Were you on duty just because of us, or do you expect others on the slope?"

"If there are others, they'll almost certainly be Erthumoi. One of us will be enough until someone actually arrives. It's Jimbo's turn to stay, and he'll call us if we're needed. Walt and I will take a swing over the Pits."

"But you can't do anything there. Those suits won't do any good at liquid air temperatures, will they?"

"No, but we can get a look—pardon the word, I'm talking about our electric field sense—at what's happening. I do like to know when something's been found."

"Did that wing of three days ago bother you?" keyed Janice. "We have no idea how you feel about your dead, and have been rather afraid to ask. It's a touchy subject with many people."

"If the owner can be identified, we'll want to take steps. How far down was it? Have you learned its age? What really puzzled most of us was how it got separated. The idea of losing a wing is—is hard to express in words, and all the ones I can think of are negative."

"Couldn't a really violent storm have done it?" asked Hugh.

"I've never experienced or imagined one that could, but I suppose that doesn't mean it's impossible. I admit I don't like to think about that, either, though I've faced my share of storms. How about the age?"

"It was four hundred eighty-one meters below the surface. The ice hasn't been kind enough to form definite layers, so we've had to use other methods of dating. The carbon 14 limit on this planet is about a hundred and sixty thousand Common Years—longer than on most worlds, because you have no magnetic field to speak of and Fafnir flares fairly often, so you have a higher C 14 percentage than usual—and all I can say is the wing is older than that."

"In our years, that's—"

Both Erthumoi engaged in hasty mental arithmetic. Hugh keyed first. "A little over two and half million minimum."

"Then we needn't worry about notifying relatives," the Habra said with no obvious trace of humor. "But I'd have guessed that such an age would have brought the fossil deeper into the ice."

"So would I," admitted Janice, "but remember the ice is moving too, probably in as complex patterns as your atmosphere and ocean. Even under this gravity, five hundred kilometers' water depth gives you something like ten thousand atmospheres, which is plenty for most of the water-ice phase changes even without complications from radioactive heating from underneath. Things happen in solids, too, just a lot slower; and at this point I wouldn't dare swear it was all solid. That's something I'd really like to know in detail. It's the most promising way I can think of for actually dating whatever we find buried here. Nice, unambiguous, straightforward—which is the last thing they'll be—time-and-distance glacial flow problems."

"It must be fun to go into the Pits and find things yourself," Ted remarked thoughtfully. "I wonder when we'll manage to modify one of our regular diving suits. The pressure is no problem, of course. We have diving fluid, too. Temperature, though— we're trying to learn more about your insulating materials. You and the other aliens who work here have been telling our chemists about the stuff you use. It should be good enough; as nearly as I can see, you need even more protection from cold than we do."

"That's no problem," Janice keyed, "but you'll have to redesign your armor to protect your wings, too. I hope you manage it soon. It will be good to have you down there; your electrical senses might be very helpful. Looking for microfossils by sending laser beams from one hole in the ice to another works all right, but you might be a lot faster."

"But you find larger fossils, too. The wings I was asking about haven't been the only remains."

"No. The ice is full of plant roots. We can sometimes trace them for a dozen meters or more. It looks as though a particular plant anchors itself and grows, maybe for years, maybe for centuries, until something drastic kills it—maybe it gets buried by an advancing dune, or something like that. While it lives, it affects the landscape around it, holding snow in place instead of letting it blow away— forget about decent stratigraphy!"

"I don't know that last word," Ted admitted, "but at least some plants let go of their roots and allow themselves to be blown away when dunes threaten to cover them. I couldn't tell you which kinds, offjaw."

"We'll have to find out from someone who does," replied Janice. "*Somehow* I'm going to get a decent dating scale for this world. But I'm tired, Hugh. Let's go—"

They went, but not to their quarters to rest. A modulated horn blast which drowned out the roar of an approaching squall took care of that.

2

AND AIR IS MADE FOR SWIMMING, NOT FOR FLIGHT

There is a difference between having fast reflexes and being easily startled. Rekchellet insisted afterward that he was responding properly and reasonably when the shriek echoed through the monitor hall and he dropped from his observation bar with wings spread. After all, if even a ground slug is in danger one is better able to help it from the air. So he claimed, firmly and permanently.

S'Nash, coiled in front of the speakers, knew that the sound must have come from one of the Pits and merely twitched before extending a fringe to flip from one visual monitor to another in search of a more precise datum. By rights it/he should have been more disturbed than the Crotonite, since the screaming voice was clearly Naxian and even more plainly, to S'Nash, carried genuine terror, surprise, and pain.

But it was not the voice of a personal acquaintance, so the sentry was able to maintain its/his calm and even to stay tactful. It/he refrained even from looking up until the Crotonite was clearly back to his perch and the burst of emotion startled from him was under control. Only then did the serpentine watch officer speak.

"Rek, do any of your screens tell where that came from? None of mine shows any Naxians in trouble." It/he heard the brief courtesy syllable indicating that the translator had done its job but got no real answer for several seconds.

"You're sure it was a Naxian?" the winged sentry asked at last. "I see fourteen on different screens, in various parts of the Pits. I can't tell in detail what any of them may be doing except for one who's polishing a new window, but none seems to be in trouble. Why don't we have more information yet? I see no one hurt or helpless."

With an effort, S'Nash refrained from taking the question as the personal criticism which it/he knew was both in order and intended. It/he *should* have called back instantly to ask what was wrong. While Crotonites tended to be reflexively supercilious toward everyone without wings there was some excuse this time—though, one could hope, the readable critical feeling *might* refer to the screamer for not being more specific. The Naxian initiated routine.

"What's wrong?" it/he sibilated into the microphone feeding the Pit transducers. It would be best, just yet, not to alarm any non-Naxians in the area. Depending on what circuits had carried the fear-laden sound to the monitor hall, these might not even have heard it and almost certainly would not have read the emotion it carried, so it/he broadcast the question directly into the liquid mixture of nitrogen and oxygen which kept the Pits' water-ice walls from creeping shut on researchers and equipment.

The answer was as wordless, as emotion-laden, and as information-free as before. It came this time as a series of ticking, hissing whispers. The source was still plainly one of S'Nash's own people, but something had to be wrong with the sufferer's vocal apparatus.

"We can't understand you," the sentry responded patiently. "If you're in monitored space, turn vertical." Rekchellet's translator got this message clearly enough, and it was the Crotonite who observed the response.

"There!" he whistled. "Screen seven! It's still trying to carry that case, but it's turned tail down. What's wrong? It looks normal to me."

"And to me," answered S'Nash tersely. "but it can't talk. Get its location! I'll check depth. We'll find out who's working closest and get help there." As it/he spoke, the Naxian keyed an alarm switch. The instant and most obvious result was a piercing howl of wordless sound. It was audible throughout Pitville and broken into a repeating sequence of long and short bursts which should have needed no translation to tell anyone that a Pit worker was in trouble, details unknown. Hugh Cedar, the Erthumoi safety chief, hearing it at the ski slope two kilometers away, would not have bet any large sum that more than half the staff could read it that completely, however.

The key also initiated other lines of activity. The pumps which fed the trickle of liquid air needed to keep the Pits filled shut off immediately. A set of floodlights flashed on, fully illuminating every liter of the two one-hundred-meter square, half-kilometer deep holes in Habranha's glacial night hemisphere. Each of the one hundred seventy-five members of the staff currently at the site immediately checked the whereabouts and status of its, her, or his assigned partner or partners, except the one who was now trying to maintain its serpentine body in the vertical attitude S'Nash had ordered. A neutrino transmitter passed the emergency signal to the Diplomacy Guild office at Pwanpwan on Habranha's ring continent, nearly three thousand kilometers away.

Robots supposedly dedicated to digging reported to Hugh Cedar, from their work stations at the bottom of each pit, in code which rode the siren frequencies and did not affect most translators, as being in rescue mode with full decision capacity engaged.

And Hugh and his wife slid toward the digs from the powdered-ice pile among Pitville's structures which served as a ski jump. When they had heard the alarm howl, they had simply glanced at each other, nodded, and without bothering to use even the briefest message to one another or the Habras they had been talking to, headed east. As they went, Hugh keyed a query to the watch.

"What's wrong?" His use of code identified him.

Rekchellet and his fellow sentry had by now learned the position of the troubled Naxian, and the Crotonite responded through the general public speakers.

"Pit One, x twenty-one, y thirty-one, z three ninety-five decreasing slowly. Naxian apparently in trouble, no clear comm, no further details."

S'Nash, presumably hoping the contradiction would not irritate its/his partner, added one item. "Subject maintaining vertical attitude by request. You should be able to identify it easily." He expected an indignant whistle, but apparently the Crotonite realized that his "no further details" had been a little hasty and was willing to let the matter pass.

Hugh acknowledged, and the couple headed for Pit One, shedding their skis and going over the edge without diminishing their speed. The fluid was only a little less dense than water—it was maintained carefully at an oxygen-nitrogen proportion which would offset the pressure of the surrounding ice at any given depth—so the impact could have been violent in stronger gravity. Neither Erthuma even noticed the shock, however; all that bothered them was a brief vision blur as bubbles of air, some carried down with their suits and some formed as the armor's heat boiled the surrounding liquid, momentarily obscured their view. These, however, lifted away or condensed again almost at once, and the couple could look around the now brilliantly lit pool. They extended fins and hand webs and swam rapidly downward toward the indicated spot.

By the time the Erthumoi had reached it, several minutes after the alarm, there were two other Naxians already there. Their snakelike shape allowed them to swim very much faster than human beings, and they had not had nearly as far to come. There was still no difficulty, however, in identifying the one in trouble, or even the basic nature of its problem.

The victim and both its newly arrived fellows were all trying to work on the same area of armor, about half a meter back of the sufferer's head. Even the wearer could reach the spot with the rather clumsy handlers installed on the Naxian suits, but no one seemed able to do anything about a stream of bubbles which was flowing from the spot.

The bubbles were collapsing again a few centimeters away, with a swirl of heated liquid rising visibly from their vanishing point for about as much farther. Clearly, there was some damage to the thermal insulation of the armor. The instrument case the being had been carrying had now been abandoned and was sinking very slowly; the two-meter-plus serpents were rising under their own buoyancy even less rapidly as the Erthumoi approached.

"What can we do?" keyed the woman.

"Do you have any insulation patches?" one of the Naxians asked.

"No." It would take too long to explain by code that Erthumoi bodies were massive enough to let them—probably—swim to the surface and leave the Pit before losing a dangerous amount of heat from such damage. In any case, the fact that no such help was on hand was the important one; excuses were irrelevant, even if Hugh Cedar was supposed to be in charge of safety.

"Can you supply energy to the area?" The question was in code, and for a moment Hugh failed to see why his wife was asking it. Of course he couldn't—then he realized that she wasn't addressing him. The robot had reached the group. How it knew the question was meant for it Hugh never asked—it was a courtesy-rooted standard procedure *not* to treat robots as rational beings in the presence of non-Erthumoi members of the Six Races, and even when people forgot this the robots themselves usually remembered. However, this one answered promptly.

"No. I am operating at ambient temperature and have only essential heaters for moving parts."

"We can't get it/her to the surface fast enough," cut in one of the Naxians, "and you Erthumoi are even slower swimmers. Sentries, can a rescue craft reach us within, say, forty seconds?"

"No." S'Nash's buzzes and Rekchellet's whistles could be heard as faint background to the translated word.

"Then the armor must be removed, as nearly instantly as possible. If H'Feer can be frozen quickly enough to forestall crystallization, it/she can be saved with suitable treatment. Can you understand me, H'Feer? Do you agree? Are you willing to face the risk and discomfort?"

The response was as wordless as it had been before, but even the Erthumoi interpreted the sounds as whimpers and thought they could read the agony in them. They glanced at each other. Fleetingly, Hugh wondered what having one's body gradually frozen from midsection to ends might feel like.

The helping Naxians received the victim's feelings far more strongly, of course, and read them correctly in spite of its/her inability to speak. For once even the Erthumoi were right on an emotional matter. The clumsy handlers on the snakelike beings' armor reached for the victim's release catches, and stopped.

"That's the trouble! It/she'd have done it already, but the release is frozen or jammed somehow! Erthumoi, your grippers are stronger than ours.

Grasp the flaps on either side of the helmet and pull straight apart. The suit should split open length-wise."

Hugh seized one of the indicated projections and Janice the other. The woman straddled the serpentine form and, bracing her feet against her husband's armored chest, pushed as hard as she could.

The suit held. Hugh was about to add his own legs to the system when the robot firmly shoved him aside, grabbed one flap in each of two handlers, made a precise incision at the front of the Naxian's helmet with one of its ice shavers, and with a single continuous motion split and pulled the armor free of its occupant. There was a brief cloud of bubbles as the air in the suit escaped and liquid contacting flesh boiled; then vision cleared and the burbling hiss died out as a swirling mass of warmer than average liquid air drifted upward from the scene.

The Naxian floated rigid in the grasp of its/her fellows, quick-frozen. It would not have worked fast enough for an Erthuma even had the liquid been helium instead of air, but no part of the slender body was more than a few centimeters from the nearest surface, and heat could escape quickly.

One of the others spoke up. "There'll probably be severe tissue damage near the injury to the armor, where there has been slow freezing going on for minutes, but at least it/she should live. We will get it/her to the surface, and—"

Hugh interrupted; he had been busy with code. "There will be an aircraft with a liquid air bath at the Pit edge in two minutes, to take H'Feer to Pwanpwan. One of your people should call ahead; I don't know in any detail the medical work needed. I believe Th'Terro would be best, but if it/she is not available there must be others at your biology station."

"You are right about Th'Terro, Erthuma Hugh. Thank you for the arrangements."

"My job," Hugh keyed. "Sorry I wasn't set up to accomplish it more quickly. I'll try to think of other ways to be ready, and will gladly welcome suggestions on other possible precautions and how they may be implemented within the Project's logistic framework."

Hugh disliked and was embarrassed by pretentious language, but had found long ago that when hampered by code restraints he usually came out ahead using longer but fewer words. It was much easier to let the translators handle vocabulary than to do his own circumlocutions by hand.

He knew that Janice was storing every precious sentence in her memory to use against him later, but didn't grudge her that bit of fun. He could usually hold his own in marital repartee.

He watched the accident victim being towed upward for a few seconds, then got back to code work.

"Report and info request from Safety One. Naxian H'Feer thermal injury, receiving help. Director, please report on task interrupted and replacement needed."

The translator responded at once.

"Cra'eth, Equipment Management. H'Feer was taking a projector to the next window site. It will not be urgently needed until the corresponding window in the other pit has been at least rough-polished, probably in another hour. I can most likely find someone to get it there; I will report within ten minutes to Watch if I succeed and to Administration if I have trouble."

"Logged at Watch," another translated voice supplemented, and then went on less formally, "This is Rek, Cedars. It looked from here as though the rescue was actually done by that robot—the digger. Should we keep quiet about it?"

"Quiet, not necessarily. Tactful, yes," keyed Janice. "Keep an honest log, certainly; we can't distort data."

"Of course. Both of us will want to talk to you when we get off watch, though."

"How long will that be?"

"A little over four more hours for me, six for S'Nash."

"You *both* want to talk it over?"

"Very much," came the translated voice of the Naxian.

"That could be a little harder. Jan and I could ski again while Rek goes flying for fun; but what do you folks do outdoors—for amusement, that is—around here?"

"I can show you—well, maybe not. I can tell you. You'd have trouble doing it, and I doubt that you'd enjoy it, but I'll explain some time if you're really curious. I'll meet you and Rekchellet at the foot of the west slope of the main waste dump at—let's say nineteen even."

"Fine."

"And please have a robot there, if you can find a way to make its presence convenient and reasonable," added S'Nash.

"Will an ice worker from the dumps be suitable?" asked Janice.

"I would think so." The translated voices from the watch station fell silent. Hugh and his wife looked at each other, frankly and intensely puzzled, but decided to say nothing even in code for the time being. They swam, not too quickly, to the surface of the Pit, found one of the numerous ladders, ramps, and scoops which allowed members of the various species working on the Project to emerge when necessary—though in Habranha's gravity there was never any real trouble about this—and made their way to their own quarters.

These were currently very uncomfortable, being full of pressure fluid, but at least the Erthumoi could remove their armor and enjoy some physical contact. They could also talk privately; vocal cords were still useless, but the microphones which normally picked up and broadcast their code through the structure could be cut off, and, of course, after a few Common Years of married companionship they could bypass code for much of what they wanted to say.

"Does S'Nash actually want to talk to a robot? It's pretty hard to believe."

"Not quite as hard as though it were Rek," Janice answered thoughtfully. "If it/he had asked for the digger who made the rescue, I could believe there was some progress here. I don't see what it/he can want that could be fulfilled by just *any* robot, though."

"Rek was listening, and didn't object. Maybe—" Hugh's code cut off, and his expressive hands stopped moving.

"Maybe what?"

"Crotonites are often good technicians, and Rek should have no trouble regarding a robot as a machine—in fact, we know he doesn't; we've known him for a long time now, and for a Crotonite he's pretty tolerant. He hasn't called either of us a slug, or even seemed to think of us that way, for three years or more."

"Habra years, you mean."

"Naturally." Hugh drifted upright in the liquid; he had removed his armor since no one would miss a chance to do this even for a few minutes, but he was wearing enough belt and ankle ballast to maintain neutral buoyancy in the dense stuff. He went on, "I don't think this is Rek's idea at all, though this sort of guessing does no good. We know him pretty well, and for my money the whole proposal is probably S'Nash's idea."

"If Rek didn't approve, he'd have made it clear when we were asked to meet them. We both know him well enough for *that*. Rekchellet has become positively fond of you and me—" Janice's signals carried no trace of smugness, but her facial expression did— "but I don't think he's extended that feeling to all Erthumoi, much less to the rest of the Six."

"Right. We're building on wind, as Rek would say. Let's eat and get out to the meeting. Much as I like this project, I wish we could spend a few days without juice. I can do without talking, but eating is supposed to be fun."

Janice nodded, and they ingested nourishment. The reflexes normally closing the human breathing passage when the owner swallows had been neutralized to allow "breathing" of the diving fluid. Eating, therefore, required extreme care, and was confined to substances loose enough not to need chewing but firm and cohesive enough to go down the esophagus together once started in the right direction. Stuff which broke up like cake crumbs could be dangerous; the coughing reflex had also been blocked since this would have ruptured liquid-filled lungs. Careful and rather skilled work with a hand pump was needed when food went the wrong way. If the person concerned was also wearing an environment suit, the problem could become really complicated, though the Cedars had now faced even this emergency often enough to regard it as more of a nuisance than a catastrophe.

They never went anywhere alone, however, while set up for deep diving, except for office or lab where help was nearby.

Funnels sealed directly to the trachea and extending outside the mouth to allow more control over what did reach the windpipe had been suggested often and tried occasionally, but so far had proved less than satisfactory.

Fed, or at least nourished, the couple resumed and tested their armor, left their quarters, made their way to the main residence air lock, checked out with the watch, and headed west.

They were not wearing skis this time; it was not necessary to climb over the piles of ice dust extracted from the Pits, and the level surfaces of Pitville were not dangerously slippery. This had not always been so, but the dust-fine water snow had now been beaten down within the settlement into a solid, almost clear ice pavement by passing feet, armored bellies, wheels, and treads. At the local temperatures, this ice was barely slippery except under pressures not likely to be provided by an Erthuma body on foot under Habranhan gravity. Powdered finely enough, though, the area of contact between grains or flakes could be small enough for moderate force to provide melting pressure; one could ski, or make snowballs.

The path was nearly dark. Energy was cheap, but lighting equipment had not been wasted except where it was considered important. The brightest object in the sky was Fafnir, currently at a distance which made it about as bright as Earth's full moon. It hung some fifteen degrees above the northwest horizon, so shadows were long. At the moment, thin clouds from the day side gave the sunlet a vague halo and hid most of the other stars.

Neither Hugh nor Janice was currently paying any particular attention to the sky. They were familiar with it, enjoyed making up constellations for it, and had even invented a zodiac for Fafnir to follow, though they did not expect to be around for the eight hundred or so Common Years it would take the little star to complete that circle. Just now, however, they were too concerned with their path and too curious about the forthcoming meeting to stargaze.

Even the footing wasn't too much of a problem; it would take a long fall to be dangerous here. Their thoughts were mostly on what was up, but neither had conceived a question or answer interesting enough to be worth the labor of putting into code.

The woman did glance up occasionally, wondering whether they might see Rekchellet on his way, but neither looked for the robot they were to meet.

Its orders had already been given and acknowledged, and its path would not cross theirs.

The ice shavings from the Pits had for the most part been taken well beyond the collection of Project buildings for permanent disposal; their total volume was expected to measure many cubic kilometers, though this would be far in the future. There were some small heaps, fifty to a hundred meters high, which had been left closer to and even among the buildings to serve as a water supply and as research material. The behavior of ice grains of various sizes at differing depths and over a range of times, under Habranha's gravity, sundry forms of traffic, and different kinds of plant cover was a key body of data to the Project, and it was on these piles that the Cedars usually did their skiing. The Erthumoi had been assured that the researchers regarded the effect of even this activity on the substrate as interesting and valuable information. The jumping ramp had been a rather private project of Hugh's which had failed to catch administrative attention until recently—it was, after all, basically just another pile of ice tailings.

The present walk, however, was to the main dump—actually to the far side of it, out of view from the settlement, an aspect of S'Nash's request which was beginning to loom larger in Janice's mind. She was not worried about the intentions of S'Nash and Rekchellet, of course. For the Crotonite, in particular, a harmless motive could be guessed; he was associating with other species, nonflying ones at that, much more closely than most of his own people would have approved.

The couple went around the Fafnir-lit north side of the huge mound. Unlike the ski slope, it was almost bare snow; only a few bushes, most of these less than fist size, had taken root and grown fast enough to escape burial as new material was added. A few stood a meter or more out from the surface,

where random winds had blown the dust away from
already deep-sunk roots.

Their path around the foot of the slope curved
southward until the buildings and lights behind them
were all out of sight, and they might have been
standing on a deserted world. The pile of ice was
larger than most of the elevations they could see, but
Habranha's night hemisphere was far from level.
The dustlike snow brought from the day side by the
upper level winds and distributed at the surface by
the even more chaotic lower ones behaved often—
not always—like very fine sand on more Earthlike
planets, and the topography consisted largely of ripples and dunes. These were not at all permanent in
spite of the vegetation; winds varied wildly on the
little planet even away from direct sunlight, and attempts to map the area around the Project base had
long been given up by all except two or three stub-
born natives who couldn't, or at least refused to,
accept the basic nature of Chaos.

Hugh and Janice were now plowing through relatively loose material which was technically snow,
though far too fine to show individual flakes to human eyes. The wind, while only moderate at the moment, was picking up enough of the dusty stuff to
block horizontal vision beyond a few hundred meters, though with the big waste pile and the companion star in clear sight neither Erthuma was worried
about getting lost.

None of the others seemed to have arrived yet,
however. There was no point in worrying about the
robot, which could locate itself absolutely anywhere
on the planet, and Rekchellet could presumably always orient himself by going high enough to see the
settlement lights; but the snakelike Naxian was another matter. One could assume that it/he knew what
to do outdoors, but a body that shape and size would
be hard to see at any distance with the blowing powder swirling mostly near the ground.

Hugh could tell himself all this and remind himself that the trip had been the Naxian's own idea, but Hugh had a job, and he couldn't help wondering what special measures he had not yet thought of might help assure the protection of two-meter-long snakes wriggling around in loose snow where they were likely to be hard to see, to have trouble seeing very far themselves, and to be easily blown away in an atmosphere whose currents were sometimes strong enough to pick up much heavier objects against the local gravity.

He was brooding over this, probably more seriously than he need have been, when the robot and S'Nash arrived together.

The former was of fairly standard make, its body a cylinder about a meter high and slightly less in diameter. The top was rimmed with alternating handlers and eyes, half a dozen of each; most of the body, the Erthumoi knew, housed the power unit and machinery for handling and traveling equipment. Its "brain" was little larger than that of a human being, not one of the ten or fifteen liter "Big Boxes." Just where the designing engineer had decided to put it, under the conflicting demands of easy service access and maximum protection, neither Hugh nor Janice knew or greatly cared. The robot differed from the digger which had performed the rescue a few hours earlier mainly in its locomotion system; instead of hydrojets it possessed three small sets of caterpillar treads, each forming the "foot" of an insectlike leg mounted near the bottom of the cylinder. It was hard to visualize any solid surface on which the system would not find traction.

Both Erthumoi were quite accustomed to such devices and should not have had their attention strongly attracted by its approach; but *something* prevented their noticing the Naxian until it/he was beside them. S'Nash simply appeared, sheathed in brightly gleaming full-recycling armor, scarcely a body length away. The wind eddying around its/his partly coiled form was making swirl patterns in the snow beneath it as though it/he had already been there for seconds.

One did not make exclamations of surprise in code, even if exclamations were needed with Naxians. In any case, before anything had been said by anyone at the foot of the snow hill, another voice cut in with evidence of irritation which even the Erthumoi could detect in translation.

"Doesn't anyone have the sense to wear a light if you're not going to stand out where someone can see you easily? I don't suppose any of you knows what hummocky ground looks like from above under slanting light, but I thought imagination was supposed to be part of intelligence. Where are you, anyway?"

"Sorry, Rek," keyed Janice. Hugh silently turned on his suit lamp, set it on wide beam, and swung it to follow his gaze aloft.

The rays could be followed easily enough in the blowing ice dust, but for a moment none of those on the ground could see the Crotonite. Then his wings showed darkly against the Fafnir-lit upper haze as he swung back toward them from farther west, fifty or sixty meters up, rocking slightly in the turbulent air. Hugh swung his lamp toward him to reveal their own position.

The reaction was less than grateful, they could tell, though more than half the words for the next few seconds were no-symbol-equivalent codes from their translators.

A single term, "Dark adaptation," came through mixed with the other sounds, and at almost the same instant the broad-winged shadow plunged into the hillside above them. A cloud of ice dust rose, spread, and swirled up the hill on the wind; coarser material hung around the impact site, settling slowly in the weak gravity and thick air. Rekchellet's tirade ceased, and for a long moment only the wind could be heard.

Nobody wasted time; even Hugh saved his self-criticism for later. He did not reject his own guilt, but with luck and quick enough action he might not have to reprimand himself; Rekchellet should be able to take care of that. The surface of the ice dust was loose and fluffy, the Crotonite couldn't possibly have hit it very hard, it was most unlikely that there was now enough weight on him to keep him from breathing, and unless Chaos had been unusually personal they should have a mishap rather than a tragedy on their hands.

Standing around watching, however, was not appropriate action. Trying to make their way up to the impact site, the Erthumoi found, was not appropriate either. Climbing was impossible. The dust was near its angle of repose, and even in what for them was scarcely one-fifth gravity, the Erthumoi slid back with the loose material as fast as they stamped and beat it downward. Their only visible achievements were to start digging a niche at the foot of the slope, which refilled by collapse from above every few seconds, and to force the Naxian to withdraw hastily to keep from being buried. Neither human being noticed its/his retreat. They realized almost at once that they would never get up the hill themselves, but decided independently and instantly that the refill wave might help uncover Rekchellet when it reached his height. They could only hope that it wouldn't as promptly bury him again with the next collapse.

The robot's abrupt unordered departure brought neither question nor comment. The Naxian saw it go, but said nothing as it vanished around the southern curve of the ice pile, and it/he remained silent even when the robot reappeared a minute or so later. The Cedars were still trying to dig, and if they noticed anything beyond the dust they were moving, they didn't waste effort or attention putting it in code. No sound had come from Rekchellet since his burial. All anyone could hear was rising wind.

The robot was no longer traveling under its own power, but riding a tracked vehicle. On this was mounted something which might on many worlds have been mistaken for a piece of field artillery, since its most obvious feature in the poor light was a slender tube some three meters long. As the machine emerged from the shadow and brought its rider into sight of the impact scar made by Rekchellet—rapidly disappearing as wind filled it with white dust—the tube swiveled upward. The vehicle halted, and a roar loud enough to drown any attempt at conversation filled the air.

Three or four meters above the Crotonite crater a new cloud rose in Fafnir's light and swept away toward the north, and another hole appeared in the waste pile. A dull red beam of light played from a point on the machine just under the tube, striking the new pit and playing back and forth over its upper side. As the seconds passed, the excavation spread downward toward the place where Rekchellet had disappeared; but unlike that made by the still active Erthumoi, this one did not fill from above.

The wind blast from the air-sweeper continued to roar, digging closer and closer to the buried flier. The mild heat beam melted the surface, and the resulting water soaked into the still undisplaced snow and froze again almost instantly into a wall which, frail as it was, supported the material above.

The Erthumoi finally realized what was going on and ceased their frantic digging. Janice, in hope of sparing the anti-artificial intelligence prejudices of the Naxian, started to key, "It's just experience, not—" and stopped before getting out the word "imagination." She knew she was right, but her own imagination had suddenly kicked in and supplied her intuition with a possible reason why she and her husband *and the robot* had been called to this meeting *by S'Nash*. She hoped Hugh would see it for himself; she couldn't tell him now. She didn't want the others to know what she'd guessed until she could watch them both closely. The knowledge should spare her husband guilt feelings about Rekchellet's accident, though she could, of course, be wrong.

It had not, she suddenly felt pretty sure, really been an accident.

She watched, much more calmly than Hugh, as the jet of air swung lower and lower, cutting its way into the heap of ice dust closer and closer to the point where the flier had vanished.

Neither Erthuma was surprised when a dark object suddenly whirled out of the Fafnir-lit surface and spun skyward. For a moment it simply blew away, then wings extended, the tumbling slowed and then ceased, and it was flying under control.

Rekchellet still said nothing as he glided to the ice beside them. The thunder of the sweeper died, and the billowing cloud of airborne dust which now extended for hundreds of meters north of the waste heap began slowly to settle as well as to spread in the rising wind.

"You're all right," keyed Hugh.

3

THE BEST PRECAUTIONS
MAY BE TAKEN LATE

"Well, I can fly!" snapped the Crotonite. "When I asked for someone to use a light to indicate your position, I didn't mean for some idiot—"

"I was a little hasty," Hugh began.

"Are you sure?" cut in Janice's code. For a moment her husband thought she was addressing him, and wondered how to get "of course I was" across with an absolute minimum of finger work. Then he realized she was speaking to Rekchellet as she went on, "What else would you have used for an excuse?" The flier hunched silently into a more relaxed position, looking steadily at the Erthuma. His beaked face was in shadow. Janice, despite her suspicion-driven alertness and personal familiarity with the Crotonite, could probably not have read Rek's expression even if the light had been better; but S'Nash was a little slow cutting off its/his speaker.

"Good for—!" came through the translators, complete with exclamation symbol.

Rekchellet produced a sound rather like a snort, which the translator passed unaltered and followed with no-equivalent-pattern. Words finally became clear. "There's plenty of turbulence up there. The wind is rising; even you must have noticed that. I could have said anything I pleased. How would you ground—" he caught himself—"would you have known if I were falsifying data?"

"*You* wouldn't be." Janice's translated code carried the emphasis clearly enough. "You knew one of us would react *quickly*, not *hastily*. Hugh did just what you wanted." The woman had clearly centered the tracker, but if Rekchellet felt either embarrassed or flattered he made no sound or motion to reveal it. "You and S'Nash, or at least S'Nash, wanted to check on robots," Janice went on. "You arranged to have one here, and set up a situation to find out what it would do without instruction. What if we'd instructed it?"

"I would have gotten in its way," the Naxian answered promptly.

"You really trust an Erthuma-built artificial mind that far? You'd risk your own life to—"

"We trust some Erthumoi *people* that far," said the Crotonite emphatically. "Not others. We understood that the robots on this project would just be dedicated machines, able to do only simple tasks like digging and disposing of waste ice. This is research, far too important to be entrusted to artificial thinking. Janice and Hugh, I trusted you. Many more trusted you because of me, whatever they may think of my taste in friends. You knew the understanding. Why didn't you keep to it?"

"Was the accident in the Pit also a test?" keyed Janice.

"No," snapped the Crotonite. "Answer my question."

"Was this second test planned before that accident, or did you two get the idea after you saw what happened in the Pit?"

S'Nash answered this time. "It was my idea when I saw the other rescue. Rekchellet disapproved, but I convinced him. Please answer his question. I want him to know."

Neither human being commented on the implication that the Naxian knew already, but both wondered briefly why it/he cared.

"In my opinion," Hugh keyed carefully, "we didn't break word or trust. None of these robots is

intelligent by our standards. You should know;
you've at least seen the Big Boxes, and probably
done some work with them even if you didn't like it.
None of these robots has anything to do with data
identification or interpretation, and no machines do
except the dedicated number-spinners you and everyone else know about.

"However, I consider it my responsibility to have
brains in any robot working where a living project
member might be in danger. Not high-class brains,
but ones capable of simple decisions. One person is
alive now probably because of that judgment—at
least, S'Nash here says the Pit accident a few hours
ago was not a setup. I don't suppose you were really
in trouble up the hill here, Rekchellet, but if you had
been none of us but the robot could have done you
any good." Hugh paused, realizing that he was being
defensive and not liking it.

"So what are you going to do about all this? Complain to Spreadsheet-Thinker or the Guild about the
robots? If they do anything negative about them, it
will only lessen the personal safety of those working
here on Darkside."

It was the Naxian who answered. "We'll say as
little as possible—nothing, if we can get away with
it, though I expect she would probably agree with
you. Let me give you our reasons." It/he was interrupted by a single word from the robot.

"Evaluation?"

"Proper and adequate, interpretation and action,"
Hugh keyed.

"Anything superfluous?"

"Most of it, but data on that fact came afterward.
Your response was proper and adequate. Back to
routine." The robot and sweeper disappeared into the
shadows south of the pile. Thoughtfully, Hugh
watched it go. S'Nash did not.

The serpentine schemer coiled into a presumably
comfortable attitude and started its/his explanation,

managing to give the impression of an educator going into lecture mode.

"I was never really worried about *your* betrayal of trust, Cedars. I don't think Rekchellet would have been either if he had thought things through carefully, but I wanted his help in getting you to the test we have just made. I had little time to think, and gave him none. I played on his feelings. I apologize, Rekchellet. I acted selfishly, crudely, improperly, discourteously, and have betrayed your trust. I am a worm and a slug, and I ask your forgiveness and a chance to earn that trust back. You may use me if you wish as I have used you."

The Crotonite had stirred uneasily, and the great wings had half spread at the first part of S'Nash's admission. They folded again hastily as a gust threatened to carry him away with the snow, and the next few sentences seemed to calm him a little. Both Erthumoi guessed that S'Nash was using its/his emotion sense to the full, trying different sentences like keys on a shop console in the hope that they would forestall or calm real anger on the part of the winged listener.

Janice also suddenly found herself wondering how trustworthy the speaker could really be if it/he were so ready to use words and promises merely for immediate effect—just to play on another being's attitudes as though an intelligent personality were a machine tool. Of course, it/he *had* confessed before seeking excuse, and the confession had not seemed necessary. Equally, of course, it might have been politic, or covered a need not yet obvious.

Janice hoped her own appreciation of the skill involved was easier for S'Nash to read than the underlying distrust which it was arousing, but this seemed a lot to hope for. The latter feeling was much stronger.

She had always known, in an academic way, that most members of the other Five Species who could get really friendly with an Erthuma would almost by definition be regarded as mildly insane by their fellows. She had kept this knowledge out of her conscious mind with, she hoped, the firmness of a flat-world believer forced to look at its planet from space; the ability to let wish color reason, so common in her species though not confined to it, was sometimes useful. How effective this might be with Naxian powers she could not be sure, however.

Like most Erthumoi, she had a personal hypothesis about the way this ability worked. She was a scientist, so her idea was essentially physical rather than mystical, but so far she had had little opportunity to test it.

At least she herself, subjectively, did not consider either S'Nash or Rekchellet insane by her own standards. There was no need to worry about what the Naxian could read on that point.

"It seemed only wise and fair to admit my deceit," S'Nash was saying, "before you came to suspect it from other cause and ceased forever to trust me. If you can't feel confidence in my word even now, please say so. I will understand and not—well, try not—to blame."

Janice wondered whether this sentence, though seemingly directed at Rekchellet, might not be meant for her; it certainly could have been inspired by a grasp of her present feelings. She became even less sure of the Naxian. She'd have to talk the matter over with Hugh when they had a chance—not that the dear fellow's judgment would be any better than hers, but they should at least try to agree on tactics.

Rekchellet interrupted her musing.

"I can see why you were in a hurry. Go on with your explanation to Hugh and Janice."

This time husband's and wife's thoughts ran in parallel. It would have been nice for the Crotonite to say definitely whether he was forgiving the deceit or not. S'Nash must know already, and only the

Erthumoi were left in doubt. Of course, one could fairly say that it was none of their business; but it would have been convenient to know just how Rekchellet might be expected to react to the next request, demand, or promise from the Naxian or how firmly he would feel bound to meet with any commitment he himself made to the schemer.

Janice forced her attention back to S'Nash's words.

"The plan to dig the two Pits, you remember, was settled only after much argument. We seek fossils and similar data to help clarify the prehistory of Habranha. There is strong biochemical evidence that the civilized beings now living here did not evolve on this world but are descended from colonists of unknown origin—possibly, and importantly to many, from the Seventh Race, whose relics have been found on so many other planets. The evidence is supported, some insist, by a *lack* of data about the general course of evolution here. But the latter really proves nothing, since neither the natives nor we visitors have done any real paleontology here. The conditions are unique. No part of the ring continent where the Habras live lasts more than two or three thousand Common Years; it is always melting at the sunward edge and on the cold side accreting bergs which have come from the Solid Ocean, as they call it.

"Darkside itself is mainly water-ice, which we hoped might contain organic remains. We know now that it does, but no standard fossil study techniques apply; we knew we would have to learn as we went along. No one minds that.

"The only remaining part of the planet where fossils might reasonably exist is the sunward hemisphere under five hundred kilometers of ocean. Darkside seemed more promising." Hugh stirred impatiently but, he hoped, imperceptibly. He had been with the project from the beginning. S'Nash's wordiness was sparing his own code fingers, but it would be nice to hear the point.

"In the other twist, there was no argument that a shaft in the ice of the dark hemisphere, eventually reaching rock some five hundred kilometers down, might well secure reasonably complete information. The dispute, as you know, was over its location. Most useful fossils were expected to be microscopic, things like spores blown to the dark side as dust. We did not know during the planning stage that many more large plants grew in this hemisphere than anyone expected. We still don't know about animal or equivalent life here. These may leave informative remains, and the wing found a few days ago offers real hope that we may some time find a more complete flier, even one of the present Habras' remote ancestors.

"However, many felt that more should have been learned about glacial movements before starting the Pits anywhere. Others insisted that such research, while useful and interesting, would take too much time and delay the actual search for meaningful remains. Attractively intense feelings were generated on both sides of the discussion, even among such placid beings as the Samians. Even more remarkably, these feelings did not smooth out after debate ended and it was decided to start digging without complete ice flow data.

"Once we had begun, of course, talk about the alternative line of action became unpopular; administrators dislike even to consider, much less to admit, that their projects may not have had optimum planning. This seems true of all the Six Races, as well as many which are not star travelers, not just my own."

Hugh rather sympathized with administrative attitudes on this point, and began to wonder whether S'Nash were simply leading up to suggesting a new site for the Pits. He himself saw no reason to keep argument alive on the matter; spending potentially useful time in the "if only we had—" mode irritated him.

"I would certainly not want to waste already expended effort, and I do expect useful and interesting results from the present dig," S'Nash went on. "I want, however, to keep track of any other work in the dark hemisphere. I want to see studies of the subsurface flow of the ice encouraged. If it does turn out that the Pits are not at the best possible place, I can stand it, of course; they'll still be useful while they last. A lot of native Habras agree with me about all this; I am not—Rek and I are not—a couple of lone malcontents. We don't want to hamper this project or lose touch it with, but we want to keep contact with any others going on."

"And this led to your test of the robot?" keyed Hugh.

"Yes."

"How?"

"Rekchellet, shall I explain, or would you rather take over?"

"You talk. I'll draw."

"Good. You both know Rek's skills." It was a statement; the Naxian knew that the flier and the Cedars had worked together before. Neither bothered to answer.

The Crotonite pulled from his harness the drawing pad and stylus he always carried. S'Nash waited silently while its/his partner made a few test marks and cleared the table again in readiness for use. Then it/he resumed talking.

"The upper winds carry water and other volatiles—ammonia, hydrogen cyanide, carbon dioxide—from the sunward side. These eventually fall as snow. In the simplest picture, this snow becomes ever deeper, compressing its lower layers and forcing them to flow back as glaciers toward the warmer hemisphere. In fact, all this motion is heavily complicated by the continuous compacting of the snow into ice, and the ice itself into various phases of differing densities, viscosities, melting points, and mechanical strengths at increasing depths." So far Rekchellet was making no diagrams; S'Nash was summarizing common knowledge.

"Most snow falls relatively near the warm edge of the dark hemisphere, the terminator, but traces of water and even more ammonia remain in the upper winds even near the dark pole and precipitate there, though much more slowly. Most of the carbon dioxide gets that far. Even if the material did not arrive as gas, gravity would make ice formed nearer the terminator flow downhill, so glaciers exist even at the cold pole, and have thickness comparable to the five hundred kilometers near the boundary—the same as the depth of liquid ocean on the sunward side. The lithosphere of Habranha has to be pretty well centered in the hydrosphere, whether the latter is solid or liquid.

"How much of that thickness stems from ice deposited near the terminator and flowing *away* from the warm side and how much got there as local precipitation, we simply don't know."

This was still obvious, but the Crotonite did a quick sketch to illustrate the situation. His reason soon became clear.

"Material from these remote glaciers also circulates, though far more slowly. The generally chaotic situation induced by phase change on Habranha seems to apply in solid as well as in liquid and gas; calculations—mathematical models—fail to agree on the speed and often even the direction of such circulation. No one has been able to decide whether fossil-bearing dust deposited far away from the terminator will or will not make up in age for what it will presumably lack in quantity. You have already found, Janice, that ordinary stratigraphy is as complex in the ice here as in the silicate crusts of more everyday planets. Many of us, as I said, felt that we should not have started to dig until this point had been clarified."

Neither Hugh nor his wife was surprised at S'Nash's increasing self-identification with the disapproving party. Rekchellet had started indicating with his usual near-magical clarity currents traveling in various directions in the deep ice of the dark hemisphere. The Erthumoi moved closer to see more clearly; the drawing surface was small.

The diagram included suggestions of flow *up* toward the surface in places. Neither Erthuma had ever heard such a possibility suggested. It was reasonable enough, though, Hugh reflected; even pure water-ice had phases of differing densities, and on Habranha it would never be pure. There'd be a fair amount of ammonia toward the center of Darkside— more than around here, certainly— and maybe—no, the hydrogen cyanide would be cleared out pretty completely long before that point by the ammonia itself.

"We could check surface ice for N-H-4-C-N," he keyed. "That would tell us lots even without boring. But how would you get detailed information of ice motion at depth?"

The Naxian's long form tightened from its heretofore relaxed spiral, and the brilliant gold-brown eyes looked out of their helmet straight into Hugh's face guard. It took no Naxian sense to tell that a point of intense interest and major enthusiasm to the speaker was coming up. There was a brief pause while only howling wind and hissing snow could be heard.

"Do you know anything about seismology?" it/he asked.

"I know what it is. A sort of quick-and-dirty method of judging the nature of subsurface strata from the way they transmit, reflect, and refract sound waves."

"Nearly correct, granting a rather broad use of the word 'sound.' Your term 'quick-and-dirty' is wrong

unless my translator badly misjudged its implications. With enough measurements, vast details about
the shapes, sizes, depths, compositions, and even
motions of the wave-carrying strata may be secured.
It's a common technique. It could be done here. Can
you imagine the usefulness of a complete chart of
the ice currents of half a world? How it could be applied to quicker, more random liquid and gaseous
circulations? What it would mean to the Habras,
who have known for ages that their population satu-
rates their world, in their endless problems with
their own environment? How it would help the project we are doing right now? Janice, we could even
predict where fossils of a given age might be found,
and recover them with minimal effort and expense,
instead of digging these huge Pits and going through
all the complexities of taking laser readings from
one to the other to study the dust motes between. We
could—"

"Surely it would call for millions of readings, and
more calculating power than you people like to play
with." Hugh had not liked interrupting, and had
briefly delayed doing so while he wondered why the
Naxian was addressing Janice so specifically, but
S'Nash's enthusiasm seemed to be getting somewhat
out of hand, if that were the right word.

"It does not require artificial intelligence, if that's
what you're hinting," Rekchellet cut in immediately.
"A dedicated number handler of appropriate power
can deal with the work. The problem is securing the
data—the measurements—the observations."

"True." Hugh decided not to argue. Basically the
Crotonite was right. However, the thought of feeding
such a mass of information to anything but a well
developed AI unit made him cringe like an astrono-
mer asked to do an asteroid orbit with pencil, paper,
and log tables. Still, this was hardly a time to dispute what amounted to a religious attitude. Maybe
the native Habras could face it; they were primitive

enough to be used to tedious labor. They built their submarines with manual tools.

More important, maybe a project like this could be put together in a way that Hugh and Janice and their fellow Erthumoi would find useful. . . .

"The equipment is simple," S'Nash continued. "Some sort of shock producer and a lot of receiving transducers."

"How many? How big an area can be checked at a time? How long would a set of observations take? How and where do you get the equipment, now that the Pits have been started and basic procedure settled?" It was a lot of code for Janice to fire off at once, but it should take a lot of answering. She, as S'Nash had done at Hugh's interruption, settled into a more comfortable stance on the snow and looked steadily at the Naxian. Something, Hugh could tell, had interested her. S'Nash presumably knew this, too; maybe it/he could even guess what it was—no, Naxians weren't supposed to be mind readers. Maybe his wife was doing some hypothesis testing of her own.

"A single shock source will do, but we'd really want lots of sources, lots of stations. For each station, anywhere from a dozen to a thousand sensors would be appropriate. The more receivers, the more quickly the data can be secured—"

"And the more complex the calculations," keyed Hugh, with his newly born thought in mind. S'Nash would only read approval, one could hope.

"Exactly."

"The realistic limit, then, is how many receivers you can get."

"Yes."

"You say such a project is going on, and you're keeping in touch with it. How many do they have? How are they handling data? Who's involved? The Guild?"

"We're trying to keep in touch informally, without interfering with our work here."

"Or your status." Hugh regretted the remark as soon as it was uttered; it was probably unfair. Neither S'Nash nor Rekchellet seemed to notice the interruption, however; the Naxian went on.

"I don't know how big the project is, or how many are involved, or just who is running it. I don't think it's the Guild, which is another reason we aren't in really close contact."

"And also why," added Hugh, "you seem to feel such a need for secrecy about all this. I don't blame you for not discussing it in detail until we got out here."

Rekchellet made a chuckling sound which, the translator indicated by a standard nonverbal symbol, actually did signify humor, and took over the explanation. "The local people who would disapprove," the Crotonite said, "quite aside from the Guild, which wouldn't really care much, are some of S'Nash's fellow Naxians. They also include the Locrian coordinator for the Project, Spreadsheet-Thinker. S'Nash feels it/he needs something to explain its/his chronic condition of anxiety, which any Naxian can sense. I'm afraid you are the villains, Hugh and Janice. While I am sure S'Nash has never said this in so many words to other Naxians, or to the coordinator, they all have the idea that you are exerting pressure on it/him to overcome the natural, healthy distrust of artificial minds which all but Erthumoi possess. I trust you don't mind being used, too."

Janice raised her eyebrows and looked at her husband. Hugh shrugged, wondering what S'Nash had read of his reaction to *that* charge. "As long as he thinks they won't know better from reading our feelings," he tapped.

"Feelings aren't thoughts," the Naxian reminded them. "You could be happy or unhappy, anxious or calm, for any number of reasons unconnected with me. I've been uneasy about this misdirection, but with your aid and that of Rekchellet there should be no more trouble. Species other than my own, fortunately, seem not to be bothered by such acts as deceptive reporting, and—"

Janice and the Crotonite objected simultaneously, but the former was hampered by her need to use code. Rekchellet's broad wings spread indignantly— but briefly; the wind was still rising—and his drawing equipment fell to the snow.

"Are you saying that all Crotonites are liars?" His fury was plain enough even to the Erthumoi, and jolting to S'Nash, they felt sure. The feelings of the necessarily less articulate woman and her silent husband were presumably also clear to it/him. For several seconds the Naxian was silent, no doubt trying to spot a path out of the verbal trap so carelessly sprung; then Janice, who for a moment had intended to object as strongly as Rekchellet, let her normal conciliatory self take over. After all, the Naxian was supplying her with interesting data.

"I think it's just that S'Nash can see that without the Naxian sense it's easier for us deceive one another," she keyed, "and that a good many of us sometimes actually do that intentionally. In view of its/his current plans, it/he can't be—" she paused, looking for just the right word—"criticizing us for the tendency, Rek. Much less for the ability."

"Precisely," exclaimed the Naxian, uncoiling and rewinding the other way. "Thank you, Janice. I chose my words very badly indeed." It/he paused and looked at husband and wife intently.

"Rekchellet has agreed to help. I can tell that you feel some sympathy, Erthumoi. Can you help without causing yourselves trouble? You are closely tied in with the work of the Project as it stands, Janice, but what I suggest interests you."

Again the couple eyed each other, and again Hugh shrugged.

"How would Administration feel?" he asked. "I should think you'd have checked that."

"Ged Barrar is a Samian. You know that as well as I do. All he'd want is for the investigation to come up with a convincing answer, so the Project will be listed as a success on his administrative record."

Janice knew there was more difference among Samian personalities than S'Nash claimed, and was sure it/he knew it, too. However, there was no point arguing the matter in code, especially since Barrar had frankly admitted holding precisely that viewpoint as part of a much more complex one only hours earlier. S'Nash had no doubt based its/his remark on something much more solid than a general attitude toward Samians.

"I don't see why we shouldn't help out," she keyed, hoping her doubts didn't show, or at least that they were blanketed by her interest, but realizing resignedly that the snaky alien would know both feelings anyway.

"It sounds like fun," added her husband. She could see a smile which might mean enthusiasm through his faceplate. She was no Naxian, but knew he was thinking about their other job, and how it might just have become somewhat easier.

If S'Nash grasped anything beyond the sincerity of the Cedars' words, it/he said nothing to reveal it. Naxians seldom went out of their way to make their own emotions obvious to aliens. Janice, who tended to think the best of everyone, assumed that the need would never occur to them, and did not suppose they were displaying Locrian-style secretiveness about their powers.

"Can you tell us more about this seismic project?" she keyed. "Is it set up anywhere near here, or haven't they actually started work yet?"

S'Nash had no chance to respond. The wind had been rising ever since their arrival, making it progressively more difficult for the Crotonite to stay on the ground even with his wings tightly folded. Now a sudden gust lifted him off the snow, and he had to spread and flap frantically for control. The Erthumoi merely staggered, but S'Nash's serpentine form was snatched out of sight, moving as frantically as the Crotonite but far less effectively. Habranha's air was dense, but not dense enough for swimming while it was gaseous.

Hugh had thought of this problem not very long ago, he told himself bitterly. Unfortunately, he had not thought of a solution. Nevertheless, he could try. . . .

"Rek!" he keyed, with his sounder at full volume. "S'Nash has blown away! Are you in control, and can you hear me?"

The answer, barely audible over the wind and through the impedance-matching equipment in Hugh's armor, was encouraging if not courteous. "The last question would have been put first by a rational being. Of course I'm in control."

"Can you see S'Nash?"

"No. It/he either has hit the surface again and dug in for stability, or is at least under the blowing snow layer."

"But you can estimate something. You can certainly tell which way the wind is blowing."

"Which way, easily. How fast, never."

"Toward the town? Will the buildings provide shelter for him—for it/him?"

"No, fortunately. They'd—" the translated voice died out in the howl of the wind, which was still mounting. Hugh had to reason out for himself why Rekchellet considered it lucky that S'Nash was not blowing toward the buildings, which were not made of loose snow.

At least, he told himself, time would be no problem; the Naxian had been wearing full-recycling environment gear. As long as the armor itself suffered no injury, of course; the memory of the Pit event a few hours before was not encouraging. Still, the present temperature was well above that of liquid air.

But well below that of freezing water. S'Nash had better not blow into anything much harder than a snow hill.

Hugh had radio equipment of a sort, since he had to talk to Habras. He didn't like to use it since he lacked the Habra senses which went with its use. The natives could detect each other at up to three or four kilometers, and their radio "voices" were varied in volume according to need. Hugh lacked the electrical senses and had no way of knowing whether his transmitting volume was uselessly weak or painfully loud unless he could see the other participant in the conversation. Trial and error was seldom satisfactory and sometimes uncomfortable for the natives when Erthumoi impatience or Habranhan occupation delayed an answer until after the next trial.

There were no Habras in sight at the moment, however, and the safety chief faced what might be a life-and-death problem. He had spent a good part of his life in exploration; he was used to making quick decisions. More to the point, though he wasted no time in self-congratulation, he had foreseen that problems of this sort might come up and made preparations.

He turned the transmitter of his Habra communicator to maximum volume for a moment and uttered a single syllable which any of his native safety crew would understand; then he promptly brought the output back to a level appropriate for conversation at a hundred meters, set his receiver to maximum sensitivity, and waited.

It seemed far longer, but within two minutes he heard a faint Habra voice. He began repeating the alarm symbol at intervals of a few seconds, very slowly increasing his volume again, and at the third repetition received a welcome response.

"I sense you, Hugh. What's the trouble?"

Even by code, it took only a few seconds to get the main details across.

"All right. We see Rekchellet. The Naxian is presumably somewhere between you and him. I assume it's wearing armor."

"Yes. Full-recycling, plenty of metal and electrical gear. You should spot it easily."

"There's a lot of static being set up by the blowing snow, but if the armor is good we shouldn't have to hurry. Shall we bring it back to your location, or into the settlement?"

"Whichever it/he wants. Jan and I will start back now. The work here is done."

Characteristically, the Habra didn't bother to ask what the work might have been; though most of the species had a powerful curiosity drive and culturally had little grasp of the privacy concept, there was a job to be done.

The Erthumoi were more than content to leave the fliers to do it, worried as Hugh was about S'Nash. The gale was still rising, and it was becoming hard to stay on their feet. The layer of wind-borne ice dust was growing deeper, and orientation was becoming harder; only occasional glimpses of Fafnir could be obtained, and they could no longer identify the big waste pile with certainty. Horizontal vision was down to a few meters, and smaller dunes were forming and moving, not as fast as the couple could walk, but quite fast enough to make the surroundings confusing.

Finally, sure that at least one of his safety workers would be nearby above the drift, Hugh felt compelled to call again.

"Ted, or whoever is there, can you tell us which

way we're going, and whether it's toward the town?"

"This is Switch," came the prompt answer. "I've not been watching you closely. Move on a bit; I'll try to correct your course when I know what it is."

"Thanks. Just a minute." Hugh connected his armor with his wife's, using a five-meter safety line. She went ahead and he followed, keeping the line taut. "Our heading should show now," he keyed.

"It does. If you make no change in direction, you will be among buildings in half a kilometer; if you swerve a sixth to the right, you will reach them even sooner." Fortunately, Hugh knew Habra direction concepts well enough to know that the "sixth" which came through as a pure number meant a sixth of a right angle, and moved a short distance to his left to correct Janice's aim.

"Thanks. Any luck with S'Nash?" he asked.

"Not yet. We suspect it had a chance to dig in, and took it. It seems likely that this would have happened as soon as it could manage after being blown away. Rekchellet has told us where this occurred, and we are starting a more careful examination of the ground from there. If the wind would drop, there would be little trouble, but snow blowing against snow creates much friction fog. Wait a moment." There was a pause of several seconds in Switch's communication. "We think we have found it, dug in as I suggested. We can't do anything on the ground ourselves in this wind; neither can Rekchellet. Does the Naxian have Habra communication? It makes no answer to our calls."

"I'd think it/he would, but I don't know for certain, It/he may be hurt. Can you guide us to the place?"

"Yes, easily. Simply head directly to your left. There will have to be correction as you near the spot, but that will suffice for now. The distance is only about three hundred meters."

As it turned out, Switch had underestimated the difficulty of keeping the pair of Erthumoi aimed properly, and heading corrections were frequent, especially as they neared the burial site and forgot repeatedly to keep their line taut. Once there, however, actually finding the suit of armor was simple enough. Janice began calling the Naxian by code, but got no response; either the snow was muffling the sound, the wind was drowning it, or S'Nash was indeed in trouble. Hugh remembered the drastic steps taken a few hours ago in the Pit, and began to worry again even though he knew that the present ambient temperature was far above that of liquid air.

"You are there!" the Habra reported suddenly. "It is between you, a meter or so to the left of the line connecting you. Its depth is about a meter—yes, draw together as you are now doing. You are right above it. A little digging should be all you need. We'll stand by, though."

Digging in loose snow and high wind, with no tools but their armored limbs, was easier than they had expected, since displaced ice dust blew away instantly. The hole they produced tended to fill almost as fast, but this time they did not have a hillside sliding down on them. Both pairs of hands met the tube of Naxian armor almost simultaneously.

Hugh raised one end, strongly relieved to find it not frozen rigid. A quick glance showed that he was not at the head, and they both hand-over-handed to the other end, raising it to look anxiously into the transparent helmet. A pair of gold-brown eyes looked back at them.

"You're all right!" exclaimed Hugh for the second time in less than an hour.

"Quite," came S'Nash's calm response. "My armor is in perfect shape. My thanks for an efficient job of rescue; I was expecting it to take much longer."

"You weren't worried?" keyed Janice.

"Of course not. The wind would not last indefinitely; even if I were not found, I could easily dig out when it ended."

"Unless a five-meter dune had stopped right over you," keyed Hugh.

"I didn't think of that. Neither did Janice, I perceive. The danger was worth the reward."

The Erthumoi had no chance to get this remark clarified.

"Trouble!" roared the settlement's danger horn.

4

AND ICY DEATH CAN COME FROM SUNLIT NIGHT

The modulations giving details of the emergency were hard to make out over the wind, but listening carefully the Erthumoi read most of the message.

"Not the Pits this time," keyed Janice.

"No specific location—something or someone missing!" agreed her husband. He called Switch, presumably still overhead. "Where and what? Can you get in touch with Central Watch? Who's on duty there?"

"Missing person. Reported from Supply Arrival by Third-Supply-Watcher. Naxian Th'Fenn is on watch, its companion was not identified."

The distance to the supply warehouse on the other side of Pitville was over two kilometers. Hugh thought quickly.

"S'Nash, can you wrap around one of us so you won't blow away again?" The Naxian coiled about his waist without verbal reply.

"Switch, or one of you, please steer us toward the town. We can find the warehouse once we're among buildings."

"You should not need our help for more than another minute or two," the Habra replied. "The edge of the squall is almost here. Snow is settling very quickly only half a kilometer to your west. If you wait briefly, you can make the trip on your own, without having to listen to heading corrections."

"Good. Thanks. We'll wait. Is Rekchellet still with you up there?"

"Yes," the Crotonite answered for himself. His own translator was also radio-equipped, as he had as much need as his chief to talk to the natives.

"Good," keyed Hugh. "Please get over to the supply depot and learn what you can. Do whatever seems in order. I'll head that way until I hear from you again, but if you can manage the whole thing by yourself I'll be glad to take S'Nash back to the quarters first. Keep me posted, please."

"I'll be there as soon as the squall gets past the depot. I'm over it now, but can't go down. I'm having the horn cut."

Hugh acknowledged and stood waiting with some relief. The last few minutes had been fatiguing, and the alarm horn, whose howl ceased a moment after Rekchellet finished talking, carried subsonics designed to be disturbing to the Erthuma safety chief.

Supply vehicles from the port, where ice gave way to ocean, regularly parked by the largest of the settlement buildings, a half-kilometer-square, two-story structure used primarily as a warehouse. This was not quite a kilometer east of the Pits.

Most of its personnel were either Locrians, able to examine the contents of containers without opening them, or Erthumoi with their high gravity physical strength, recruited mainly for that quality. Hugh knew none of them very well personally, and hoped that Rekchellet would face no problems demanding tact by either party before he and Janice got there.

Another thought crossed his mind as the wind began to slacken.

"Switch, or whoever is up there?"

"It's Ted, Hugh."

"Fine. Have the sentries reported who is missing, or at least what sort of person?"

"No. I asked, and Th'Fenn replied that it, too, had asked and been told that the supply chief didn't know."

"That seems strange."

"So I thought. I wanted to investigate myself, but you told Rek to go and I thought I'd better stay here in case you had further orders."

"Good. Thanks. I think I'll head for the warehouse anyway as soon as we can see. Janice can take S'Nash home."

"I don't need to go home. My armor is in perfect condition, and so am I. I have no duty scheduled for many hours and am as curious as you are about the disappearance. I will come with you, and Janice wants to come also."

One did not question a Naxian's reading of emotion, and Hugh knew his wife's feeling anyway; assigning her to serpent care had been unavoidable, in his own opinion, and if she hadn't shared it she would probably have spoken up even more quickly than S'Nash had.

It was some minutes before the air cleared, and many more before the trio reached the site, the Erthumoi's diving fluid roaring in their ears, the other showing no signs of exertion obvious to its/his companions.

Rekchellet was already there. So were two other Crotonites, three Erthumoi, and three Locrians. Moments after Hugh, his wife, and S'Nash arrived, half a dozen natives including Ted settled out of the sky around them.

Beside the building, its power unit melting the snow beneath it and ice encrusting its hull and cabin windows, stood a tracked cargo carrier. Its doors and hatches all seemed to be sealed, at least on the side which Hugh could see.

"What's happened? Who's missing?" he asked of the world in general.

A Locrian gestured to indicate that she was the speaker, and answered. "This truck arrived a short time ago. It was not scheduled, but that's not unusual. It was obviously on automatic control as it approached, which is not surprising, but it parked itself which, as you know—" the voice of the vaguely humanoid and less vaguely insectile speaker took on a perceptibly prim tone even through the translator—"is less usual. We waited for a minute or more. There was no communication from within, and no one emerged. We examined it closely and there is no person or other living being aboard. I therefore reported missing personnel to the Safety Watch."

Hugh decided to face what was presumably going to be the music.

"Is there a robot?"

"No." Hugh and Janice looked at each other; one of the other human beings, whose thoughts had apparently paralleled the Cedars', gave a grunt of surprise. "Just the automatic controller, which I judge to be of Crotonite manufacture," the Locrian concluded.

"But you know that someone has been there." Hugh made it a statement; after all, the missing-person alarm *had* gone out.

"Yes. There are food containers which seem to have been recently used; at least, the traces they still contain have neither dried nor decayed noticeably. There are two sleeping units which appear to have been used and not repacked. Waste recyclers—"

"What species?" cut in Janice. She was not squeamish about waste receptacle contents, but felt that the Locrian had made her point. She wanted more useful information.

"Crotonite—"

"Nonsense!" the tone was indignant. "Why would any flier ever travel in a crawling machine, and how would he even get into a—a *sleeping unit*. Fliers don't wrap themselves up to sleep; they perch or hang, ready to fly!"

The Erthumoi wondered how Rekchellet was reacting to this outburst from his fellow. Privately, Hugh thought he would try to find out from S'Nash, later on. The determination strengthened with the Locrian's calmly unhurried reply.

"If one allows himself to be blown away instead of flying, one strikes obstacles." The translator carried no sarcasm or other feeling that Hugh or Janice could detect. Possibly the Crotonite did read something, however, for he fell silent. "I am only Counter-of-Supplies, but I am not blind. I am certainly not as blind as beings whose vision is cut off by walls and armor. I have told you some of what I saw inside this carrier. I will tell you the rest, such as seems important, if you give me time. If you prefer, you may open it and see what your limited senses permit for yourselves. You must eventually do that in any case, since translated words are of admittedly limited value. Shall I continue?"

"Please," said Rekchellet, to the interest of Hugh and Janice. They had not been sure his language contained an equivalent for the word; they could not remember his using it in their hearing in the Common Year they had known him. The other Crotonites said nothing, but their heads turned sharply toward him as the word was uttered. The beaked faces remained expressionless as far as the Erthumoi were concerned, but once again Hugh hoped he might get information later from S'Nash.

"I did not mean to imply that *only* a Crotonite was on board. I had not completed my remarks, you will remember. The nature of the food remnants indicate a Flier of that kind, but the control station is configured for Erthumoi hands, body shape and size, and senses, though Locrians could operate it easily. However, such a being must have been wearing recycling armor, as no food or wastes of that species can be seen. There is also the frozen body of a native Habranhan."

Hugh's job responsibilities took over. He knew none of the natives present by name except Ted and possibly Switch, who might be one of the others, but two were carrying translator units and would presumably understand his questions.

"Can your people survive being frozen, with or without advanced medical treatment?" he asked, with the recent Naxian incident in mind.

"No," came the definite answer. "If Counter-of-Supplies is correct, there is nothing to be done. I take it," the words were now clearly addressed to the Locrian, "that you were speaking literally, and did not merely mean 'extremely cold.'"

"The body is embedded in a block of ice, and the body fluids also seem solid, I fear. I am not familiar enough with your anatomy and physiology to say what other damage, if any, there may be, and it would take a very long time to make a detailed comparison of the body with one or more of you. It would be more practical to have an examination made by one of your own medical specialists, even if his or her own senses are stopped at the surface. You presumably have techniques for dealing with that problem."

Hugh, the sense of urgency gone, let his mind go back to what seemed to be the central problem.

"Counter-of-Supplies, does the truck's fuel cartridge provide any information?" he asked.

"Not to me. It's depleted enough to have made many trips between here and the ocean since last being charged, and still holds enough for many more. The truck could have spent much time, and gone anywhere on this hemisphere, since its last servicing."

"Thanks. Is there evidence of any other people having been on board?"

"Nothing direct. The food evidence indicates a Crotonite, the sleeping equipment at least two Erthumoi. It seems likely that the latter were using recycling armor, and there is nothing to show whether or not there were more than two, or whether or not still other species, also in self-contained suits, were present. It seems unlikely from the size of the cabin that there were many, unless a large number of Samians were for some reason riding close-packed, without artificial bodies."

"But you have seen no evidence of that."

"None."

Neither Hugh nor his wife had a clear idea of the Locrian sense's limitations, nor how it worked. Unlike the Naxians, the beings were deliberately secretive about its nature. Janice, like many others, had asked one of them the reason for this and been answered frankly enough.

"If you Erthumoi learn how we do it, you will be moved to develop means of blocking our sight. Most of you value what you call 'privacy' on occasions. We don't want it blocked, any more than you would like to be blindfolded without warning."

Janice was not alone in having her scientific curiosity turned on by the situation, and had done much thinking. Her husband, however, was more concerned with clarifying the present situation.

"Then, to keep things simple, we're missing a Crotonite who was riding instead of flying, and two Erthumoi."

Hugh had a strong interest, quite aside from the clumsiness of code, in keeping the summation terse. There was one well known reason why a Crotonite might not be flying. Some nations, some whole planetary cultures, of the species had the grisly practice of amputating the wings of those assigned to deal diplomatically with "slugs"—the various nonflying species, held in contempt by conservative Crotonites. The custom was far from universal, and neither Hugh nor his wife wanted to mention it, since to many Crotonites it seemed as repellent and uncivilized as it did to Erthumoi. Rekchellet, they knew, was one of these; they didn't know about the others.

"Check the port for what they know of Carrier ABBI-THTHIN-11," Hugh keyed the sentry group, knowing that microphones scattered through the town could be counted upon to relay his code. The Guild symbols were visible, not too clearly, under the coating of ice. "If its recent route can be determined, equip fliers, with good lights if necessary, to cover it—aircraft, Crotonites, Habras, anyone not busy at Level B or higher work. Send me whatever new information comes in. Coordinate as usual."

"I thought Erthumoi dropped everything when life, especially Erthumoi life, was at stake," remarked one of the previously silent Locrians.

"We have that tendency," Hugh admitted, "but I don't yet know that this isn't simply a group who sent the carrier here unmanned for their own purposes and are in no trouble at all."

"Why is it carrying the body of a native?"

"I don't know. My first thought was to check the port to find out about the truck itself, which is already being done; my second is to ask Habras if there is any objection to our lab's trying to date the body. If the problem doesn't resolve quickly, I'll either appoint a boss for it or get rid of this diving juice and do my own bossing. Let's open up this truck and see if there's anything inside that Counter missed."

The crust of rime ice which obscured—to the non-Locrians—the view through the control compartment windows also covered most of the upper body of the vehicle, and had to be scraped away from hatch rim and outside controls before ingress was possible. It was two or three minutes before the string of white warning lights which outlined the hatch began to blink and the bottom-hinged section swung slowly out and down, presenting a rampway ridged for traction and negotiable by feet, wheels, tracks, or bellies. This led into an air lock occupying almost the full five-meter width of the truck body, with inner doors in both fore and aft walls. There was ample room even for the Crotonites and Habras, and all swarmed up the ramp. Counter-of-Supplies made sure the entry was clear, closed the outer door, and, without asking Hugh, opened the forward inner one. The safety director and his wife led the way to the control section.

One of the other Locrians opened the other door and, accompanied by most of the rest of the group, went aft to the living and cargo sections.

Counter-of-Supplies had been quite right; there was no living being, and no robot more complex than the built-in automatic driver, on board. The body of the native was in the cargo space. It was rather smaller than any of the Habras present, about three and a half meters long and under thirty centimeters in diameter at its thickest. Its general structure was similar to that of a Terrestrial dragonfly, with distinct head, thorax, and long abdomen. The head had about the same volume as that of an Erthuma, and the four eyes mounted equally spaced around an imaginary circle a little forward of the midpoint of the skull could, given adequate backup nerve wiring, provide stereoscopic vision in all directions except directly behind. The three pairs of wings, only a little over half a meter long, were attached to the thorax and now folded back against it and the forward part of the abdomen. The body plates had the typical random patterning in shades of red, with wings a barely visible transparent yellow.

Still without checking with Hugh, the three Erthumoi supply workers began carrying crates to the air lock. Rekchellet stopped them.

"Wait. Do you know what's in those crates?"

"They're standard food containers, going by size, shape, and label," answered the largest of the human beings, rather impatiently. The Crotonite stared at the boxes for a moment. He was at least as imaginative as Hugh, and shared the Erthuma's responsibility for general safety. Then he gestured with a wing tip to one of the Locrians who was standing silently by. He was casual about using the Locrian ability, though he understood it no more than Janice did.

"Look inside." The being addressed had already uncovered her single eye for deep-penetration work, not because she knew that Rekchellet was Hugh's deputy but because it was part of her routine supply-handling job.

"The labeling is correct. This," she indicated one container, "is food for Samians. The other two now being transported are for Crotonites. One has been unsealed, and six of the unit packages originally inside are gone. The wrappings of two are—"

"Hugh!" Rekchellet did not wait for the rest of the report. The Erthuma acknowledged from forward, and he went on, "Crotonite food is missing from the cargo."

"How much?" the coded response came at once. The Locrian answered before Rekchellet, who opened his beak and then realized that he didn't know how much a unit package represented.

"Packages for six normal work-and-rest cycles are gone from one of the crates. However, only two sets of wrappings are in the waste receptacles on the truck."

"Suggesting that a Crotonite spent two days or so on the truck, going Reason knows where, and then left with food for four more."

"A reasonable inference, I would say."

"How about Erthumoi food?"

"The evidence is that any Erthumoi aboard were using recycling suits," Counter-of-Supplies' translated voice reminded him.

"True, but please check food anyway—and any other points you think might tell us anything. Even emergency supply food tastes a lot better than the stuff from a recycling suit, and it's worth looking for signs of nibbling.'"

"There is another object of possible interest on board."

"Who's speaking?"

"Third-Supply-Watcher. The truck has a tech-specialized translator supplement containing four modules."

"I'm coming. Open it up and we'll see who can read their labels. Maybe we'll have to put them in the main—"

"That won't tell us, if no one here uses any of the languages," pointed out Rekchellet.

"One move at a time," tapped Hugh as he entered the compartment. "Do you have it open yet?"

The Locrian silently indicated the small, rectangular metal container, one of its sides now folded back on a hinged edge. The modules were hexagonal prisms about three centimeters in length which might have been cut from a lead pencil, though none of those present would have used that simile. They were shiny black, and could have been made of any of half a hundred of the common information storing materials. All could see the four mentioned by Third-Supply-Watcher, resting in holes in resilient packing material. There were two more holes of similar size and shape, empty. There was no way of guessing whether these had been occupied when the truck set out on its journey. Hugh dismissed the point as unworthy of worry.

Everyone silently examined the prisms as Third-Supply-Watcher removed them from their housing and handed them around. Janice and Rekchellet started to speak almost at once; being a practical person, the woman yielded the floor.

"This one holds a Crotonite language, but I don't know which world or group. I don't recognize the coding after the main set symbol." Hugh nodded, which was much easier than acknowledging by code; Rekchellet was familiar with the Erthumoi gesture, the Naxian wouldn't need it, and it didn't matter for the moment whether the others grasped it or not. Waiting a moment to be sure her winged

friend had no more to say, Janice keyed in her own
point.

"Two of these have Erthumoi main set symbols,
but hold different languages. One I can't guess; the
other is almost surely one from Earth itself—low
code number; look, Hugh." Her husband looked, and
nodded.

"I learned a little Swahili in required Human History, never mind how long ago, but I don't know its
translator symbol. We could try it," he keyed. "Do any
of you others know any of the Mother Tongues?"

One of the Erthumoi started to answer, but
Rekchellet cut in abruptly.

"The research would be interesting, but it would
be more straightforward to ask the people themselves when we find them. We now seem to be certain that one Crotonite, two Erthumoi, and
one—what is the other module? Has anyone recog-
nized it?" Two or three negatives punctuated a background of silence.

"Do you all know the set symbols for your own
translator codes?" This time the affirmative answers came from the four star-faring species represented. "Then there could also be a Samian or a
Cephallonian—"

"Surely not without other traces of its presence!"
S'Nash spoke up for the first time in many minutes.

"Well, maybe just Samian—or pardon me; no
doubt a Habra could have been present in recycling
armor." Hugh and Janice smiled to themselves. A
Crotonite's apologizing was a memorable event,
though, of course, Habras were fliers and thus not
subject to "ground slug" prejudice. "Anyway, this
sort of guessing is pointless; what we know is that
people are missing and need to be found. Even if
they're missing and in no trouble, and merely failed
to tell where they were going, they need to be
found—if they're stupid enough not to file travel

plans, they're stupid enough to get themselves in trouble later."

"And you don't really have to be stupid to get in trouble," added one of the Erthumoi. Rekchellet ignored her.

"When we find them, our questions will, no doubt, be answered easily."

"Where to look?" keyed Hugh.

"We start along the route of the truck, of course."

"Ocean four hours away. Crotonite passenger consumes two days' food before disappearing. What was the truck route?"

Rekchellet's face could not show a smirk, and the translator failed to get one into his voice, but both Hugh and his wife read the body attitude.

"As Counter-of-Supplies mentioned, the mechanical driver of this vehicle is of Crotonite manufacture. It will have recorded the path taken—unless," Rekchellet slowed uneasily for a moment, "unless it was specifically set not to. I'll check. We should be able to trace its path, including such details as halts along the way."

"And whether any hatches or cargo doors were opened?"

"Well, probably not. That would not be considered a navigation matter. However, there should be traces at any place people emerged."

"In blowing snow?" keyed Janice. Rekchellet shrugged, his wing joints brushing the carrier's ceiling.

"If we seek carefully enough, yes. Hugh, I can handle this; it's far too much trouble for you to do everything in code. I'll arrange the search after checking this driver and finding out from Pwanpwan and the Port whatever we can about this vehicle's recent doings and who was using it and why. You and Jan are full of pressure juice and set up to handle problems in the Pits, which are more likely to need quick answers anyway. You could hardly go hunting all over the Solid Ocean, even if Spreadsheet-Thinker could be argued into releasing an aircraft for you. We fliers can do the job much more safely and efficiently. What would they say in Pwanpwan if we lost a flying machine on a search job?"

"What would they say if we lost a person without searching?" countered Hugh.

"That would probably depend on the person. We've already lost some, it seems, but as far as we know now it was their own fault, not ours. I'll do the checking. You can stick to the Pit work. If Pwanpwan is so worried about the missing people that they want machines to look for them, too—all right; if they care so little they don't even want to risk people from the Project, well—it's not all right, but I don't know what we can do then. I'll keep whistling to you."

The Erthuma pondered. Objectively, Rekchellet was quite right on every point. Hugh sometimes had trouble being objective, but decided he could manage for now, at least until he learned so much about the missing truck occupants that he couldn't help thinking of them as people. Janice was probably already worried about them, but—

Rekchellet, who had been on his way to the control section for much of his recent speech, began talking again. "The route has been recorded inside the driver guide. I can have it print a trip table for you, but it will be quicker simply to set it to backtrack and start at once."

"Who can go? We'll have to check with Administration. Also, we don't have information from the other end—"

"Supplies aren't unloaded yet—"

"Wouldn't it be better to examine the record and shortcut to places where the truck stopped?"

The remarks and questions almost drowned each other out. All were vocal; neither Hugh nor Janice attempted to say anything in code. Both were still thinking.

"The supplies don't matter," snapped the Crotonite. "They can be unloaded later. They may not even be ours. I am free for ten hours, and Kesserah here can take my next sentry call. That will give me another six. If the search takes longer than that, we can make more involved arrangements—oh, Lightning. The truck has no neutrino transmitter. Shortcutting won't work—"

"Why not?"

"If they did this on purpose, there's no way of telling at which stop they actually left; they could have set others into the control before they left. We'll need to—"

"If they left on purpose, and are concealing themselves on purpose, why are we bothering to look for them?" asked the same being who had suggested the shortcut procedure. "It's obvious that you *want* to find them and *want* to know why they did what they did, and I can understand that; but what good reason can you offer for risking your own safety and the Guild's property, and possibly slowing Project work, to satisfy irrelevant personal curiosity?"

The Crotonite hesitated, and Janice cut in.

"Maybe not all of them are acting on their own, or in good judgment. They could need help. I agree that Rekchellet should go, and at least one other who can drive the truck or fly or both so that they can search near the track as well as along it."

"I can set it to drive itself, and do the flying as well, Jan," was the slightly indignant response. "But we'll have to get a transmitter. Is there one here in the warehouse we can use without disturbing Spreadsheet-Thinker?"

"There are several here," said the Locrian supply chief, "but it seems unwise to—"

"I'll clear it with Administration. This is certainly a safety matter," Hugh cut in. "Let Rekchellet have it, please. He'll need it to get his information from Pwanpwan anyway." The Locrian gestured silently to two of her Erthumoi assistants, who promptly disappeared into the building. Hugh turned his attention to Rekchellet.

"Of course you *can* go, as far as time is concerned, and I certainly won't stop you if you think it's best. But should you go alone? In *your* best judgment? As a safety specialist?"

After a moment of silence Rekchellet shrugged again. "No. Of course not. Who else can come without upsetting routine?"

Realizing that she'd better speak quickly or not at all, in view of Rekchellet's tendency to get any given task under way as quickly as possible, Janice keyed in a matter which had taken her interest from the first. She didn't know where the frozen body had come from or who might consider it personal property, but it was the largest and most complete object Habranha had provided so far bearing any resemblance to a fossil.

"Hadn't we better unload the body?" she asked.

"Why?" asked Rekchellet. Before the woman could key an answer, he provided one himself. "Oh. I see. A very good idea. If we find the missing people and they don't want to answer questions, the fact that we possess their specimen may make them cooperative."

"We'd better find out whether it's a specimen," Hugh pointed out. "Ted, is it likely that this could simply be an accident victim, or someone who's missing from a Habra project?"

"I see no way to tell. I agree with Janice that we should unload it before sending the truck off. Later I or one of us can examine its ornaments more closely and try to identify it."

Minutes later the truck was trundling eastward toward the ocean on automatic control. Its cockpit windows had been cleared by heaters, and Third-

Supply-Watcher was looking out through them. Rekchellet and two Habras were swooping back and forth above the vehicle. The rest of the supply personnel had returned to their building, while Hugh, Janice, and S'Nash were walking and crawling, this time with no haste, toward the residence area.

Hugh still felt a little tense, and wondered what word might come from the other end of the road to the ocean. He relaxed only a little when the Locrian's first promised report from the truck reached the safety office on schedule.

"We are still following the road. The truck's air sweepers are operating much of the time, but the snow has not been very heavy. The fliers are remaining in sight most of the time, as agreed."

Establishment of a routine calmed Hugh enough to let Janice get him away from the office. The Erthumoi left their snakelike satellite for a brief visit to their own quarters, and for a few minutes seriously discussed whether they should get rid of the pressure fluid to free themselves for more varied activity. Both of them felt that this might prove necessary, but both knew that the feeling might be subjective, fed by the general discomfort and inconvenience which went with diving juice and by the curiosity generated by the unoccupied truck. Both taking on and getting rid of the fluid were operations needing hours and calling for much discomfort and reorganization of body mechanics; neither step was ever done lightly, to be reversed again shortly. If they "de-pressed," either an untrained Erthuma pair would have to take on the duty or part of the Pit work would have to be, by Hugh's standards, inadequately covered. He could accept neither.

There was, of course, another solution, but none of the other races would accept it. Not yet. Neither husband nor wife felt that the time for *that* sales pitch had come. Even S'Nash's robot interest hadn't reached that level.

They were still debating when the second report came in from the truck.

And the third. Rekchellet spoke this time.

The information from Pwanpwan had arrived. The truck had left the Port ten standard days before, but was not involved with the Project. The Guild knew only that the vehicle had been taken for unspecified Darkside research by a Samian whose identity could be supplied if necessary and that it had been boarded by a Samian, presumably the same one, by two Erthumoi, and a Crotonite just before its departure. There had been some surprise at the presence of the flier, but like the others he or she had been wearing environmental armor and there had been no way to satisfy casual curiosity about identities.

Hugh was intrigued by the confirmation of their earlier ideas, and its addendum.

"A Samian, too? That's interesting. It couldn't have traveled far from the truck without special gear, so—" he fell silent for a moment. "You're still following the road, I take it?"

"Well, not exactly. I was about to tell you."

"You're off it? Which way? How far?"

"Well, not very far. The autodriver pulled us off to the left, which is north, about fifteen minutes ago. It went about two hundred meters, started up a hillside, and the engine stopped. I can't seem to get it going. Third-Supply-Watcher can't see anything wrong with it, but of course she doesn't know very much about these machines."

"Do you?"

"Of course not."

"Can you tell whether it's power or control?"

Rekchellet hesitated for a moment.

"Well, sort of. If I turn off the automatic driver, I can start the engine and move the truck around, but the moment I engage the auto the drive simply cuts out."

"You're sure you're not at the end of the recorded path in the automatic?"

"Nowhere near it. The record readout shows it's been far into the dark hemisphere, to a point about a hundred and fifty kilometers north of the Cold Pole. It's clear and unambiguous, and I don't see why the driver can't make the truck follow it."

The Erthuma looked at each other but found no inspiration. There was no more reason to expect Rekchellet to be familiar with Crotonite guidance devices than for Hugh to have expertise in Erthuma-made vision transmitters. The identity of the manufacturing *species* was irrelevant.

Their minds ran on parallel tracks that far. Then Janice began to smile.

HERE HILLS MAINTAIN THEIR STANCE NO MORE THAN WAVES

Hugh could see his wife had thought of something, probably something which would annoy or embarrass the Crotonite. He was a little surprised when she leaned over to bring her code sounder near the microphone of the neutrino transmitter, since she usually got no pleasure out of irritating people; then he relaxed when her fingers fell away from the keys. She turned toward him, the smile replaced by a thoughtful frown.

"Hugh, I can't tell him. It's too silly. Didn't he, or someone, say that the autodriver was Crotonite equipment? I'm sure I remember that."

"Right. They didn't say what world, though. Rek hasn't mentioned any trouble with using it, but that doesn't prove it's labeled in his own language. It could be a model standard on any number of their planets. Why?"

"Why would a Crotonite *ever* design or build an automatic controller for a *ground* vehicle, let alone make so many that it's a stock item in galaxy-wide use?"

"Why should this one have been made for a ground— Oh!!" A slow smile, similar to his wife's moments earlier, spread over his face; then, like hers, was replaced by a more serious expression, and Hugh looked consideringly at the microphone. After a moment he keyed a message.

"Rek, I take it the instructions on that driver don't help."

"I don't know the language they're in, much less the abbreviations. And don't bother to ask about instruction manuals. I don't see one around, and if there's anything certain it's that it wouldn't be in any language I know."

"But you said it had produced a record—a readout—of the route the truck had followed."

"That's in numbers, on a map which is simply a vector diagram. No terrain, just coordinates."

"You can read the numbers."

"Sure."

"Then that language can't be too far from your own. Still, I suppose reading tech in it might be a bit—well, never mind. Could you follow that course and drive the truck manually?"

"I suppose so. So could Third-Supply-Watcher here, I expect, with about a five-minute lesson in reading the numbers. It would be a nuisance. We'd have to identify vertical coordinate information and ignore it and—oh!" The next few seconds gave only no-symbol-equivalent signals from the translators. Husband and wife smiled at each other. At least, they hadn't had to mortify their friend by explaining the trouble themselves, though this didn't mean that he wasn't mortified.

"I suppose," Hugh cut in finally, "there's some way of making the autodriver ignore elevation instructions."

"Why should there be?" Rekchellet's voice didn't actually snarl recognizably, but both Erthumoi were quite sure of the feeling. Janice tried to be soothing, though this was difficult through the translator and doubly so in code.

"Wouldn't anyone ever want to get back *over* or *to* a particular place, without necessarily following the specific dips and swoops of an earlier trip?" she asked.

"I suppose so," came the grudging answer, "but if there's any way of telling this mess of defective diamonds to do anything of the sort, I can't read it off its key symbols."

"Then we'll have to follow the readout manually. Will that slow things down too much?" queried Hugh. "Are you listening, Third-Supply-Watcher? Do you think it will take long for you to interpret the driver's record?"

"I am listening. It should not be difficult to learn the number symbols; the ease of actually following the chart will depend on the nature of the path. It will probably be easiest for Rekchellet to interpret the whole chart to me now, so that I can work from memory instead of stopping to read whenever the direction changes."

"You can remember the whole thing?"

"Of course, once I understand it."

"Then you and Rek please take care of that. If you can tell about where you're going during any given hour, please let us know. Rek said something earlier about a place near the Cold Pole. I'm not expecting to lose track of you and the truck, but if only the expected happened I'd be helping Janice full-time at specimen dating, or be out where you are, studying dune motion."

"Of course. We'll keep sending the information in whatever form seems clearest once I understand it myself," the Locrian promised.

Hugh nodded, meaninglessly as far as the truck crew were concerned. There should be no problem expressing locations on Habranha; the world was only a little over three thousand kilometers in radius, but quite large enough for its own gravity to keep it decently spherical. It was tidally locked to Grendel, as Falgite-speaking Erthumoi called its red dwarf sun, in an almost perfectly circular orbit with its rotation axis at right angles to the orbit plane. Tidal forces had done all they could over perhaps twice the age of the Solarian system, and those of Fafnir were negligible. Hence there were no complications from libration, and longitude as well as latitude could be defined objectively without an arbitrary prime meridian. This was fortunate, since all the "land" on the sunward hemisphere was floating ice and the stability of the Solid Ocean glaciers was open to doubt.

Hugh again fought down the urge to get rid of the diving fluid and take an aircraft out to the truck himself. He knew he wasn't needed. Rekchellet was much better qualified physically to do search work over the Fafnir-lit snow hills than any Erthuma. Hugh didn't know Third-Supply-Watcher or all the Habras who were along, but he had no reason to doubt their abilities either. He and his wife had a natural desire to find out what had led up to the truck's arrival at Pitville and the source of its grim cargo, but so, presumably, did the others. They had as much right to satisfy the emotion as the Erthumoi, and could be trusted to pass any information along when it became available.

And there was a bright side to staying. They were also curious about the frozen corpse still lying outside the warehouse, and any answers to that problem were likely to be found right here at Pitville when dating and other analyses could be made.

Maybe.

The real trouble with the safety job, Hugh frequently told himself—he didn't waste code effort repeating the point to Janice—was that it was interesting only in spurts. The rest of the time he had to spend trying to think up things that might go wrong and arrangements he might reasonably make to forestall them. That, at least, was what the job description implied.

There were actually other things to think about. Rekchellet's half-joking remark that S'Nash was distracting its/his fellow Naxians by suggesting that the Erthumoi were plotting to popularize the use of artificial intelligence had not been funny. It was very close to the Cedars' actual basic responsibility on Habranha, a fact it would be better for the Guild, or at least its local personnel, not to know. It would be naive to suppose that S'Nash, at least, hadn't figured it out by now; the words to Rekchellet could easily have been meant to tell the Erthumoi this. The Naxian, Hugh was sure, was quite subtle enough. Even if they hadn't, S'Nash must have sensed his and Janice's emotional response to the Crotonite's words, and there could be very few reasonable explanations for those feelings. No mind reading would be needed.

Of course, S'Nash it/himself seemed a bit—liberal?—by Naxian criteria; one could hope for tolerance of such activity.

Also, it/he had been using Rekchellet and the Erthumoi for personal convenience, and had given the former permission to return the attention. This might not have been meant literally, but taking it so could hardly be resented by a reasonable being.

Hardly.

Wishful thinking, Hugh. Let Jan get in on it, boy; she's better with non-Erthumoi than you are.

"We're starting." It was the Locrian's voice. "We cannot use full speed, since my attention will be divided between chart and surface now that we are off the road, and the surface itself is far from level. In a way, that will help since it will give the fliers more time to examine the region to either side, but I am more doubtful now about their chances of seeing anything. The hills seem to move fast enough to keep this machine from retracing its way in all three dimensions even after what I assume must have been a fairly short time, so it seems likely that traces left by anyone who went outside, or which were left by the truck itself when it stopped, will be covered."

"That would depend on chance," keyed Hugh. "Some stuff might be left clear for hours or days, depending on which way the dune was traveling. Keep

your eye ready for tracks; the truck is heavy enough to
have welded snow or melted its way into ice if it
stopped for more than a few moments, or perhaps even
if it didn't. A long stop should leave an ice sheet where
the engine melted the ground under it. Is there any spot
on the map which looks special? Something they
headed toward for a long time, or away from for a long
time?"

"Yes. After many short legs starting at the Port, it
indicates a great circle path of forty-two hundred
eighty-three kilometers to a point two hundred
ninety-one kilometers north of the Cold Pole, and
from there a similar one of even greater length, four
thousand four hundred ten kilometers, followed by a
dozen more short legs ending at the point where we
left the road."

"And, I assume, a final leg along the road itself to
here."

"Of course."

"Well, I suppose the long sections are as likely to
be meant to deceive as the short ones. Better not
shortcut."

"That was Rekchellet's opinion and mine."

"Good. Remember, the best indication of a stop
will probably be a patch of melted and refrozen surface."

"That may well be. I will watch."

"You especially," added Janice. "Even a thin
cover of blown snow would hide that from the fliers."

"True. I will watch carefully. That was why I expected to have to divide attention so much."

"It's worth any lost time, I'd say," keyed Hugh.

"I agree."

The Erthumoi leaned back from the microphone.
There was little they could do until more information came in from somewhere. Hugh almost hoped
for another emergency signal, which would at least
have made him feel useful. His wife could always

fall back on lab work, of course. That thought gave
birth to an idea.

"Say, Jan," he signaled, "Do we really need anyone's permission to go to work on the Habra body?
You only want tiny samples, and if it's anything like
as old as that wing, no one would mind anyway."

"But if it's a modern casualty, someone might. We
don't have any idea how old it might be. It's like a
fossil bought from a wandering dealer—no provenance. We can't even *guess* how old it might be because we don't know how long this species has been
around on Habranha in its present form—that's the
main reason for this whole project, after all. What
we could see in the ice *looked* modern, and Counter-
of-Supplies didn't mention any differences—"

"But she did say she wasn't very familiar with
Habra insides. We can't weigh that very much.
Come on. You could use a regular microcorer on the
ice slab, and get a bit of body plate or even some inner tissue, and no one'd be bothered. They wouldn't
even have to know. You wouldn't have to check out
special equipment from anywhere; you have everything you'd need in your own lab right now."

Janice frowned thoughtfully.

"Did all the Habras who saw the body go with
Rek?" she asked after a time.

"No. Only two."

"Can you get in touch with any others and ask if
the body ornaments on it showed through the ice
well enough to help with identification?"

"I guess so. I don't know who else was there, off-
hand, but Counter should be able to tell us. She
knows—no, maybe not. The Erthumoi and Locrians
were supply people, but the Habras came from outside about when we did. I think Switch went with
Rek; Ted was there, too, but would have stayed
around. Still, I'll ask her." Hugh turned back to the
microphone. He wasn't seriously bothered by his

wife's scruples; he shared them, actually. It was merely that his curiosity was overpowering them.

It took over a quarter of an hour to identify the natives who had not gone with Rekchellet; Hugh, in fact, had to conceive the notion of calling the truck and asking, when Third-Supply-Watcher could get its attention, one of those who had. The call and conversation were quick enough, but the gestation of the idea had been embarrassingly long. Another sixty seconds of relaying through the Habra community—it was nice, the man reflected, that *someone* could use radio freely here—had him in touch with a being the translator called Miriam.

Janice put the question to her, not because she expected to get more sympathy from a female but because Hugh's hand was getting cramped again. Miriam, winging somewhere near the settlement on her own affairs, answered readily enough.

"I could see the ornaments. The ice was fairly clear, and they caught my attention because I'd never seen anything like them. I couldn't even tell whether it was a man or a woman."

"Not even from the body?"

"Well—I—" Janice was quick-witted and hardened to many local customs. She guessed the likely cause of the hesitation.

"Sorry. I didn't mean to be rude. The ornament pattern, though—that was completely unfamiliar?"

"Completely. It corresponds to no age group, sex, or social organization I have ever seen in my life."

"And like most of your people, you've been all over your world."

"That's right, as far as the continent goes."

"Then it's reasonable to guess that this person has been in the ice for a long time."

"I can't think of any other explanation."

"And—please forgive me if this question is also discourteous—will anyone be bothered if we use a very tiny sample of his or her tissue to try to find out how long ago death occurred?"

"That would be all right even if there were known relatives, unless they were very odd people indeed. There are such folk, but I really wouldn't worry. All of us here would very much like to find out how long ago this person froze, and where and why; but I suppose some of that will have to wait until we find the people who were in the truck."

"And maybe longer," was Hugh's contribution to the close of the discussion. "Thanks, Miriam. Jan'll let us all know as soon as she has anything to tell." He turned to his wife and gestured, not using standard code, "All right, darling. Do your job."

She came as close to expressing affection as environment armor allowed, and headed for her lab.

Hugh thought briefly of bumping someone from a tour of watch duty which demanded a different sort of concentration and was, in its way, a sort of relaxation, but the seed of another idea was starting to sprout. He decided to stay where he was, as undisturbed as possible, to let it grow.

The truck had come to Pitville some undetermined distance from some undetermined point somewhere on Darkside, apparently under automatic control. The last seventy or eighty kilometers of that journey had followed the regular road from the sea. The rest had apparently been cross-country.

Why had it followed the road? Why had it not come into the settlement straight from its point of origin? Because someone wanted that point to remain unknown?

But then why allow the autodriver to make a record of the trip? And why set it to follow the road, even briefly? Any random direction of approach would be just as deceptive. Could the driver's chart have been falsified in some way? One of the people on the truck had been a Crotonite, who might very well have been able to make the device sit up and talk—and lie. So could the Erthumoi who had apparently been there, or any other passengers; it was a matter of learning the foibles of that instrument, not of belonging to a particular species. Any technically trained member of the Six Races, or, for that matter, a Habra, could probably have learned the requisite skills from a competent instructor in, at the outside, an hour or so.

Should he, Hugh Cedar, call Rekchellet and Third-Supply-Watcher and their companions and suggest that the search was a waste of time? Not yet. There's a broad gap between even the most reasonable hypothesis and the weakest real theory, and a good chance still remained that people were actually in trouble and needing help somewhere out there in the chilly half-light of setting Fafnir. Or somewhere where Fafnir had already set.

What was needed was a bit of testing. Someone, as a first step, should go out to the point where the truck had left the road and look for—what?

Well, for evidence of whether the machine had stopped there and for how long. It would have melted snow under its body, which would have frozen into a sheet of ice almost at once when it left. With luck, the sheet would even bear marks of its treads, and possibly other tracks.

Who should go?

Agreed—by and with himself—that the truck shouldn't be called back. It should continue what it had started.

A Habra or a Crotonite could get there from Pitville far faster than Hugh himself, even in the low gravity. Unfortunately, the only Crotonite to whom he could explain the whole matter quickly enough was Rekchellet. It would take too long to get any other even to start listening. The Habras were both pleasant and bright enough, but he didn't feel for the moment that he knew any of them that well, even Ted. Janice couldn't go any faster than he. S'Nash . . .

Maybe. The snake could travel fast enough. Janice, however, had shared with her husband her mixed feelings about the Naxian's trustworthiness, and Hugh had already felt much the same; his thoughts during the meeting at the ice dump had closely paralleled hers.

Strongest point of all: the ice sheet, if it had been produced at all, had not been noticed by any of those now with the truck. It could easily have been covered by blown snow, or even by an advancing dune. Third-Supply-Watcher would have seen it only if she had been looking for it, and she had presumably had no reason to do that. Or had she? Hugh remembered that something had been said about examining each place the truck had stopped for clues.

He hesitated; he rather liked the idea he was developing, and didn't want it to die too young, but common sense won. He called the truck. The Locrian answered.

"Did you make a really close examination of the place where you left the road before you started climbing hills?" asked the Erthuma.

"Not a deep one. There seemed no reason. There was no evidence of a prolonged stop, and it seemed unlikely that one would have been made so we checked only the surface. Is there reason to have gone deeper?" answered the Locrian with evident concern.

"No strong reason. I had an idea, but not a very well supported one. Not enough reason for you to turn back. Have you found anything of interest?"

"Not to the search. Judging by the differences between our actual height and readings on this chart, the hills move quite rapidly at some points and much less so at others. I have failed to find any systematic relation so far."

"If you do, put in for an advanced degree. Thanks." Hugh signed off, thought for another minute or two, and called Ged.

* * *

Janice had picked up a coring tool at her lab and made her way to the warehouse. The slab of ice was lying where it had been left; not even a Habra was watching or guarding it. Miriam's casual attitude toward the dead, or at least dead who weren't personal acquaintances, seemed to be shared by the other natives. In the interest of statistical reliability the Erthuma took two dozen specimens from points scattered the length of the body, though mostly from its upper surface—even here the ice slab was hard to turn over for a single human being in armor. She included some wing tissue for comparison with the specimen already found in the Pit.

The operation was simple enough, but had to be done carefully, with each item separately stored and labeled; the whole procedure took nearly half an hour. Absorbed in work she liked, Janice took no real notice of the variations in weather which occurred during that time—a spell of clear calm, with Fafnir shining on the work area to lend his small assistance to her own lamp; another howling snow squall which forced her to bend close to see what she was doing; a mass of slow-moving, nearly saturated, bitterly cold air which threatened to hide subject and equipment in quickly growing frost. She was used to Habranhan weather and paid attention to it only when its demand was insistent. She had checked her armor properly and trusted it.

Back in the lab, she started a nondestructive examination. Like the Locrian, she was not familiar with Habra internal machinery or tissue structure, and it took her some time to realize that what she was seeing was not entirely animal tissue. When she began to suspect, it was easy enough to check, though she had to go outside once more for a comparison specimen—not, of course, from the body. Not even from a living native, which might have demanded more diplomacy than she yet felt ready to use. She found her specimen quickly enough, immediately outside the building, and spent more time with the microscope.

Then she called Hugh.

"I don't think we'll need to notify relatives with this one, either," was her greeting.

"Another fossil, if that's the right word here?" Her husband's eyes lit up.

"It's not a fossil. It's a frozen specimen of original tissue. Don't make me get technical in code when you already know. It's certainly been buried, though."

"How old is it?"

"I haven't dated it yet. The point is that the tissue is riddled with microscopic threads which are turning out to be roots."

"You're sure they're not nerves?"

"I wasn't at first. Then I found them in parts of my ice cores which came from outside the body, and I've matched them from plant samples I took right at the lab door."

"Matched? Same species?"

"I wouldn't know. Same general structure. That body's been under the ice long enough for bushes to grow above it and through it. I'll run some dates now."

She signed off without formalities, and Hugh resumed thinking. Ninety seconds later he called his wife again.

"Can you save some of your ice for Red, or should he get his own scrapings?"

"I hadn't thought about microbes. Silly of me. I can supply him. Shall I call him?"

"I will. You're busy, and it'll take some explaining. He'll be annoyed if we can't give him an age, so get to it, Hon."

"Right."

Hugh got in touch with the Erthuma biologist who currently specialized in Habranhan microorganisms and explained matters as tersely as his listener would allow. His thanks consisted of a loud complaint that Biology had not been informed of the Habra body. Hugh pointed out that it had been in their possession less than three hours, identified as a specimen rather than a casualty for less than one, and that if Respected Opinion McEachern knew how to tell the age of such an object at first glance both Cedars would be delighted to hear his opinion. Meanwhile, Janice was attempting a carbon date and would let them know as soon as she could. He was welcome.

Hugh leaned back and flexed the fingers of his code hand.

Then he called the office of Spreadsheet-Thinker and asked whether he could have the assistance of a Locrian of third or lower skill rank for at least twelve hours. The problem would be explained in detail in a written report which Safety Chief Cedar would submit within the next hour to the administration office. He also wanted use of a land-traveling robot and an air-blast sweeper, but expected that this might take longer. It had occurred to him that there was no real need to go on foot.

Hugh then went to a writing keyboard with what would have been a groan of relief if he had had the use of his vocal cords. It was *so* much easier to write than to send verbal-substitute code. It was a pity that people doing complex and dangerous tasks couldn't take their eyes off them to read . . .

The report was done in a quarter of an hour; the brevity which code constraints had been forcing on him seemed to be carrying over. He transmitted it to Administration and three minutes later was informed that sweeper and Locrian would appear when the latter's sleep period ended, which was very shortly. Where did Safety Chief Cedar want them in half an hour?

"At the warehouse—the terminal where the road comes in from the port."

"You will be there to provide instructions, or should we relay them?"

"I'll be there."

The Erthuma frowned thoughtfully over the communicator. He would also need a Habra, of course.

Fortunately, Hugh could use one of his own safety people without having to clear through any higher office. There were senders, tied to his own desk, scattered throughout the settlement which would broadcast brief please-check-in messages at inoffensive volume to Habra safety watchers within two or three kilometers.

There was only one other decision to face.

Once again Hugh Cedar was looking at the pumps and condensers of the pressure-fluid equipment. He didn't look long. He and Janice had spent one period, over half a Common Year before, with only one of them set for deep diving. It had seemed a good idea at the time, but Janice, who had been the diver, had gone back to air breathing well before that project had ended. Little had been said later, but there was a strong mutual feeling that henceforward it would be neither or both when it came to pressure treatment.

Janice was currently far too busy to waste time in changeover, and Hugh could do what was now necessary easily enough with his armor full of liquid. Being less agile might be some hindrance, but being twice as heavy could only help.

Hugh filed a plan of his proposed activities for the next few hours. He didn't actually call Administration and tell them, but Spreadsheet-Thinker or Ged Barrar or any of their staff would be able to find him if they had to. So could any of his own safety people, especially a few minutes later when he made contact with Ted.

The Habra came plunging out of the dimly-lit

haze above the settlement before the Erthuma had
gotten fifty meters from his door, and swept in
graceful patterns above the street as Hugh made his
way slowly toward the warehouse and the start of
the Port road. He listened with interest as his chief
shared ideas. He listened again, with no obvious
urge to interrupt, as Hugh repeated them to the Locrian and to S'Nash who were waiting at the warehouse. The Naxian had apparently been examining
the frozen body but did not actually explain its/his
presence.

"Eleventh-Worker, we're going out to the place
where the truck which is being back-traced left the
road—you know about that?"

"I know about the truck which arrived under automatic control. I heard nothing of an investigation,
but I am not surprised that you are making one."

"I have an idea that it stopped at that point and
was deserted by the last, or perhaps by all, of its living occupants there. If it did, it should have left an
ice patch similar to that." Cedar indicated the spot,
now partly covered with drifted snow, a few meters
from where the ice-shrouded corpse was lying. "It's
likely that any such trace will be covered by now, either by blowing snow or a moving hill. We might
find it by digging, but obviously you can save us a
lot of time, especially if it's *not* there."

"Of course."

"The robot will use the sweeper to clean any area
you indicate, so that I can examine it too—"

"And I," S'Nash cut in.

"Sure, if you want to come."

"I find myself most interested, even though there
seem to be no Naxians involved in the Truck Mystery." The listeners could almost hear the capital let-
ters. "There does seem to be a Crotonite, and there
are reasons which I'll be glad to explain when you
have enough time why I am trying to understand the
flying ones better than I now do."

"No need, unless Eleven or Ted wants to hear. I suspect we all feel much the same on that point—though maybe Ted, as a flier himself, has no problem."

"You star travelers are all strange to us," the Habra admitted, "the Crotonites no less than the others. The fact that they can fly makes no real difference."

Hugh smiled at the thought of how Rekchellet would have reacted to that remark. "We ground types can ride on the sweeper," he keyed. "You're welcome, too, Ted, but I suppose you'll be more comfortable in the air. The distance is fairly short, and we could all make it under our own power, but it will be much quicker if we ride. Just a minute; I'm thinking like a glacier today."

He left the group without worrying how the translators might handle the simile, and entered the warehouse, where he remained for some time. When he finally emerged, two other Erthumoi were with him, carrying a neutrino transmitter. This they settled as firmly as they could on the sweeper carriage, received Hugh's coded thanks, and disappeared inside once more.

"Climb on!" keyed the safety chief. "We're on our way, unless someone else has an idea we can use. You all know what we're looking for, and my brain isn't working well today."

No one spoke up, and all but the Habra clambered onto various parts of the carriage.

"I'll stay within hearing," were the native's words as he lifted away from the group. Hugh gave the robot a quick code briefing, and the machine set the sweeper carriage in motion. The Erthuma watched his Naxian and Locrian companions narrowly at first, but neither seemed bothered by a robot chauffeur. After all, automatic pilots were used by everyone; they had been steering aircraft and surface vessels, spaceships and wheeled carriers for all the

Six Races, except perhaps the Crotonites, for ages. Artificial intelligence was something else entirely. Even the fact that this driver had taken verbal instructions could be rationalized; following a road was simple enough, even if the road might sometimes be blocked by a creeping hill of ice dust. They did, after all, have a sweeper with them, and neither the Locrian nor the Naxian considered the road's slope a problem. If the ground changed altitude, they might have noticed if they were walking or crawling, but certainly not while riding.

Hugh gave no thought to the possibility of road blockage; he knew it had been clear up to the point where the truck had turned off, since the vehicle's autodriver had given them no problem until then. Of course, something might have drifted into the way in the last hour or less, but that could be dealt with when and if. He was concerned solely with finding the turnoff spot, and had little doubt that the robot would be able to do so. Information from the truck had been adequate and precise.

6

AND CLEAREST TRAILS THE KEENEST MINDS MISGUIDE

"What's the strangest thing your people see about star visitors, Ted?" Hugh asked when they were well under way. "Or would you rather not tell us?" For once, he had no ulterior motive behind the question, except perhaps an urge to learn something before his wife did.

"You don't seem to *expect* to find each other different," was the prompt response. "You appear to be— well, an Erthuma is surprised when a Crotonite thinks differently from him, and a Samian is surprised when a Naxian thinks differently from *him*, and so on. Even Naxians, who are supposed to read feelings, seem to be surprised at some of the feelings they read. You're not blatant about it; consciously you do expect each other to be different, but you're still visibly startled, even the Naxians, when it happens. Why? You're from different places, with different foods and different comfortable temperatures and different ideas of what smells good and what's polite. Some of you lose consciousness part of the time—you can't seem to help it—and others get impatient about it and complain about the inconvenience to *them*. They don't consider the inconvenience it must be to those who—'sleep' is the word, I think."

"But we know that we're different, and allow for it!" insisted Hugh.

"You know it consciously. Somehow you don't seem to know it down where your minds really work. It's as though down below those levels where you know about your own thoughts, you're sure *you*

are *right*. That's a little frightening. We're glad
enough to have you here, of course. We spend a lot
of our time just keeping alive, diving to the ocean
floor for mud to fertilize the continent and working
out ways to take care of people whose farms are
melting away on the sun side without being unfair to
the ones who work to fertilize new land on the
colder shore; but we've liked to think about causes
and other abstractions as far back as our history
goes. You're certainly giving us new things to think
about."

"How far is that?" asked S'Nash instantly.

"What?"

"Your history."

"Currently, three hundred twenty two thousand
seven hundred seventy years."

"Habranha years, of course."

"Of course. We've been here and about the same
for a lot longer, we're sure, but every now and then
records get lost during transfer from the melting to
the growing side of the Ring, and sometimes records
are a little ambiguous because nothing much has
happened out of the ordinary for a few thousand
years. The arrival of you aliens will help enormously
with that problem for a million years or so, anyway."

The aliens all fell silent as they tried to work out
the time period in their own standards. For Hugh, it
was not quite twenty thousand Common Years. A respectable recorded history, better than any Erthumoi
world he knew of. But then, with a single planet-
wide culture, what could happen to make history?

It occurred to Hugh that thinking carefully about
the sort of mind now being displayed by Ted, who as
far as he knew was a perfectly ordinary working cit-
izen and not a professional philosopher, might answer that question. He'd have to make time for that
later. He'd also like to arrange to listen in on a
lunchtime conversation, or its equivalent, between a
couple of Habras.

Or better, half a dozen if his translator could handle it.

Keeping to the road was getting difficult. Another snow squall was blocking vision for Erthuma, Naxian, and robot. Ted was, as far as they could tell, still circling overhead; whether he was above the blinding stuff or relying on his other senses Hugh didn't know, and the wind at the moment was too loud to let him ask. Eleventh-Worker had made himself familiar with the packed-ice structure of the road itself under the drifts, and assured Hugh that he would know if they strayed off it; but the robot's inertial sense was probably enough to forestall that. The way was known to be straight as far as the turn-off.

"I hope we don't overshoot," Hugh remarked after what seemed months of blind travel. The robot promptly answered the implied question, in spite of the presence of non-Erthumoi passengers. It must have interpreted the words as an order, missing the implications that the ability to do this might bother the aliens. Fuzzy-logic systems could do that; Hugh hoped they wouldn't do it too often just yet.

"Seventy-four point three kilometers from the truck's starting point by the shed is the road distance I was told. We have three point four to go." If S'Nash and the Locrian read anything more than the literal information in the message, they failed to show it.

By the time two of the kilometers had been covered, the snow had stopped, but the wind had not. It was a biting, turbulent blast from their right—the south—which threatened at times to tip the carriage off its treads, had cleared every particle of loose snow from the road and left its solid surface visible to all, and was making it hard for the three living passengers to keep from blowing away. Above them, Ted was still flying, but his natural skills were being taxed near their limit and his strength even more so.

Every minute or two he would be swept out of sight to their left, to reappear seconds later as the wind eased a little.

Fortunately, the squall lasted less than ten minutes. When it abruptly ended, the Habra settled toward his companions, embraced the tube of the wind-sweeper, and folded his wings.

"I'm not as surprised as I was about that detached wing you found in the Pit," he remarked. "Mine feel as though they've nearly pulled off. Someone who ventured here alone and met turbulence like that could easily have trouble, especially if he wasn't protected from the cold. Did you find any trace of armor or clothing with that wing?"

"None," replied Hugh. "I was there when it was excavated. The wing itself was surrounded by the usual bits of plant root you find all through the ice, but nothing artificial."

S'Nash cut in.

"Did Janice date the plant material as well as the wing tissue?"

"Sure. She's been doing bits of root all along. The age was the same, as nearly as she could measure."

"Why would there be only bits, and not complete plants?" asked the Locrian. He was hard to hear; they had passed the region cleared by the wind, and the sweeper was in use again.

"The guess at the moment is that plants like those we see around here put down roots as far as they can to hold themselves in place, until some ice dune covers them and kills them—"

"It doesn't always kill them," pointed out S'Nash. "Some of them seem able to separate from their roots and blow away when threatened with burial— the tumbleweeds."

"True. Well, we've found a few complete bush specimens in the ice at various depths. Jan's been trying to make a depth-against-age table with them and the root fragments she's dated, but it hasn't been very consistent so far. Whole plants are usually older—hundreds of Habra years, even a thousand—than the root fragments at the same depth, and the bits themselves vary quite a lot at any given level, and, too, we only have specimens from this particular dig—the stuff the lasers have spotted between the Pits, and the occasional things we've actually run into directly as the Pits deepened, like that wing."

"Precisely." S'Nash uttered only the single word. Hugh felt sure it was meant more for him than for the others. He would have continued lecturing gladly had he been able to speak, but his fingers were getting tired again, and there was silence for a time as the sweeper carriage trundled along. He wondered how much Eleventh-Worker had taken in.

Hugh knew little of Locrians and their social systems, and couldn't guess at the interests and mental abilities of someone presumably fairly low on their labor scale, judging by his name. His one question so far had been very much to the point; it would be best to assume that he was grasping everything unless he indicated otherwise, and risk the possibility that embarrassment would prevent his revealing ignorance. It was easy to regard the being as a person, despite his vague resemblance to a four-limbed insect.

"We have two hundred meters to go, if the distance you supplied is correct," the robot interrupted Hugh's cogitations at this point. Eleventh-Worker did not wait to be instructed, but peeled back the outer lids and exposed his single eye for full penetration, not bothering to rise or shift position to get a clearer "view" ahead. Hugh watched closely, indifferent to S'Nash's knowledge of his efforts, but failed to observe anything which he and Janice hadn't discussed before. The Locrian sense was still a mystery to him.

"Slow down, please," Eleventh-Worker requested after a moment. "I want to examine everything

within twenty meters on each side, and we're going
much too fast for a careful look."

The robot obeyed without consulting Hugh; he
wondered how S'Nash and Eleventh-Worker felt
about that. They showed neither surprise nor revul-
sion nor any other emotion Hugh could read. The
Naxian, it seemed likely, had merely recorded the
event as another bit of evidence; it/he was, one
could reasonably infer, gathering data on how intelligent the "limited decision" robots Hugh had acknowledged using in Pitville might actually be.

"You suspected that the truck stopped for a time
in this area." Eleventh-Worker's words were a statement, not a question. Hugh agreed. "Stop here.
Sweep the snow away for the next fifteen meters
along the left side of the road, and an equal distance
away from it."

Again the robot obeyed without waiting for
Erthuma confirmation, and the roar of the sweeper
battled that of the wind. No heat beam was used this
time, and Hugh felt sure that S'Nash was noting the
fact and considering its implications about the robot's intelligence. There were more items for it/him
to think about in a few seconds; the loose snow billowing from the surface where the jet of air struck
was swept back toward the watchers by the wind,
and still without consulting anyone the robot cut off
the blast, moved the sweeper around to the upwind
side, carefully keeping its tracks off the area described by the Locrian, and resumed operations.
Within a minute the patch of bare ice predicted by
Hugh appeared from under its white covering, some
of the blanket sticking and resisting stubbornly for
seconds before flying away in fist-sized chunks.

The exposed surface was not perfectly smooth.
Examining it closely, Hugh and the others decided
that it must have stayed slushy long enough for
blowing snow to be caught and build odd-shaped

mounds and towers which had frozen to the substrate far too firmly for the sweeper to remove.

Among these shapes, however, tread marks could be seen and even some motions analyzed. The truck had not come to a stop, paused, and gone straight on; it had made a turn, and Hugh felt he was not yielding too much to wishful thinking in deciding that the turn had been toward Pitville. S'Nash, more objectively, insisted that the truck could have been going either way—that they could, in fact, be examining marks left by Rekchellet more recently.

"We can call him and check how long he stayed at the roadside," Hugh pointed out. "That's why I brought the transmitter. We'll feel less silly, though, if Eleventh-Worker looks around for more signs of stopping, first."

"I suggest you make the call, Eleventh-Worker make the examination, and I look over this area more broadly," answered S'Nash. "That should make the best use of time."

Hugh was at the transmitter before it occurred to him that S'Nash could do the talking much more easily, but both the others were now invisible in the fog which had been thickening in the minutes since the wind had died down. It seemed too much trouble to look for the serpentine form, and obviously the Locrian had to do the examining, so Hugh energized the signal equipment.

Third-Supply-Watcher responded; Rekchellet and his Habra companions were in the air. She was able to assure Hugh that they had not paused at all at the roadside; the automatic driver had guided their truck away for some two hundred meters before reaching a point where surface elevation had changed enough since the vehicle's earlier passage to make it go on strike over failure to follow its vertical guidance—or less figuratively, had probably interpreted the failure as a malfunction and responded to a built-in stop command. Third-Supply-Watcher could tell precisely how far this was from the road and from where they had left it, if necessary. Hugh decided that it was not, and signed off with appropriate thanks.

He looked around to find himself still alone.

The fog had thickened. He could see for some three meters; nearly all of the sweeper and its carriage, but little else. S'Nash, Eleventh-Worker, and, he suddenly realized, the robot were all out of sight.

He had given the machine no instructions, which made its disappearance interesting, to say the least. One of the two possibilities which came immediately to mind was also disturbing. Hugh had been sitting on the sweeper carriage; now he slipped to the ice, stood up, glanced around carefully, looked at his left wrist, and for the first time realized that he was not carrying an inertial tracker—something he had solemnly sworn, half a Common Year ago, never again to be without on Habranha.

Going back for one now would be neither practical nor productive. Fafnir was intermittently visible, now much nearer the horizon than when it had illuminated Rekchellet's dive into the snow, and would furnish direction for a while yet if visibility grew no worse. The road surface itself was fairly easy to distinguish—clearance by wind was roughly up with coverage by precipitation for the moment. Looking for people might not be safe, but it was important.

And his code sounder should be audible; the wind was down for the time being, too.

"S'Nash? Eleventh-Worker? Are you close enough to hear me?"

The Locrian answered at once.

"Yes. I have covered about one hundred meters of the north side of the road, to a width of fifty meters and a depth of about three. Should I work the other side, or increase the width or length of my search pattern on this?"

Hugh thought briefly. "Width on that side, I'd

say," he finally pronounced, mentally filing the possibility that the depth represented a Locrian limit. "That's where things seem to have happened, if anything did. Can you see S'Nash?"

There was a pause, presumably while the worker looked around. "Yes," came the answer at length. "It/he and the robot are thirty meters to the south of the road, and about fifty to the east of your position, apparently examining something on the ground."

"Thanks." The Erthuma took another look at Fafnir and set out toward the still invisible pair. He would have been kicking himself had his armor allowed. So what if he hadn't brought a tracker? The robot had a built-in location system, and the Naxian had had the sense to use it. There had been no need for the safety chief to worry about losing personnel on this trip—where was Ted? He hadn't been on the carriage when the talk with the truck had ended.

Well, Hugh hadn't called him. He'd surely stay within range of the Erthuma's translator, unless—

He had. He responded at once, and Hugh's professional worries ceased for the moment. The native assured his chief that all of the party was obvious to his electrical sense, though he couldn't always actually see them through the fog.

"Can you tell me whether I'm heading toward S'Nash?"

"Not exactly, but you'll be close enough to see them in a few seconds."

"Did I start out right, or are they moving?"

"I didn't notice your start. They aren't moving now. The Naxian is examining something on the ground."

It/he was still examining it when Hugh came close enough to see distinctly. The robot was standing a meter or so away, motionless. The man tried to make out what was attracting the other being's attention, but between the fog and the poor light saw nothing. He turned his own lamp on the surface.

"What's there?" he keyed. Ted hummed to a landing beside them. S'Nash continued to examine the ice for many seconds before answering.

"I'm not sure," it/he said at last. "The marks are faint, and many of them obliterated. We're beyond the edge of the patch melted by the truck, but something has either chipped or melted or pressed small dents in the road ice—little cup-shaped openings. I don't recognize them at all. What do you make of them?"

"I can't even see them," Hugh admitted. "Ted?"

"Nor I."

"How big are they? I didn't know your people could see smaller things than mine, but maybe that's the problem."

"They're just over five millimeters across. There are a lot of small bumps and pits made by snowflakes which stuck or liquid drops which froze when they hit, and these are mixed in with them. I distinguish them only by their regularity. They form a pattern—so." A handler extended from the tubular armor and indicated, one after another, a row of dimples in the ice which answered his description. Hugh shook his head.

"I'd never have made those out from the rest of the marks. You think they're a track of some sort?"

"Can you see the pattern, Ted?" asked the Naxian. The Habra answered negatively.

"That's interesting. I don't know what they are, Hugh. A track is the best word I can think of, but I have no idea what made them."

"How far have you followed them?"

"They start at the edge of the melted surface left by the truck and end here."

"And they're perfectly uniform all the way? That's—oh, thirty meters or so?"

"About that. No, they're not all exactly equally spaced, and they're not all along perfect lines, but they're all—I can't come up with a word. They're *related*. That's the best I can say." S'Nash looked briefly at the robot, but if it/he had planned to address it, the intention was dropped before anything was said.

"Do you think someone or something left the truck at this point?" asked Hugh bluntly.

"I have no opinion. Something could have, certainly. This could be a trace, but so far it's no help. I don't know what it could be a trace of."

The Erthuma hesitated, then turned to the robot.

"Make a record, to hundredth-millimeter precision, of the marks pointed out by S'Nash."

"I fail to distinguish them from the other marks."

"S'Nash will indicate the strip in which they lie. Record the entire strip."

The Naxian extended its/his gleaming armored body in a straight line. "Parallel to this, near side thirty centimeters to my right, twenty wide, starting at my tail and moving forward to my head. You should probably include my image for scale."

"That will not be needed. Absolute measurements will be included in the record."

"All right. When you reach my head, stop, and I'll go forward to mark the next segment, and so on."

The robot made no verbal response to this, but followed the instructions. Within a minute it reported the record complete.

"All right," keyed Hugh. "We could spend hours here, but I doubt we'd find anything more. Can any of you suggest anything specific before we go back to town?"

Ted spoke up rather diffidently.

"We seem convinced that the tractor stopped here for a time, after traveling to some part of the Solid Ocean. Right?"

"Right." Code and translated words mingled.

"Then some of the melted ice might contain plant remains from wherever it had been earlier. Should we not collect some of the frozen material, to be checked for root varieties?"

"We don't know how species vary on the different parts of the dark hemisphere," objected S'Nash.

"Not yet," answered the Habra. "If what we gather here shows any difference, we will have something to look for."

Hugh and the Locrian agreed eagerly, while S'Nash acknowledged its/his own error with less enthusiasm. They were not equipped with proper containers or labeling materials, but they were only about seventy-five kilometers from Pitville. Ted winged eagerly away, and returned, having exceeded by a wide margin what Hugh had thought was his species' speed limit, in less than two hours with a sack carried in his handlers.

This proved to contain fully a hundred small transparent envelopes, each already numbered, and a large recording sheet. The others had filled the time by extending the search area, but not even Eleventh-Worker had found anything except the place where the autodriver had stopped the truck. This had left another sheet of ice, but no markings of the sort S'Nash had found at the road.

"Janice says to fill every one of the bags, and if any record is ambiguous you know what she'll do," the native reported to Hugh. "She says that any clue to what part of the truck anything fell from will be helpful. She also wants at least twenty chips of plain ice from the melted area, with no plant remains visible in it."

"That shouldn't be hard," answered Hugh.

"Visible to whom?" queried Eleventh-Worker.

"I'm sure she meant me," replied the Erthuma. "I doubt there's anything on the planet in which you couldn't spot impurities."

"You flatter me. I have no reason to believe that my resolving power is any better than your own. I am merely less hampered by what you find to be obstacles." Hugh filed this remark as well.

"All right. Let's dig. S'Nash, point out one of those track marks, or whatever they are, please; I'll chip it out complete for the lab, too."

The Naxian complied, and in due course the envelopes were filled. "Due course" meant a fortunate twenty minutes of absolutely still, clear air; another twenty of rising fog, while Fafnir slowly sank behind a hill to the northwest; and ten of increasing wind which cleared the view again but threatened to broadcast the collecting envelopes over the snowscape. Two of them were indeed snatched from unprepared hands to vanish against the dimly lit whiteness, but they were of nonconducting material, quickly picked up a frictional charge as they blew across the snow, and were found easily enough by Ted.

Hugh suspected that the Naxian was a little disappointed by this, and that it/he would have liked to make another test of the robot's powers. The Erthuma was just as glad that nothing of the sort had happened. He didn't want things to go too fast.

They restored the envelopes to Ted's bag and sent him back to the settlement and Janice. The ground travelers boarded the sweeper caisson and returned more slowly. It would be half of another Common Day before Fafnir really set, but the sunlet was now behind hills nearly all the time, and the road was almost completely dark. The organic members of the group were tired and hungry, but still reasonably alert. Hugh called the truck twice during the trip to learn whether Rekchellet had found anything.

The first answer was a simple negative from the Crotonite himself, who chanced to be inside and resting, though about to go out again.

The second, a little over an hour later, was answered by Third-Supply-Watcher. Hugh was exhausted enough to react only very slowly to the report that all the fliers were out of sight and had not communicated since Rekchellet's last departure from the vehicle.

However slow, the reaction was violent enough. The robot's inability to get more speed out of the caisson they were riding made it worse. For an instant, Hugh considered taking it on the track of the other vehicle. Then sanity prevailed. The trail was unmarked, and even though both he and S'Nash were wearing recycling suits Eleventh-Worker was not. They were simply not prepared for an indefinite trip. There were supplies on the truck itself, but no assurance that they could find it; the communicator, as a by-product of its near-instantaneous signal speed, could not be lined up—all direction-finding devices from the earliest radio days had depended basically on the fact that the carrier impulse reached one side of a loop antenna or similar structure measurably earlier than the other. The Habras with Rekchellet and the truck also seemed to be gone even if Ted could get close enough to talk to them directly.

Hugh ordered the robot to take them back to Pitville at the greatest possible speed.

A little later he explored the idea of sending the robot alone to the truck's aid. The machine, however, had only auditory communication, understood only Hugh's own language and code, and carried no translator. Also, it was probably not a good idea to entrust an artificial intelligence with that much responsibility in front of S'Nash and Eleventh-Worker.

The Naxian and Locrian had heard the message from the truck. Ted presumably had not. Hugh now called the Habra down and explained the situation. The native, not surprisingly, responded with a plan of action.

"I'll head over in the general direction they were going and try to get in touch with Walt and Crow," he said promptly. "If you keep that light on at its present power and spread I can find you again more easily than by field alone. I can't hear you or talk to you from very far, of course, but as long as the air is clear I can see that light from many kilometers away, and I'll have no trouble sensing the carrier and robot from three or four at least. Ask Third-Supply-Watcher to call you right away if any of the fliers reports in, so you can tell me when I get back in touch."

"All right. If possible, come back over us to report, even negatively, every few minutes, please. It may help to know what areas we *don't* have to cover with an all-out search."

"I understand."

Hugh turned back to the transmitter to send Ted's request, and found himself getting no response from the truck. After several minutes of this, he rather foolishly asked the robot whether they were going as fast as possible. He was told that they were. The machine did not add anything like, "Of course," or, "As you ordered," but Hugh was sure that S'Nash was reading the embarrassment which washed over the Erthuma's sense of anger and helplessness.

Frustratingly, the air remained clear; visibility was hemmed in only by the surrounding snow dunes. At first, some of their tops were still brightened by the last rays of Fafnir, but these became fewer and fewer until only a few high cirrus clouds were illuminated.

After about a quarter of an hour they heard Ted's voice.

"I've covered only about twenty kilometers. I stayed low and looked closely. Have you heard from anyone?"

Hugh reported that the truck seemed to be missing, too.

"Would it be wise for me to climb to, say, a kilometer, which is about my limit in these clothes, and sense only for the truck, and examine it when I find

it, then report back to you, before looking further for
the fliers—who may be moving around anyway?"

"That seems a good idea, Ted." Hugh glanced up
and caught a brief glimpse of the slender figure sil-
houetted against the faintly lit clouds.

If the truck were really missing, something worri-
some was going on. Hugh had refused to let himself
get really concerned about the fliers, who might
merely have found something interesting and be trying to find out what it was before reporting, but a
dozen tons of surface-bound metal had no business
vanishing, or even letting itself get buried, which
was the easiest way for it to disappear. It might conceivably have been lifted off the planet by a spacecraft, but surely the Locrian would have considered
that worth reporting. If she could.

Hugh made four more efforts to call Third-
Supply-Watcher before the caisson brought them
back to the warehouse. None got any answer. By arrival time, Hugh had a formal search fairly well
planned. Finding Ged Barrar checking out the frozen
Habra body was extremely convenient. He saw no
reason to wonder about the administrator's activity,
which seemed perfectly in character. The Samian
had no obvious special observing or measuring
equipment on or in his skeletonlike walker, but this
meant nothing; Hugh knew nothing about the species' natural sensory equipment, and couldn't even
identify the "eyes" of the machine.

The Erthuma wasted no time on courtesy.

"I'm going to commit all my fliers to a search,"
he keyed as the caisson came to a stop. "We'll have
to reschedule some sentry assignments. Also, I may
need one of the transport aircraft—possibly; I don't
know yet whether I'll have to go along myself."

"What has changed?" came the slow response.

Hugh summarized the events of the last few
hours. Barrar said nothing for half a minute; the

Erthuma impatiently let the slow Samian thoughts wind to their next question.

"Is it necessary to find the truck? We know whose it is, and they are not really our problem."

"Third-Supply-Watcher *is* my problem. So are Rekchellet and the Habras with him, though I admit they may not be with the truck and are likely to turn up by themselves. The Locrian needs to be found, in my judgment."

There was another pause. "I agree. I approve your commitment of the flying personnel. Whether I can free an aircraft is another matter; I will have to get back to the office to check their status."

"Can't you just ask Spreadsheet-Thinker from here?"

"I prefer not to interrupt her cogitations. I'll let you know as quickly as I can." Barrar strode deliberately away.

Hugh had to be content with this, or at least to make the best he could of it. He unloaded the transmitter from the caisson by himself, dismissed robot and sweeper, left the communication device at the warehouse door, and headed slowly back to his own office—even more slowly than the Samian; so slowly as to be striding almost erect, instead of with the forward slant of an Erthuma in low gravity. His mind was very busy.

S'Nash writhed along just behind him, also silent.

There was a neutrino transmitter in the safety office, and Hugh made another futile attempt to get in touch with the truck. He decided against calling Barrar, who was presumably doing as much as he could to fulfil his promise. Hugh could have demanded one for emergency use, as he had at the time of the Pit accident, but he was not quite sure that this, even now, was a life-and-death emergency.

Not quite. Third-Supply-Watcher had a communicator at hand; *why* hadn't she used it?

Perhaps she couldn't.

Perhaps she didn't want to.

And any imagination, especially if freed from the chains of normal discipline by the acid of worry, could produce an indefinitely large set of possible reasons for either situation.

Hugh firmly welded the chains back together, and began calling his safety people. He also put S'Nash to work rescheduling the sentry assignments of the nonflying members of his staff. If the Naxian preferred hanging around in what should be its/his free time, it/he might as well be put to useful work, especially if Naxians were going to form almost the whole of the sentry crews for some dozens of hours to come.

Moments after he started calling, a Habra appeared at the office air lock and cycled himself through. Hugh didn't look carefully enough.

"Ted! What have you found?"

"This is Walt. We haven't seen Ted. Hugh, there's something strange going on."

The Erthuma recovered from his surprise, resisted the temptation to respond sarcastically in code, and confined his reply to "What?"

"Rek was flying well ahead of us and higher than we can go, when he called to ask if we could see a light coming our way. We did, and he said to watch but not get too close while he looked it over. We agreed. We couldn't see very well, of course, but could sense a dozen or so people flying with the light. We were expecting him to tell us what was happening. After he closed with the group, he said they were all going down. We followed, and they landed far ahead of the truck. A few seconds later his translator cut off. Then the whole group suddenly left in many different directions. We went in immediately but couldn't sense Rek's equipment, and it was too dark in the shadows to see him on the ground if he was there, and it was starting to fog in. We neither saw nor sensed anything. We spent a long time searching a five-kilometer radius, since the fog turned to snow. Then we decided it wasn't wise to stay out of touch so long, so we went back to the truck. We couldn't get in."

"What?"

"The outer door controls wouldn't work. It had stopped. We could see into the driver's section, and a Locrian was there, but we couldn't tell who; they all look alike to us."

7

A CLOSELY FOLLOWED ROAD
NO DISTANCE SAVES

Fafnir was a little higher above the horizon from
Rekchellet's viewpoint, since he was both farther
west and much higher than Hugh. Actually, he was
too high for ground searching and knew it perfectly
well, but he had no intention of staying there. There
had been pleasure in lifting himself into the clear
upper air, and there was some excuse, since it gave
him a chance to see and memorize a vast area of the
wrinkled ground below. He had no plans to map the
entire dark hemisphere mentally. Between his normal flier's nervous system and his trained drawing
skills he might indeed have managed this, but right
now he was only trying to match the route printed
out by the truck's autodriver with topography ahead.

He had done this several times since the back-
trace had started. Each time he had spotted valleys,
hollows, and clefts near the mapped line which
might have concealed people or objects which had
left, or been removed from, the vehicle along the
way.

Close examinations had turned up nothing so far,
but the surveys still seemed worth making.

And only he could make them. Thanks to his
smaller body and broader wings, he could fly much
higher than the natives, with or without protection
from the cold. A cynical Erthuma might have suggested that he had adopted this search technique to
make the fact clear to his companions. This was not
true, at least not consciously; the Habranhans were

fliers, too, and it had never occurred to Rekchellet to feel for them the ordinary Crotonite contempt for nonflying races. Also, his general attitudes had been bent—twisted, many of his own people said—by long association with Erthumoi like Hugh and Janice Cedar.

But still he soared high, examining the rippled surface below in the light of setting Fafnir, ignoring the fact that even he could study the spreading shadows much better from nearby. He also ignored the biting chill, which grew worse as the search carried them farther and farther into the little world's night hemisphere. Like his companions, he was wearing protective clothing on his body; like them, his wings were uncovered. Unlike theirs, his wings were living tissue, carrying circulating blood, rather than sets of thin, resilient, horny plates which grew only at the roots.

It didn't matter yet. In flight his body generated plenty of heat; the skin covering his wing membranes was full of insulating air cells, and only by deliberate inflation of the underlying blood vessels could he lose much body heat by that route.

Nearly five kilometers below him and about as far to the east he could see the lights of the truck, lumbering along its planned path. His companions were invisible since they carried no lights, but they would be within a hundred meters of the surface and a kilometer or two of the vehicle, contour-chasing, subjecting every irregularity near the mapped track to the attention of their eyes where possible and their other senses elsewhere. So far, they had passed two places where the printout showed sharp changes in direction, but neither of these had revealed any sign that the vehicle had either stopped or discharged anything. Third-Supply-Watcher had also made a careful examination at each site, looking specifically for any hole which might once have contained the frozen Habra body, but she, too, had found nothing.

With all he could see from this height firmly in mind, Rekchellet began to glide downward. He would do more good, until they had traveled another score of kilometers at least, sharing the work of close search. He targeted a hill a good deal higher than most, a few hundred meters to the left of the truck's intended path, as the center for a new sweep. Presumably the others hadn't reached it yet. Fafnir and the unmoving stars watched his descent.

He was still a kilometer above the hilltop, however, when he saw that one of the stars to the west was not motionless. It was not very bright, but easy enough to see. It was shifting very slowly upward and to his right.

He had no way of judging its distance, and for a moment thought it might be one of the orbiting stations which four of the Six Races now maintained over Habranha. He discarded this idea almost at once; all of these satellites were in the planet's orbital and equatorial plane, and the thing he was watching clearly was not. It must also, if in low orbit, be deep in Habranha's shadow to be in that direction, and presumably too faint to see. Even before he considered the possibility of an approaching spacecraft his great wings had tilted and swung his small body toward it.

Almost simultaneously its angular motion ceased. Straight away from him now? Or straight toward him?

A few seconds gave the answer and eliminated the spacecraft hypothesis. It was growing brighter too quickly. It must already be close, and small, and approaching.

Why straight toward him? There seemed only one reasonable explanation. It had detected him. How? He was carrying no light. Habra sense? What would Habras be doing here? His own companions had no lights, either. He called; like Hugh's, his translator carried a minimum-power radio transmitter, and Rekchellet knew some Habra speech himself.

"Walt! Crow! Can either of you hear me?"

"Yes, Rek. Have you found something?" came Crow's voice.

"I don't know. Do you see a faint light, getting brighter, approaching from nearly west?"

"Yes." There was some heterodyne squeal as both natives answered at once.

"Can you see or sense anything about it? It's still a little above my altitude, but seems to be descending slowly."

"I see only the light," Walt spoke alone this time. "Should we go up to see, or keep searching down here?"

"Come on up."

"Shouldn't one of us tell Third-Supply-Watcher?"

"Don't spend the time now—one of you would have to land and get her attention. You can't talk through the truck hull. If it turns out to be important, one of us can report when we know what to say."

That was a tactical error, and Habranha's chaotic nature took full advantage of it—though, of course, the planet itself could not be blamed this time.

The light seemed almost upon Rekchellet now, far brighter than before; bright enough to show him his own wings and body, bright enough to hide in its glare whatever might be carrying it. Walt and Crow were still far below, and could make out no details even with their nonvisual senses.

"Who's there?" called the Crotonite, transmitting on both his feeble Habra radio and the much louder sound waves of his translator's speaker. Rather to his surprise there was an answer; less astonishingly, it consisted entirely of no-symbol-equivalent sounds. The speaker was using a language Rekchellet's equipment couldn't handle. The chances were that the same was true in the other direction. One definite fact had come through, however.

The being carrying, or accompanying, or hiding behind the light was a Crotonite. The translators assigned a different class of tone patterns to each of the Six Races as standard policy. The information might or might not be helpful, since there were two or three thousand different Crotonite languages in use on more than that many worlds; since they were a flying species, a given Crotonite culture was usually at least planet-wide.

Besides his own, Rekchellet could just make himself understood in one other. The existence of translating equipment had not helped general linguistic skill, though there were philological specialists who could *produce* translator modules for use with newly discovered races.

He was not surprised a few seconds later to see the vague outline of a pair of Crotonite wings against the sky beyond the light. He gestured irritably to have the beam directed away from him; it was only much later that it occurred to him to be surprised that the gesture was obeyed. The lamp was not only aimed away from him but changed in adjustment; it ceased to produce a blinding glare, and allowed him to see the other flier fairly clearly.

There was little surprising about its appearance. Like Rekchellet, it was wearing a body sheath against the chill; unlike his, the protection seemed to include the wings, which reflected the dim Fafnir light with the sheen of polymer film. *Wing protection which doesn't interfere with flight is a new one,* Rekchellet conceded to himself. *Where is this fellow from?*

The newcomer made two more attempts to speak, apparently to convince himself or herself that it was futile, and then made a downward gesture.

"Walt, Crow, it's a Crotonite. He wants me to go down for some reason. I'm assuming he has something to show me, so I'm going. You two stay close enough to watch what's going on, but not too

close—if you can help it, don't let him know you're
here. If you see any reason, get away fast; one of
you warn Third-Supply-Watcher on the truck, the
other head straight for Pitville and Hugh with the
best report you can put together."

"Where is he taking you down?"

"I don't know. You'll have to watch."

The stranger was leading the way in a long but
quite steep dive, not merely gliding; there was evidence of a feeling of haste. Rekchellet followed. At
about one kilometer altitude a group of natives appeared around them both, crowding as closely as
wing freedom would permit. He could not see his
own Habra companions, but trusted that they were
following his instructions. Presumably, since anything they said to him would be broadcast in their
own speech and only translated at Rekchellet's end,
it would be heard and understood by these people.
This might be either quite harmless or quite awkward since there was no way to tell what the newcomers wanted or intended. Rekchellet was far from
paranoid, especially by Crotonite standards, but he
was fully as far from sharing Janice Cedar's tendency to assume the best of everyone. She was insane,
he knew; a very nice person, but quite out of contact.

They were ten kilometers or more from the truck
when the group at last swept over a low hilltop,
touched down on the slope beyond, and folded
wings. The Habras surrounded the two Crotonites in
a close ring, barely leaving room for lift-off if
Rekchellet had wanted to. The carrier of the light
was facing him, once more attempting to communicate by voice, this time not using the translator. A
few of his words—it was now evident that he was
male—aroused a vague feeling of familiarity in
Rekchellet; there might have been some historical
affinity between their languages. No ideas got

across, however. It was his actions which made the situation clearer.

He took a small case from his harness and opened it. The light revealed fully a score of what appeared to be translator modules. Pulling one of these out from among the rest, he gestured for Rekchellet to hand over his own translator unit. It did not occur to the normally suspicious explorer until much later that it would have been easier for him to take the cartridge and insert it in his own equipment without detaching the latter; quite unthinkingly he obeyed the gesture, removed the device from his own harness and handed it to the other flier.

At the same instant he felt his wings seized. Not painfully, not even very firmly, but solidly enough and for long enough. The modules flicked back into their case, his own translator unit was snapped to the stranger's harness, the light went out, and the Crotonite, as his Habra cohorts opened out to give room, spread and raised his wings and with a combined downward beat and thrust of stubby legs went airborne.

Rekchellet stood for just a moment in shocked surprise. In that moment another Habra snatched the tracker from his harness and was also gone. The remaining ones also left, each in a different direction, and the Deputy Safety Chief of Pitville found himself standing alone on a Solid Ocean hill with no means of judging what was occurring or why.

It had been a long time since he had been so angry, and for several minutes he was incapable of clear thought. He could only wonder what the purpose behind this silly attempt at stranding was— silly, since obviously he could get back to the truck or to Pitville; they hadn't done anything about his ability to *fly*. Was someone trying to annoy him for being friendly with Erthumoi?

Not likely. He was certainly unpopular among some Crotonites—had been ever since he had exhibited his painting of an Erthuma with wings, widely regarded as obscene—but there were few who would translate that into concrete action. They were civilized people. Their very superiority over the unwinged would keep them above that level.

There were Trueliners, of course—the ones who insisted fervently that Crotonites were direct descendants of the Seventh Race, and therefore were automatically entitled to all the relics of that species found by anyone anywhere. Could any of these be on Habranha and interested in Rekchellet? Conceivably; he had occasionally expressed disdain for their ideas quite publicly. But, again, what could even a Wildwinder expect to *gain* from this trick, however extremely and universally the colonists of that world might resent doubt of their mythical ancestry?

Then, as his temper cooled, Rekchellet wondered what might have happened to his companions. Would his attackers have tried to do anything to them, too? There was no way to deduce this; it depended on the reasons for doing what they had done to Rekchellet himself, and he could only speculate on that. He could no longer call the Habras, and with his equipment gone they could sense him only from nearby. Walt and Crow—and perhaps Third-Supply-Watcher—would have to take care of themselves.

No, that wasn't quite true. He could warn the Locrian; he could get back to the truck—he certainly remembered the way!—and tell her what happened. Deciding what to do was, after all, the important thing; hunt for explanations and theories later, you hatchling; *act* now.

Back to the truck.

Or back to Pitville? The distances differed by only a few tens of kilometers; the back-trace had led them east along the road, but since then they had been heading pretty much northwest, though there had been jogs in the path. Rekchellet visualized the map. Yes, distance meant little. Would wind make any difference to flight time? No doubt it would, but there was no predicting how much or which way on Habranha.

From Pitville, Third-Supply-Watcher could be warned by neutrino transmitter, but she'd still be alone. If Rekchellet went back to the truck, he'd be able to help physically and could report to Pitville just as well.

But how much help could he actually be to the Locrian? He'd been of little use to himself just now.

That thought made up his mind for him. He'd go back to the vehicle and try to make a better showing this time—if these whatever-they-were made trouble there. He didn't know whether they'd try, and he—forget it. That's back to premature theorizing. *Get into action, Hatchling.*

He swept into the air, beat his way upward, and quickly spotted the truck light. It was many kilometers away, but he knew just where to look. He flew toward it with all the power his great wings could use, but before he had gone halfway Chaos put in its bit. The light vanished in another snow squall. This one was deep, dense, and extensive enough to hide the hill-and-dune patterns which he had memorized so thoroughly, and for long, long minutes he circled impatiently over the general area waiting for the inevitable clearing to take place. It seemed like hours, and might have actually been over an hour—he never knew—before the winds died and the ice powder settled enough to let him match his memory once more with the view below.

The match wasn't perfect, of course, less because the dunes had moved—they hadn't, significantly—but because now Fafnir was almost at the horizon, shadows were far longer than they had been, and many of the smaller humps were no longer visible at all. Rekchellet had known what to expect; changing surface illumination was nothing new to him. Still, it took time to reorient himself, and to identify with fair certainty the valley which the truck should be traversing.

When he had managed this, he had to face the fact that no light could now be seen. That forced still another decision: should he remain at altitude and examine the surrounding valleys since he could just possibly have picked the wrong one? Or should he go down and make a really close examination on the assumption that the truck had stopped and become buried, had lost its lights, or had been interfered with by his recent antagonists?

The last possibility decided him. He went down.

There were numerous bumps and ripples in the fresh-blown snow, many of them quite large enough to have buried the vehicle completely. For a while, Rekchellet feared he might have to dig into thirty or forty individual dunes, with no tools and no certainty that any of them was the right one. He almost reconsidered his decision against reporting first at Pitville. Then he noticed that a strong wind, unusually steady for Habranha, was blowing along the valley and sweeping the piles of ice dust before it at respectable speed. The larger ones, close examination showed, were traveling westward at a rate of a meter every three or four minutes. If the truck were actually inside any of them, it should be uncovered in half an hour at the most, and with any luck much less.

Chaos helped this time. Ten minutes or so after he had started patrolling the most probable section of the valley, as figured from his memory of the original topography and the truck's speed, the shallow upwind slope of one of the larger dunes began to display a small projection. A few more minutes revealed this to be the hind end of the truck, now being left exposed by the advance of the wind-driven powder. Why it should have stopped and allowed itself to be buried in the first place Rekchellet refused to consider; there were too many possibilities.

He tried to land on it, but the smooth body offered nothing to grip; he was promptly blown away, and regained his equilibrium only after a second or two of mad fluttering. He did land behind it, and within a minute or two found that enough snow had gathered on his windward side and been scooped from his lee to topple him into a growing hole and start to bury him under a new embryonic dune. He was able to spread his wings and avoid burial only with difficulty. He settled finally on a nearby hilltop which seemed to be packed hard enough to promise some kind of permanence, and watched as the truck slowly emerged into view, or such view as there was; Fafnir had reached the horizon and the whole floor of the valley was now immersed in shadow.

When the main hatch was clear, though the front of the vehicle was still buried almost to the control room windows, the Crotonite flew down to the truck again. He was worried; not only were the outside lights off, but the control chamber was dark.

Total power failure in such a machine was rare enough so that he gave it only a passing thought. Why had Third-Supply-Watcher shut things down? Or had she been the one to do it? Were the ones who had stolen his communicators, or others of the same group, already inside, perhaps waiting for him? Maybe it wasn't wise to show himself—no, forget that, they'd have seen him already and have been expecting him before that if they were there. All he could do was get in fast, if that were possible, and do whatever seemed in order. . . .

A single wingbeat carried him to the door, and his small hands operated the opening mechanism. This was purely mechanical and should work even if the power had failed or been shut off. It did; the door swung out and downward, and Rekchellet was inside the lock instantly. He hit the switch which should close the door again, much less certain that this would work.

The portal promptly closed, however; there was
power. He groped in the darkness for the controls of
the forward inner door—he had been in this vehicle
only once before, and never in another like it, so he
was not familiar with its detailed operation—and
presently found them. Warm air, good air, with de-
tectable traces of ammonia and hydrogen cyanide,
enough to be homey without being dangerous to
Erthumoi or Naxians, swirled around him as the way
to the control room opened. The air had not been
like that before, and he had no trouble guessing what
sort of person would be in the control room.

As he shuffled forward on his stumpy legs, lights
suddenly went on. They were neither numerous nor
very bright, but adequate to let his eyes confirm his
sense of smell. A Crotonite stood by the controls
Whether it was the same one who had robbed him a
little while before Rekchellet couldn't tell, since he
had never had a good look at the thief, but he was
wearing the same sort of clothing.

There was no sign of the Locrian, but the room
was orderly; loose equipment was all where
Rekchellet remembered its being. He could hope
there had been no violence. There seemed only one
way to be certain, however.

"Where's Third-Supply-Watcher, my driver?" he
asked.

There was a brief answer, of which he understood
no word. The other gestured with a wing tip, however, toward the rear of the truck. It could be hoped
this meant that the question had been understood and
that the Locrian was back in the cargo section. It
could also be hoped that she was unharmed; it
should not have been necessary to use real violence
on the relatively frail being. Of course, a typical
Crotonite might not have been very careful with a
nonflier; Rekchellet turned aft, determined to make
sure. Third-Supply-Watcher was not a personal

friend, but her welfare and safety were part of his job.

A snarled monosyllable whose transmitted feeling was clear enough even if its precise meaning were not made him turn back to face the intruder. Two or three more sentences hissed and clacked from the other's beak; then all question of his identity disappeared. A flight harness was dragged into view from a shelf which had been hidden by one of the film-covered wings. A hand groped in the pouch attached to it, and Rekchellet's own translator unit was pulled into sight. He reached for his property, but the other gestured him back with another snarl, and groped once more in the pouch. A module was pulled out, examined in the dim light, and inserted in the equipment in place of one which the Crotonite extracted from its socket and tossed aside, to drift unregarded to the floor. Then the unit was handed to Rekchellet, who clipped it back in place on his own harness. It began to speak at once.

"You will stay and listen to me until I dismiss you, crawler with aliens. I know who you are."

"I have never denied who I am, and never expect to," snapped Rekchellet. His indignation was mixed with another emotion. In the improved though still dim light, he could see that the other's wings were not clothed but were partly prosthetic; the polymer film he had glimpsed in flight was not covering the membranes but replacing them.

"Don't talk to me as though you had self-respect. I tell you I know who you are. I have heard you deny your own hatch right. You have spoken of the Seventh Race as though you were a Cephallonian or a Samian, denying that there are only Six Races Between the Stars. You deny that your own people are the ones whose ancestors left the cities and machines we find on so many worlds, and to which we are entitled because we are their descendants."

"I deny only that it's been proved," Rekchellet replied firmly. "I'd like to believe it as much as anyone would."

"It's obvious! They were fliers—"

"Possibly."

"Certainly!"

"There are many flying people. The natives of this world are one set, for example."

"But the Habras are not related to us! They can't possibly be descended from the same ancestors!"

Rekchellet was about to point out the fallacy of this reasoning, but paused. He had never encountered a religious or political extremist, though Trueliners had been described to him, and only now began to realize what he was getting into. He could not bring himself to agree with someone he suspected of being from Wildwind, but he could see that outright disagreement would certainly interfere with his own job. He still wanted to know what had become of Third-Supply-Watcher.

Rekchellet had developed rudiments of the art of tact in the last Common Year or so, trying to keep on living terms with his own people and on friendly ones with Janice and Hugh Cedar.

"That's true enough, I must admit," he made a gesture indicative of accepting a social superior's opinion. "I didn't mean to deny such an obvious fact. I was worried about the Locrian who was driving this vehicle a short time ago; her safety is part of my assigned duty, and you wouldn't ask me to shirk a responsibility."

"I could easily criticize your accepting responsibility for the welfare of creepers." The other did seem mollified, Rekchellet noted thankfully. "However, your charge is unharmed. I removed it from the controls of my vehicle and placed it in the passenger section. I fear there is no Locrian food there, but it will do for a time."

"*Your* vehicle?"

"For the time being. I and a colleague arranged with the Guild for its use, and it is *my* responsibility. You wouldn't interfere with that, of course."

"Of course not. If it's yours, we have nothing to worry about—or disagree about, I hope. It arrived unmanned at Pitville, and our safety people were worried about those who had obviously been aboard. We had reason to believe that a Crotonite and two Erthumoi, and possibly others, were missing. It was assumed at first to be one of our own supply carriers, until we studied the record of its autodriver. Some of our crawler-workers even started to remove supplies." Rekchellet deliberately avoided mentioning the frozen Habra corpse which had been aboard; he wanted to hear what, if anything, the other would say about it on his own. He was not really suspicious yet, but increasingly curious.

"You spoke of knowing my name," he added after a moment. "You probably know also that my world of hatching is Tekkish. Is it at all likely that I have heard of yours? I am most known and active in the visual communication field, as you must be aware."

The other stared at Rekchellet silently for several seconds, making him wonder what could have been tactless about such a question. Surely this fellow didn't expect the whole galaxy of Crotonite worlds to know his name—or did he?

There was no sign of anger or other emotion in the answer when it finally came, however.

"My name is Ennissee. I feel sure you can guess my hatching world, but lest I embarrass you, it is Wildwind. You have heard of it."

"I have," agreed Rekchellet. "More relics of the—the Ancient Ones have been found there than anywhere else in the galaxy, I understand."

"Quite right. One of our reasons for being sure we are their descendants, naturally."

"I see." Rekchellet refrained from pointing out that Wildwind was known, on the basis of well documented history, to be a third-stage colony world and not the one on which the Crotonites had originally evolved. That planet had been well and solidly identified from its fossil record, besides being covered by documented history extending back before star travel.

This was a point one could safely infer that Ennissee would prefer not to discuss.

"By the way," said the Wildwinder in a voice which suggested that he was willing to drop controversial subjects for the moment, "I have been supporting some research here on Habranha much like that of the group you are working for. We've been digging with experimental equipment for remains of ancient life on the dark hemisphere. At first, I didn't like the idea of associating with—you know. However, it has occurred to me that your workers could be helpful. Your group is equipped to date specimens, of course."

."I understand so." Rekchellet accepted the implied truce, though uneasy about the sudden change of attitude.

"Good. We have found only a few traces of once living material until recently, but a few Common Days ago encountered the buried, frozen body of a native. We went to some trouble to conceal the discovery—you know how primitive people sometimes feel about disrespect for their dead—but it's in the cargo section of this truck. Perhaps we could smuggle it to your laboratory, when no Habras are around, and you could find out for me how long it's been buried."

Rekchellet thought rapidly. He doubted strongly that Ennissee had failed to notice the absence of the corpse, but was not surprised at the elusive language since he, too, was a Crotonite. He could now see a reasonable explanation for the sending of the unmanned truck and cargo to Pitville. Ennissee could take it for granted that the team there would examine the specimen in every way possible. His problem would be in learning what they found out about it.

An Erthuma or a Locrian would simply have brought the body in and asked, but that would have involved the tacit assumption that the Pitville workers were equals and conversing with them on that basis, something certainly very difficult and quite likely impossible for Ennissee. Rekchellet's presence was a convenience, obviously; he could get the information the other wanted, being on familiar terms with the aliens. Naturally, it would be necessary for Ennissee to make his own superiority to the grub-lover perfectly clear before voicing his own needs; it would be demeaning to ask a favor from, rather than give an order to, such a renegade.

Rekchellet was almost, but not quite, amused. He even thought fleetingly how his ability to be amused rather than bitterly indignant stemmed directly from his friendship with Janice Cedar. He was not objective enough, however, even to pretend to accept the suggestion of his own inferiority. The other's damaged wings were enough to save any Crotonite from that danger, even though they could still be used for flight.

"I'm sure they will respond to courtesy," was his answer after a bare moment of hesitation. "Naturally you'll be glad to discuss the source of your specimen. Its provenance will be of great importance to our own investigation."

S'Nash, had he been present, would certainly have been interested and possibly frightened; Rekchellet could perceive the other's indignation, but had no idea of its intensity. He was rather glad to have scored.

It was several seconds before Ennissee spoke again.

"You may follow me to my site," he said at last. "I must set the truck's driver to bring it back there as well." He seemed to have forgotten his earlier remark suggesting that he supposed the specimen still to be aboard. "Though it is a long way, we will fly to save time."

"How about my driver? I don't believe there is any Locrian food aboard."

"It will have to eat what there is. I do not choose to waste time carrying it back to your work site. Later that may be convenient." He turned to the autodriver and began to manipulate its keys, shielding the console with his wings. Rekchellet was not at all surprised to learn that the vertical record which had forced his own group to drive the vehicle manually could be cut from control, but felt rather annoyed at not having a chance to see how it was done. He used the time, however; the map was within reach, as was his stylus, and he quickly scribbled a few words, hoping someone would be able to read them.

"You may release your driver from the back compartment. You should also tell it that any attempt to cut off or change settings on this control will shut down all power. I will come back to recover it later, but it may be quite cold inside by then."

Rekchellet was not too disturbed at having an obvious maneuver foreseen and forestalled. He went back through the air lock section as the truck resumed its travel, and opened the door for Third-Supply-Watcher. She was not surprised at his arrival, naturally.

The Crotonite quickly passed on Ennissee's warning, adding no comments of his own. It was quite likely that they could be heard from the control section. Third-Supply-Watcher was equally cautious, merely acknowledging his words and following him forward. Ennissee paid no attention to her.

"We'll go now," he said briefly. "I've set the hatch to open for half a minute as soon as the inner lock door closes. You will follow me out. The truck will reach my site before I expect to need it. I assume you have warned your—your responsibility about the driver setting as I instructed."

"Of course."

"Do you consider it intelligent enough to heed all the implications?"

"Of course."

"Then come along." Ennissee led the way back to the air lock, waited until Rekchellet had joined him inside, and closed the forward door. As he had said it would, the outer hatch promptly started to yawn. The moment it was wide enough, Ennissee leapt through the gap. Rekchellet followed, and was meters away by the time he heard the panel close behind them. He cast only a quick glance at the moving truck, feeling pretty sure what the Locrian would do, and concentrated on keeping Ennissee in sight. The artificial wing membranes seemed no handicap; Rekchellet began to realize how long it had been since he had rested or eaten.

Inside the truck, Third-Supply-Watcher waited calmly until the two winged beings were out of sight. Then she went to the cabinet where the neutrino transmitter had been kept.

It was empty, and S'Nash might once again have been interested; but the Locrian said nothing even to herself. There had, after all, been no reason to suppose that Ennissee was completely stupid. She looked briefly to make sure the equipment was nowhere on board, wondered how far back he might have jettisoned it, and spent a few minutes examining the driver connections. This took enough of her attention to make her miss the natives who swooped briefly past outside during those minutes.

She was not expert in electromechanical matters and could not be sure of what she saw, but not even S'Nash would have detected any uneasiness in her manner as she stood motionless in front of the control console, thinking carefully, for another minute or two, and then shut off the autodriver.

8

AND CLUES MAY OFT BUT
LITTLE HELP PROVIDE

"Like Erthumoi, I suppose," Hugh keyed, not worrying whether his cynicism showed.

"No, you're easy. Your faces move. But what do we do about Rekchellet and Third? If it was she in the truck we should find out why, and if it wasn't we need to find out what's become of her."

"And where the new one came from. Right. So you checked in here. Good. I wish I knew what was best, but—where's Crow? Did he come back, too?"

"No. We thought of that, and then decided it would be smarter for one of us to keep track of the truck. It might start traveling again, or get buried, and be hard to find even for us unless we got within three or four kilometers; and the whole problem started with that truck, didn't it? And there are a lot of square kilometers on the Solid Ocean."

"It did. You were right. Are you tired, cold, or hungry?"

"I'd be glad to eat."

"All right, go ahead. Then tell every other flier in Safety what's happened. Send a pair of them out to find and relieve Crow so he can come in, too; you can tell them where to start looking, at least."

"Should I report to Administration?"

"I'll take care of that. Go eat." Walt left the office without further questions, and Hugh retuned the transmitter.

In spite of his recent conversation with Barrar, he first told Spreadsheet-Thinker's office what he was doing and why, delivering the information as a statement rather than asking permission. Since he was using code, they knew better than to ask for more details just yet, but Hugh was sure that his sudden monopolization of so much workpower would not go unchallenged for long. Barrar's calm acceptance of the situation had rather surprised him; Hugh doubted neither the Samian's willingness nor his ability to back him up, but felt better having the whole matter formally on record. He was not an experienced administrator even yet, but was learning.

He then retuned the communicator, and with rather more complication managed to reach Janice's lab.

"Hon? I think I've talked Spreadsheet-Thinker out of an aircraft, but it may take a while to materialize. There are things to do out there in the dark. Have you found out anything more about our iceberg?"

"Yes. Age. Tell you when we're together."

He confined himself to "That all?" His wife presumably had reasons for secrecy.

"H'Feer came by the lab with thanks. It/she's back at work. Wants a job in Safety."

"Good. See you."

Hugh was perfectly willing to have more and different people under his charge if Administration didn't mind, but was not going to discuss the matter without knowing more about the Naxian, especially about how well it/she had recovered from being frozen alive. That was something else which could wait. He signed off and left the office, still planning.

Janice was a thoughtful and foresighted partner. Hugh had mentioned wanting an aircraft. She knew as well as he that Administration would have to approve the request and, at reflex level, probably wouldn't. She greatly enjoyed the sense of accomplishment when it could honestly be experienced, and did some planning of her own.

By the time her husband reached their quarters,

she had called around and unobtrusively determined the present official location and assignment of all four of the aircraft used by the Project, just to provide Hugh with ammunition he might need.

She was not too surprised at his worried state when he detailed the situation to her; he was a responsible person, and Rekchellet a good friend. She showed him the information she had gathered about the aircraft. He looked at it, grinned, and did the best job of kissing her that a room full of diving fluid allowed.

"Beautiful. There are two they could spare without hurting a thing. I can surely talk them out of one, especially since some of our own people are now unaccounted for."

"Will they blame you for their getting lost?"

"Why? They approved what we were doing."

"What they knew of it."

"Spreadsheet-Thinker wouldn't like to admit there was anything going on here she didn't know about. It would reflect on her administrative efficiency. Come on; I'll have the use of that machine in five minutes."

Actually it was nearly five hours. Hugh had misjudged something. He thought some bad language, arranged for communication with the flying searchers he had so hastily sent out while on the way back along the road, and calmed himself with a meal as Janice had done. They even slept, briefly; he had not realized how tired he was, and she had been in the lab through most of his absence.

The hours were fruitful only in determining a fairly large area where Rekchellet did not seem to be. The truck had not moved, but the watchers could now see no one inside. They had not tried to enter or attract attention, judging that the search for Rekchellet was more important; the slow vehicle could be found easily enough, they now felt, even if it did resume travel.

All this was reported to Hugh by relays of his own personnel, and he in turn dutifully reported the details to Administration with ever louder insistence that he be given the use of a flying machine. He never understood with any certainty what caused the delay; Spreadsheet-Thinker remained noncommittal. The Erthumoi suspected that in spite of Janice's earlier research, one or more of the vehicles was being used without authority and the administrators simply didn't know where it was. Hugh almost mentioned this to S'Nash, when the Naxian appeared and asked how the search was progressing, but decided against it. The snaky being would already be aware of his irritation and coded complaint would be conversational overload.

Finally, however, clearance came. Hugh sent out a relayed message for one of the Habras or Crotonites on the search to come back toward Pitville to meet him and act as a guide. Husband and wife had been wearing most of their armor all along. Now they donned helmets, checked out, and made all possible speed to the hangar. S'Nash was now there, and while Naxians had no reputation for *radiating* their emotions, both Erthumoi felt a shade of self-satisfaction when it/he spoke.

"About the best we could get, I'd say." It/he did not amplify, and neither Erthuma went beyond casual agreement; but both wondered a bit.

Hugh had asked for the services of another Locrian, and there was a further brief delay while they waited for this one's arrival; naturally, he had not been released from regular work until after clearance of the flyer. The being appeared with what under any other circumstances would have seemed commendable speed and climbed into the ten-place machine, introducing himself as Plant-Biologist.

Janice and he talked quiet shop about Habranhan vegetation while Hugh lifted off and headed slowly northwest, blinking his lights in the standard here'sheadquarters pattern of the Safety Office. S'Nash, who had come aboard without asking administrative clearance, curled up behind the pilot seat and said nothing.

The truck, they knew, was nearly a hundred kilometers from Pitville. The flier could have covered the distance in moments, but not safely; there were too many living searchers in the air, many of them not carrying lights yet in spite of Hugh's efforts in that direction. The Habras were cooperative enough, but their eyesight covered nearly the full sphere and no one had yet designed a running light, other than a rather useless one pointing straight to the rear, which they could carry without the glare's interfering with the bearer's vision. From their own point of view, of course, their electrical senses made such equipment superfluous; they could detect each other and Hugh's ship with no trouble.

But if the craft were moving at anything like its full speed, they could never spot it in time to dodge.

After endless minutes, the radio receiver picked up a Habra voice. "I see you, Hugh. Descend to one kilometer, and slow down to comfort speed." This, to Habras, was about fifty kilometers per Common Hour. "Good. I'll be with you in a minute or two. You're heading in almost the right direction. I will come close enough to let you see me."

There was a pause. Then Jan jumped slightly as the crimson-patterned cylinder of the Habra's trunk suddenly appeared a scant two meters—less than its own length—above the pilot canopy of their craft. As usual, the wings were invisible, partly from their transparency, partly from their rapid motion; the cockpit light was bright enough to have shown them had they been in glide mode, since it was bright enough to show the body's color. Harness ornaments which both Erthumoi knew to signify maleness glinted.

Hugh gestured to indicate that he saw, and the

native drew smoothly ahead and down until he was directly in front of the cockpit and level with it.

"Follow. You'll see the truck in about five minutes," his voice came again. "When you do, tell me and I'll cut over to one side so I can watch you better. We'll both stand by in case you have anything for us to do. We just relieved the last pair, and can stay for a couple of hours with no trouble."

"I'll watch him," said Hugh to the others aboard. "You keep your eyes on the ground. Let me know when you see the truck." A mixed murmur and buzz of agreement allowed the man to focus his attention on his leader, and for the promised five minutes nothing more was said.

It was the Locrian who spotted the truck first, partly because the native led them directly over it and neither Hugh nor his wife could see straight down. Plant-Biologist, his vision not blocked by the floor of the little craft, calmly reported the sighting.

"The truck is below us. You will have to fall back or go to one side to observe it through any of your windows."

Janice was mildly annoyed, but tried to retain her scientific objectivity. They were still five hundred meters above the hilltops, and the Locrian's words had just invalidated her favorite personal theory of how their penetrating vision worked.

She pushed that thought into the background, as Hugh called to the Habra, slowed abruptly, and swung around in a tight circle to let more conventional eyes confirm the report.

It was correct. Dark as the landscape now was, with the rime-covered body of the vehicle little different from the ice dust around it, even human eyes could see it.

He went down as close as he could, but still could not see satisfactorily. The vehicle was in a narrow valley; if he flew low enough beside it to get a look through the driver's window, dividing his attention to take the look could be disastrous. There was no reason to suppose that the local hills were as loosely constructed as the waste pile at Pitville.

Still, he had brought Plant-Biologist along for a reason; he might as well use him. Hugh hovered over the truck and asked the Locrian to examine it as thoroughly as he could, with special reference to who and how many were aboard. The other settled more comfortably in his seat, unshielded his eye, and went to work.

"There is only one living being there," he said at last. "The Locrian is alone in one of the after compartments, apparently relaxing. There is no one else in that chamber, in the lock, or in the driving section."

"Is it Third-Supply-Watcher? Or are you acquainted with her?"

"Yes to both questions."

"Can you talk to her?"

"We cannot hear each other. If we can attract her attention and she sees me, we can signal."

"Good. Our obvious questions are why she stopped and what has happened to Rekchellet. I don't really expect an answer to the latter. I'll try to get to a position where she can see you—I'm surprised she hasn't noticed us already—and you can start your arm-waving or whatever the signs involve."

Third-Supply-Watcher remained motionless and apparently uninterested in her surroundings for several minutes, until Hugh asked the Habra to pound on the shell of the truck. This produced results.

"She has noticed our ship and looked at it several times. I don't know why she hasn't looked inside— wait; she sees me now."

Plant-Biologist fell silent. He made no motions that either Erthuma could see, but with Locrian eyesight there was no need for motions to be external. It seemed best not to interrupt, and Hugh waited as patiently as he could for the next few minutes. The scientist finally reported.

"She was told that if she turned the guiding equipment off, the main power would also be cut. She doubted this, but took the chance in order to make the truck easier to locate. As you can see, she does not have full-recycling armor. She does not know her precise location, but did not want to get any farther from Pitville. There is no Locrian food aboard, and stopping here seemed better than allowing the vehicle to proceed as it had been set. I agree with her."

"Her armor will let her join us here," pointed out Janice.

"True," agreed Hugh. "I'd have her come over in a shot if I thought she were in immediate danger."

"She is very hungry," remarked Plant-Biologist.

"Oh. Of course. Sorry." The man pursed his lips, and hesitated. "I'd love to know where that thing is supposed to have been going, but there's no one here who can set the autodriver up again if we do anything but simply turn it back on."

"Rek did," his wife pointed out. "There are other Crotonites in your own crew, some of them probably within fifty kilometers. Why should Third have to—"

The biologist made a querying sound.

"Sorry. I meant Third-Supply-Watcher."

"She shouldn't," admitted Hugh. "Tell her to stop worrying for now. We'll land, and she can come over here. Have you any food with you?"

"Of course." This time the biologist, or his translator, had no trouble with the address ambiguity. He fell silent once more as he signaled his fellow on the truck.

"We'll have to get out and work the lock controls from outside," Janice pointed out. "They're mechanical, and Third-Supply-Watcher may not be strong enough to handle them."

"Wait a minute. Something's funny," returned her husband. "She said the power would go off, but the drive cabin lights are still on."

"She is operating the inner lock, and passing through. Now she is closing it, and has operated the switch of the outer hatch." The three watched as the door swung out and down as the Erthumoi had seen it do before. Hugh hastily grounded the flier as the lightly armored insectile figure emerged. He opened his own air lock, and Plant-Biologist reached for the pack he had brought aboard.

Third-Supply-Watcher did not remove her helmet after coming aboard; Habranhan air was crushingly dense for her species, and Hugh had not bothered to drop the ship's pressure, since he, Janice, and S'Nash had long been used to it themselves. However, her armor had a feeding lock and she promptly made use of it. Presumably she thanked the other Locrian, but neither Erthuma could detect the communication. Hugh, not wanting to interrupt her meal, went through the lock to check the truck out himself. Two winged figures promptly landed beside him. One was a Crotonite, which could be helpful. He beckoned them to follow him inside.

The power, in spite of what had been said, was still on; it had not been a matter of some emergency exit device operating. The outer hatch closed behind them as Hugh tripped the switch, and the forward lock door opened with equal docility. The inside was comfortably warm by both Erthumoi and Locrian standards; it was only as this fact tapped on the door of his consciousness that Hugh realized what a chance Third-Supply-Watcher had taken. If the power had actually been cut, she could easily have frozen before being rescued.

There was only one difference that Hugh could see from the way things had been when he had previously examined the vehicle, not too much more, he realized with a start, than a Common Day before.

This was a sheet of printing fabric half a meter long and a third as wide fastened to a set of clips on a side panel. He looked at it closely.

It bore a zigzag pattern of short, straight, continuously connected line segments. From one end of this pattern there extended a longer line for a distance of about three centimeters; from the other a still longer one, nearly the length of the sheet, almost parallel to but diverging slightly from the first and broken into dashes for about the middle third of its length. Each segment was marked with tiny characters, and close examination showed that the lines themselves were made of almost microscopic writing. After a few seconds, Hugh decided that this must be the chart Rekchellet had persuaded the autodriver to print and which he and his companions had been trying to follow back to its end. The larger symbols were presumably location data and the tiny ones a continuous record of height. The spot near the Cold Pole which Rekchellet had mentioned was presumably the terminus of the longest of the lines, and the second longest must end at Pitville if the Crotonite's interpretation had been sound.

He turned to the two fliers and told them his suspicions. He knew the Crotonite slightly though he was not sure whether she hailed from Rekchellet's home world.

"Kesserah, can you read these? Rekchellet said they must be numbers, and claimed they were enough like his own to be legible. He said this point," Hugh indicated, "was near the center of the dark hemisphere. That means this thing can't be all to one scale."

"It isn't," replied the Crotonite. "The dashed section implies ellipsis. Rekchellet was probably right. I interpret the characters as he did." She turned the sheet over. "That's Rekchellet's writing."

"What does it say?"

"It makes no sense to me. Just, 'Make Ennissee pay before you tell him that date.'"

"Who is Ennissee?"

"I'd say it was a Crotonite name, but it doesn't call up a wing pattern to my memory. Has Rek met any Crotonites since you saw him last?"

"Apparently yes, Walt told me. Something funny has happened to him, and it started in the air, I'm told. But if that involved this Ennissee, Rek must have been back on the truck since. I hope Third-Supply-Watcher has finished eating; I'll have to ask her right now."

Hugh emerged as quickly as the lock system allowed, followed by his winged helpers. All entered the flier, where there was plenty of room for everyone. Third-Supply-Watcher was still eating, Hugh saw, and he made suitable apologies, but could not wait with his question.

"Please! I'm sorry to interrupt, but I must know. Did Rekchellet come back to the truck after you reported his absence to me?"

"Yes, but not at once. The outside hatch controls were operated by someone of whom I only caught a glimpse. That showed a Crotonite, and I looked only casually, assuming it was Rekchellet. Then the one who entered came to the driver's cabin and dragged me away from the controls. He stopped the truck, then pushed me back to the cargo section and locked me in. Then he waited, while snow covered the truck. Presently another Crotonite, who did prove to be Rekchellet, found the buried vehicle and entered. He met the first one, and they talked—argued, it seemed to me—for a long time, though I could neither hear nor understand. Rekchellet was not at first carrying his translator, but the other gave him one.

"Eventually, after much discussion, they set the truck going again. The other Crotonite adjusted the autodriver, and while he was doing that Rekchellet wrote something on the back of the map we had

been using. Then he came back and unlocked my
door and said that he had been told what I told
you—that the autodriver had been set to shut off the
main power if it were interfered with. Otherwise, the
truck was supposed to follow where the other
Crotonite was taking him. The other was listening,
and his translator could certainly handle
Rekchellet's language, so I judged Rek didn't want
to say more, and I waited for a chance to read what
he had written.

"They opened the main hatch and set it to close
after them, and left by wing while the truck was in
motion. I looked at Rek's note, but couldn't read it,
and saw nothing to do except stop while I was still
reasonably near Pitville and hope I'd be found before I starved or froze. When the truck didn't cool
down, I tried some of the light circuits and realized
the story about total cutoff was false, but I still
couldn't see what to do except wait. I could have
driven without the automatic, but wasn't sure which
way to go, and staying here seemed to offer the best
chance of being found before I starved. I'm not sure
I would have been if I'd wandered at random."

"Nor I," answered Janice. "Rek must have been
pretty sure we'd be along, though. I know he's a
Crotonite and you're not a flier, but he's a pretty
good fellow."

"Perhaps. What now?" asked Plant-Biologist.
Hugh pursed his lips again.

"If both you Locrians are willing to come, we're
looking for Rekchellet and then for something a bit
north of the Cold Pole," answered Hugh, "and we
can certainly use you."

But heading for the Grendelian antipodes wasn't
quite that easy, and not yet the right thing to do.
Hugh saw his wife's raised eyebrows through the
faceplate of her armor and paused to think.

The cold pole of Habranha was nearly 4900 kilometers from the terminator, over 4500 from their

present position. That meant nothing to the machine they were flying, but a great deal to two other groups—their winged and unwinged helpers, and Rekchellet and Ennissee, if the unknown Crotonite had actually been that individual. Rekchellet could not have flown the distance equipped as he was. The other—

"Third-Supply-Watcher, could you see clearly what sort of equipment the other Crotonite was carrying when they left the truck?" Hugh asked.

"Just ordinary Crotonite warmth harness, with very little decoration, and one or two small items of equipment. A translator, of course."

"Any sort of breathing mask?"

"No."

That disposed of recycling equipment; Crotonites, like Erthumoi, exhaled large amounts of water with their breath, and any efficient recycler had to trap that.

"Was there anything else noticeable about him?"

"Yes, definitely. His wing membranes were artificial. He had lost the natural ones in some way, and those he had were of artificial film."

"How about the bones—the framework?"

"Quite natural. He had lost only the membrane."

Hugh turned to Kesserah. "Have you ever heard of such an injury, or how it could have been suffered? Do you know of anyone who has been injured that way?"

"No to the first and last. Wing membranes are tough but not impossible to tear. Also, they carry blood. If one were torn, I can imagine a surgical need to replace it completely if it failed to heal properly—and possibly to treat the other side to match, though I'm no medic and don't know that that would always be needed. It's also possible that they could be lost to frostbite, though we have alcohols in our blood which give it a low freezing point."

"Thanks. At least, even I should be able to recognize this one if we meet him. The trouble is, there's no way he and Rekchellet could fly on their own over four thousand kilometers over this dark hemisphere, is there?"

"None that I can imagine. I certainly wouldn't try it."

"Then either he lied about where he was going, as he did about shutting down the autodriver; or he had another vehicle hidden somewhere within flying distance of here; or he had caches of supplies which would let him stock up along the way. In any case," Hugh chewed his lower lip reflectively, and looked around at the others, "in any case he's told us in too many ways about this place near the Cold Pole to leave me in much doubt that he wants us to go there. I wonder why. Any ideas?" He glanced around once more.

"The note Kesserah read for us mentioned a date we might tell him," Janice said slowly. "I can think of only one date we could know which has any connection at all with that truck. That's, of course, assuming the Crotonite with the damaged wings is the Ennissee Rek wrote about; nothing seems to make sense otherwise."

"What is the date you mean?" asked S'Nash.

"The age of the frozen specimen we found on the truck. I don't see anything special about it; I took samples, and made the usual checks, and it's not as old as the wing we found in one of the Pits a while ago, but it's certainly not current."

"What is the age?" asked the Naxian.

"I'm wondering why it's important, and why Rek wrote that we should make this Ennissee pay for the knowledge," the woman answered obliquely. "I wonder if he meant simply payment in the ordinary, literal sense of exchange tokens or service obligations, or in some more figurative fashion—as though this person had already contracted an obligation, and owed us something because of whatever he'd done to Rek or to us or to someone else."

S'Nash did not repeat his question. He must have known that, whatever her reason, Janice did not intend to answer it right then and didn't care how obvious she made the fact. She was quite sure he didn't know her reason; she wasn't completely sure she knew it herself yet. She could not see what harm the information would do, but intended to follow Rekchellet's guidance until the matter became clearer. It boiled down to the fact that she trusted the Crotonite more than the Naxian, though she could give no objective basis for the feeling. She certainly did not dislike snakes—at least, no more than bats. She had never seen either in the original, but their ecological niches were well filled on Falga and traditional images from the mother planet had carried over. She did not think of Naxians as snakes and Crotonites as bats, or of Locrians as mantises or Cephallonians as fish or dolphins; she had grown up regarding them all as people.

None of this crossed her conscious mind but whatever feeling was underneath kept S'Nash quiet.

Hugh was thinking again, and for fully a minute no one spoke. It was he who finally broke the silence.

"All right. This machine's points are speed and carrying capacity. It will take a small group of people and a good supply of food to the Cold Pole. Most or all of the group will be Habras, because I expect what we seek will be under the snow. It better be all, so we can concentrate on their food—no, I can't do that. I'll have to carry Crotonite supplies, too.

"The Crotonites will please study this chart—here, Kesserah—and use it as a guide. It may not be a very good one, but it's all we have to go on for the great circle route to the place we hope Ennissee and Rekchellet were going. You will follow along that course, looking for signs of the two we hope we're following. Every five hundred kilometers I'll leave a cache of food for you, well lit so you can see it from a good distance and with a neutrino communicator so you can tell me when you've reached it and what you've found. You all have inertial trackers, don't you?"

"Most of us."

"And lights."

"Of course."

"All right, you can start now from here. Get your group together and tell them what I want, and *look carefully*. I'm not sure this Ennissee person really cares much what happens to Rekchellet once he's sure we're heading the way he wants. Third-Supply-Watcher, did Rek have his translator when he left the truck?"

"Yes, definitely."

"But not when he arrived, you said."

"No. The other Crotonite apparently had it, and gave it back to him during their argument."

"We don't know how he got it away from Rek in the first place, though, so we don't know he didn't do it again. Kesserah, I'm more and more worried about Rekchellet all the time. Look *carefully*, please. I know that sounds silly along a four thousand kilometer search line, but I mean it."

"We'll do our best. I suggest you recruit more people—fliers—to help."

"If I can get them. Everyone not in Safety supposedly has a job schedule which may interfere and which I can't override, but I'll do what I can." The Crotonite gestured understanding and made her way to the air lock.

Once again Hugh's hands were aching from code transmission, and once again he was wondering whether it might not be better to get out of the diving fluid filling his armor. It seemed likely that he would not be in the Pits for some time, as things were now going.

But such a move would waste time, and there might not be time. Rekchellet had no food or water.

Hugh turned to the Habra. "You heard all I said to Kesserah."

"Yes."

"Please have four of your people ready to come with me on this machine. You can all return to Pitville now; those who don't accompany me had better stay there and resume routine duty. Things could still happen in town, after all. Please tell Ted he's in charge until Rekchellet or I get back. Tell everyone to stay below one kilometer going back; I'll be above three, at full speed until I'm near town. What's your name?"

"I'm Holly."

"Good. Thanks. If you'll get outside and start spreading the word, we'll go for supplies." The Habra operated the air lock without assistance. Hugh waited until the indicator showed the outer portal safely closed, went to the controls, and lifted off cautiously. He was reasonably sure that none of his safety crew would be directly overhead, but had developed professional habits of his own.

At one kilometer he nosed upward and applied more power; at three, eight seconds later, he leveled and began to tear through protesting air. Even at Habranha's nightside temperature, the feeble gravity kept air pressure and density from dropping quickly with height. The aircraft's shell warmed significantly in the few minutes of the trip.

There was, of course, more delay than he had hoped at Pitville. This did not originate with Administration this time; Barrar was extremely cooperative, to the extent of deciding to come along himself, though a little later he reported that Spreadsheet-Thinker had issued a veto on that plan. Hugh, however, had forgotten to assign Pit safety duty to

anyone. The only species who had developed the
pressure fluid were Erthumoi and Habras, and
the latter did not yet have protection against liquid
air temperatures. The Naxians could stand the
pressures reached so far in the digging. So could
Cephallonians, but the only members of this race attached to the Project or, as far as Hugh knew, on
Habranha were otherwise occupied and certainly
elsewhere on the planet. Two of the Erthumoi in
Pitville had expressed willingness to serve a pressure term, but Hugh didn't consider them well
enough trained yet; and after explaining this to them
as tactfully as he could, he assigned a pair of
Naxians to Pit safety. After all, a majority of the
workers in the liquid air were of that species anyway, and would be until a depth of two or three kilometers had been reached. Erthumoi were being
recruited for the remaining nearly five hundred kilometers, though it was hoped that adequately insu-
lated armor for Habras could also be developed in
time. The natives, at least the many who had worked
at mud collection in their submarines, were by far
the most experienced performers under high pressure.

But Hugh could not get Rekchellet out of his
mind, and worked in a state of frantic irritation
while he set matters up to take care of themselves,
or be taken care of by Ted, or—reluctantly on his
part—by higher administration officials while he
was gone. The top office seemed perfectly content to
allow Ted to take over the job; Hugh was not sure,
down at the emotional level, how he should feel
about this. Of course, if Spreadsheet-Thinker decided to make the change permanent, Hugh could always keep himself busy in the Pits.

At least there was no trouble about the food he
was taking. Counter-of-Supplies did not, as far as
Hugh could tell, even check with Administration;
she set her muscular Erthumoi workers loading ev-

erything Hugh requested onto the aircraft, including transmitters.

Four Habras, presumably the ones Holly had been commissioned to locate, were orbiting over flier and building as the loading went on. Hugh paid no attention to them until the job was finished. He was learning another administrative skill, to avoid worrying about a task delegated to someone else. Only when the last of the food cartons and water tanks was aboard did he address the natives.

"Ready to go, I think." They swept to the snow before the open air lock instantly, and the Erthuma gestured them inside.

9

CLEAR SIGHT MAY NOT PROVIDE
THE CLEAREST VIEW

His four Habras came aboard happily enough. Early metal aircraft brought to the planet by the starfaring races had given them claustrophobia, since the walls had blocked their electrical senses; this machine had been built of nonconducting synthetics with natives in mind. As passengers, they chattered eagerly at the view from heights they could never reach under their own power, and admitted Janice and S'Nash freely into their discussion.

They worked quickly and efficiently at the first stop, setting up the light and transmitter Hugh had promised the Crotonites, stacking cases of food beside them, and flying around to scout the region within a forty or fifty kilometer radius to learn whether they could sense any evidence that Rekchellet and the other had actually come that way.

The Erthumoi were rather surprised when they did. A dozen kilometers north of the just completed cache a single empty Crotonite food package was detected just under the ice-dust surface, its material charged differently enough from the surrounding material to reveal it to Habra senses. The discoverer brought it in for detailed examination, assuring Hugh and Janice that nothing could be read from the surrounding surface. If S'Nash felt any skepticism, it/he kept it private.

The interesting part of the container itself was that it bore markings in addition to the machine-impressed label, markings definitely not made by machine, though they were more regular than either of the Erthumoi could have produced by hand.

S'Nash insisted after a glance that they were Crotonite writing in the same language Rekchellet had used in his earlier note. It/he could not read a symbol, but was completely certain of the pattern. Janice was willing to believe it/him; she had already been impressed by the Naxian pattern-analysis ability shown at the point on the road where the truck had stopped. It fit her favorite hypothesis about the way the emotion-reading worked, now all the dearer since the collapse of the one about Locrian deepsight.

Hugh was less certain, but willing to accept S'Nash's opinion as a working hypothesis. After a moment's thought, he took the wrapping outside and carefully placed it under a food carton. When the Crotonite searchers got that far and reported to him, he could tell them where it was and ask for interpretation, meanwhile hoping that the group included someone familiar with Rekchellet's language. The interpreting devices were designed for oral and to a lesser extent gestured speech, not for writing.

They had reached and were setting up the fourth cache, some two thousand kilometers from Pitville and not yet that close to their putative goal, when the flier's communicator asked for attention. Janice answered.

"This is Velliah. We have reached the first food cache. We found it with no trouble, and there is plenty of food for all of us. I am sorry to say we found nothing on the way."

"We may have," answered the Erthuma. "Under the carton at the west end of the pile you will find the remains of what seems to be an ordinary Crotonite food pack, open and empty. There are marks on it which look to us like Crotonite writing. Would you examine them, tell us whether or not we are right, and if anyone in your group knows the language used, read it to us?"

"Of course. One moment." There was a pause of only a few seconds. "It is a food package. I can't read the marks, or for that matter the printed label, but there are universal standard symbols for the contents. I will ask whether any of the group can read it." The pause was longer this time, and broken by a new voice.

"This is Reekess. I'm not from Takkish, Rekchellet's hatching world, but I know its written language fairly well; it was colonized only a few hundred years apart from my own. This note is signed by Rekchellet. It says he has no tracker and no useful communicator, that he is extremely hungry and tired, that he knows Habras can find the wrapping and should be able to find him the same way. He will fly as long as he can to keep warm, going straight west by the stars. When he has to stop it will be in a valley to keep from being blown away, so he may be buried. Tell the Habras to scan carefully. That's not verbatim, but is the sense of it."

"Nothing about someone named Ennissee?"

"No. Strictly survival matters."

"All right. Stay there, and stay on the ground. We're coming back at high speed. We have four Habras on board with us, including the one who found that note. Watch for our lights."

Janice did not sign off formally; with Hugh at the controls, there would be only a brief pause in the conversation. As the craft roared through the dense air, she brought the natives, who had been too far back in the cabin to hear everything, up to date on the results of their find.

"You found the wrapper because of its charge difference, I suppose, Fibb?" she asked.

"That's right."

"Is Rekchellet right in believing you can find him the same way?"

"Probably. I'd doubt it if he were flying, but buried in snow or with snow blowing against him he'd show a bright—I expect your translator will call it 'color,' but I'm sure you know that's not the right symbol."

"I know. It will have to do. The main thing is that you should be able to detect him."

"I'd expect to. Very well, he said he'd fly straight west by the stars—"

"Straight west from where? I know where I found the wrapper, but am not at all sure that was where he left it. It could have blown far before being buried."

"Drat. You're right, of course. All right, wider pattern and slower search. I hope he's not too close to starving or freezing."

"As do we." The native's voice offered no suggestion of how much hope he really held. Not even the Habras knew this hemisphere of their planet at all well. As Hugh settled toward the light which marked the cache, all of them seized the opportunity to eat. Food was energy, needed both to travel and to keep warm.

As the air lock opened, Hugh restrained his winged assistants with a gesture and preceded them outside, where a small group of Crotonites waited.

"Is any of this food of yours liquid, or otherwise suitable for someone injured or unconscious?" he asked.

"It's not liquid, but if you find him unconscious just push a pellet of—" the speaker indicated one of the containers—"this down his throat. It will digest quickly; it's an aminated carbohydrate—quick energy."

"There's no risk of choking him?"

"Why? Oh, I remember—Erthumoi breathing passages are cross-connected with the swallowing channel. It would make one wonder about evolution if it didn't make one wonder even more about the intelligence of the designer. No, no risk. Have each

of your natives take one of these packages. That
way—" the speaker gestured—"is west. I can't
guess how far Rekchellet might have flown; even if
he were extremely tired and hungry, anger or des-
peration might have kept him going."

"My Habras covered the region within forty kilometers of here pretty well at the time Fibb found the
note," Hugh pointed out, "but we don't know what
the weather has done. As Fibb says, the note may
not have been where Rekchellet left it, and Rek himself may have had his course affected by wind,
though I haven't seen any signs of a real storm here
lately. He had no tracker, remember."

"Nor have we seen storm signs. But that proves
little on this world."

The natives were off, each carrying a package of
restorative, within the minute. After another few
minutes' discussion, it was agreed that the
Crotonites would also go aloft and keep somewhere
near the Habras, carrying lights. Their translators
would allow them to hear the natives' radio speech,
and most of them could understand it after a fashion
even without the appropriate language modules—
Crotonites had been on Habranha a long time. Hugh
and the other two nonfliers took the aircraft aloft
and went highest of all, hoping to keep all the lights
in sight at once and be able to respond to any positive report.

With Fafnir gone, the landscape looked nearly
featureless; the hills, wrinkles, dunes, or whatever
one chose to call the irregularities simply didn't
show. The starlight was too nearly uniform to provide any distinct shadows; even clouds and high-
blowing snow could not be distinguished from the
snow-covered surface. Occasionally some pillar of
white powder riding a topography-guided column of
dense air—Coriolis force was negligible with
Habranha's slow rotation—would build up enough
charge to reveal itself to Naxian and Erthumoi eyes

by bolts of lightning. Sometimes there would be several of the whirlwinds in a few hundred square kilometers, some spinning in one direction and some in the other. They might either attract or repel each other, cancel or reinforce when they met. Hugh shook his head slowly as he watched. There were still Habras who hoped to be able to predict their world's weather patterns in detail.

All he himself could hope was that Rekchellet was not hidden in one of the squalls, where even the Habras could hardly fly, or buried too deeply for his individual charge pattern to be perceptible to them.

The four natives had arranged a pattern reaching fifty kilometers to each side of the line running west from the point where the wrapper had been found. With their sensory range and flying speed, they were moving along it at less than ten kilometers an hour. This was a discouraging speed; it seemed quite possible that even a starving Rekchellet might have flown on for well over a hundred. Time and again Hugh felt tempted to suggest a narrower sweep, and each time told himself firmly that the Habras should know what they were doing. If anyone was qualified to suggest a change, it was the Crotonites, not he. They should be best able to guess what the missing one might have accomplished; but even they could only guess, and the natives *knew* what their own senses could do.

Two hours. Three hours. Four. The low-flying searchers came in for food, finished it quickly, and launched themselves once more from the air lock; the Crotonites went back to the cache in shifts for the same purpose. Hugh had almost definitely decided to order that the pattern be narrowed when a message was relayed back through one of the Crotonites that the natives were *widening* it; they were now so far from the originally unsure starting point of the lost being that this was the only reason-

able thing to do. The Erthumoi digested this for half
an hour.

Hugh was about to enforce his own emotions anyway when a light blinked far to the flier's left. Others repeated the signal closer to the aircraft and he
dived toward the nearest, slowing to match veloci-
ties a few meters from a Crotonite. The latter's voice
was picked up by the outside microphones.

"They've found something. It's buried. It can be
uncovered faster if you get over there. Go to the farthest blinker, and follow its carrier down."

Hugh obeyed without answering, hoping silently
that all the Crotonites at this level were carrying
lights, and was at the indicated one in a few seconds.

"Where?" he asked the single word. The broad
wings tilted and began a steep glide even farther to
the left of the original pattern. They were down to
half a kilometer—two hundred meters—one
hundred—a Habra was suddenly visible in their own
lights, and the Crotonite spoke as he or she peeled
away to circle, light blinking a new pattern, above
the area.

"Follow Holly."

The native led them only a few more meters, into
a narrow cleft between two unusually steep hills.
She paused, hovering, over a spot not much wider
than the flier itself. Hugh settled the machine under
her, and all three emerged. Holly's voice had started
before they opened the lock; the flier's hull did not
block radio.

"I'd almost bet this was the right place. The hills
to either side are solid ice, as though a glacier had
come up and split. The space between is snow which
has blown in and not packed very closely. I guess
Rekchellet decided that any snow which blew over
him here could not bury him very deeply; any that
piled past the top of the ice would blow away."

"Doesn't it *look* like Rekchellet?"

"It doesn't look like anything. I can't see it. It's

an area of different charge—it's *colored* differently from what's around it, but you know that's a poor word. I don't know the size; it could be very small with one sort of charge difference, and very large with others. I can only say it isn't ice or snow, and we'll have to dig to be certain."

"Do we have any digging tools?" asked S'Nash, presumably remembering the incident at the waste hill. Hugh smiled grimly.

"We do. This isn't just what I expected to use them for, but we have them." He returned to the flier and emerged almost at once with two extremely broad-bladed shovels, one of which he handed to Janice. "Sorry, S'Nash, I don't know what you could use for this purpose. We start—where, Holly?"

The native took a few steps and indicated. "The center of the field is immediately under this point. As I said, I can't guarantee how far it spreads."

The Erthumoi started moving ice dust with all the speed consistent with the possibility of a living body's being at risk from their blades. After the first two or three scoops, Janice asked, "Where's S'Nash?"

Hugh looked around; the Naxian had indeed disappeared.

"Back in the warmth, I suppose," he answered. "He couldn't have blown away now. Did you see him go, Holly?"

Before the Habra could answer, an armored serpentine head popped out of the snow directly in front of the Erthumoi.

"The ice is loose all the way down," it/he said. "It's Rekchellet, or at least a Crotonite, apparently unconscious. You can dig for about a meter and a half before there's any risk of cutting him with your tools. Go to it."

The shovels moved briskly, their wielders thankful for the brief lack of wind, and within minutes part of the hidden being could be seen. Hugh laid his shovel down, gestured to his wife to do the same, brushed ice dust away with his hands, and presently had uncovered enough of the body to provide a handhold.

Crotonites are light, even in decent gravity. Hugh needed no help, once he had his arms around the still form, though there were no projecting arms or legs to seize. It was completely wrapped in its wings. With a brief, "Come on!" he started back to the aircraft with his burden. Janice picked up the shovels and followed; the Naxian went ahead, finding a little trouble with the loose ice dust but managing to reach the air lock first.

Holly hesitated, then spoke. "Shall I tell the rest we've found him?"

"Yes, please," answered Hugh without turning. "And please have someone stay near us. I'll probably want everyone to go, or come, back to Pitville, but will be too busy to organize for a few minutes."

"I understand. We will tell everyone." Even Janice had forgotten the other Crotonite who must still be overhead. She did not know his or her name, but spoke aloud.

"Please come to the flier—you who led us down with your light. We need your help. Rekchellet may be in very bad shape."

Moments later the broad wings of the Crotonite showed in the flier's lights, and their owner settled at the air lock. Janice, who had remained outside, waved him or her in, and followed.

"Your name, please?" she asked as the hatch closed.

"I'm Reekess. We've talked before."

"Yes. Thank you. Rekchellet may owe you his life, if we can save it. Hugh and I know little of Crotonite physiology, not enough for common-sense first aid." She opened the inner panel, and both entered, halting abruptly at the sight meeting their gaze.

Rekchellet, if it were he, had been deposited as gently as Hugh could manage on one of the padded benches. He was still wrapped in his wings, and there was no obvious way to unwrap them; the membranes were stiff and brittle, and cracks up to several centimeters in length showed in them. A number of small detached fragments, the largest several centimeters square, had fallen to the seat and one to the floor in front of it.

"They're frozen," said Hugh, "so I can't unwrap them even to tell whether he's alive. What can we do for him, Reekess?"

"The membranes will thaw in this temperature in a minute or two. If the cracked areas start to bleed within that time, he is certainly alive; if not, he still may be. He could have, and probably did, shut down circulation to the area before it froze. Until they thaw, there is nothing to do; we must not risk more wing damage—there has been too much already, though I could not expect you to appreciate that."

"He is alive," said S'Nash firmly.

"How do you know? Is he conscious? Can you sense his emotions?" asked Janice.

"Not exactly. He is not conscious, I am sure, but some of the factors I normally perceive in reading emotion are operating."

Janice, grim as the situation was, couldn't keep her mind from wandering to its beloved theory. She wasn't sure how this fit, but at least it was more data.

Hugh kept closer to the main problem.

"Then we get him to Pwanpwan as fast as this thing will go. We'll have to get the Habras aboard—we can't abandon them out of flying range of town—and Reekess can tell the Crotonites to go back to Pitville. There's plenty of food for them to make the trip on at the cache. All right, Reekess? Can you tell me where the Crotonite medical center is at Pwanpwan, or should I call them as I go?"

"I'm not sure anyone can handle this," was the slow answer. She seemed about to add something when S'Nash cut in.

"Get him to our facility. I'll come along. They can take care of him. Tell your safety crowd, and let's go."

Erthumoi and Crotonite looked at the serpentine speaker with surprise, but Hugh hesitated only a moment.

He remained the pilot, but S'Nash, however informally, became commander. It/he said almost nothing during the trip back to Pitville, the disembarkation of the Habras, and Hugh's terse reporting to Barrar, but those few words had carried weight, with one exception. Reekess refused to follow the suggestion that she, too, remain behind when the flier started for Pwanpwan. She declared her firm and complete indifference to what the administrative office might have to say about the matter if its members were told. Job responsibilities were real, but so were others, she insisted. The Naxian did not press the matter, and she was still aboard as Grendel appeared above the horizon ahead of them and iceberg-dotted open water began to show below.

Pwanpwan was fairly close to the cold, or growing, side of the ring-shaped ice "continent," since the visitors from the stars were in no hurry to have it reach the warm side and be forced to move when this melted, but it was a long way north of Pitville's latitude. The trip took several minutes, giving plenty of time to heat the flier's hull by friction once more.

Most of the Iris, as organisms with Erthuma-type eyes called the ice continent, was a crazy-quilt of varicolored vegetation. Much, but not all, of this was cultivated by the Habras for food, but they deliberately left many patches running wild to provide a reference base for biological information and buffering. The Cedars had been told by natives that most of the "events" in the long but placid recorded history of the world had occurred when ecological oscillation had threatened its food supplies.

Pwanpwan was rendered fairly distinct on this landscape by its concentration of buildings; Hugh would have had no trouble finding it even without the flier's instruments. He set the craft down at S'Nash's terse directions close to a shuttle of obviously Naxian build cradled in an open space among the structures. Reekess became visibly uneasy as an enclosed catwalk began to extend from the side of the shuttle toward their flier.

"You're taking him off planet?"

"Yes. Our medical laboratories are in orbit, with available free fall."

"But what can you do? Do you really know anything about Crotonite physiology?"

"A great deal, I guarantee. We can heal him, even to restoring the destroyed wing tissue. We can give similar help to any of the Six Races. I don't mean that Naxians in general can, but my own world's people are noted for such skills. That's why we have a lab here; we are on the point—may have reached it by now; it's not my personal field, and I haven't checked for a while—of being able to do tissue regeneration for Habras, too."

"Why should you be interested in the health of other races?"

"I'm not sure we are, in any personal sense. Why are *you,* yourself, on a world other than your own? There are many kinds of exploration, and curiosity is an aspect of intelligence." The Crotonite was silent for a time, while the air lock connection was sealed to the extended catwalk, and a powered stretcher accompanied by half a dozen lightly armored Naxians came through.

"I'll have to go with him."

"You will find the air unsuitable. We're prepared to keep him in appropriate atmosphere, but not his entire surroundings."

Hugh spoke for the first time since they had left Pitville. "They'll take care of him, Reekess. Won't it be better to go back to Pitville with us and let work ward off worry?"

"*You're* going back?"

"Yes. I've done all I can for Rekchellet now, and have other responsibilities. What do you expect to do here, or up in the Naxian station?"

Crotonites tend to be outspoken beings where other races are concerned, especially nonflying ones, but this time Reekess actually seemed a little embarrassed. She didn't quite want to follow her feelings and say that she distrusted the Naxians and regarded crawlers' abilities with contempt, since her mind told her that neither remark would be justified. Her feelings, however, were hard to fight down, especially since she knew that every Naxian in sight was aware of them, and she couldn't help resenting that fact. Erthumoi were not the only beings who resented invasion of privacy under some conditions.

S'Nash broke the impasse. "Did Rekchellet ever tell you that he was doing work for me—had responsibilities to me?"

"No."

"Well, of course he wasn't supposed to. However, he has done many things in the last Habranha year or two which should convince you of this if you think them over. I have responsibilities to him, myself."

"I don't know what he's been doing. I don't know him that well. We aren't really close personal friends. I just don't like seeing a flier helpless in the—you can't even call them *hands*—of crawlers." She hadn't meant to be quite that free with her words, but she couldn't apologize. Neither S'Nash nor any of its/his fellows seemed bothered, and they certainly could not have been surprised.

Hugh spoke more urgently.

"I think we're delaying Rek's treatment. Will you

compromise? You can stay here in Pwanpwan and check in with your own people at the Guild. I can make that reasonable with Administration at Pitville. You can call me there when you've either found out enough to satisfy you, or decided that you want something else done, though I admit I don't see what else it could be; could your own people repair Rekchellet's wings?" The Erthuma nodded toward the cracked and torn membranes, now warmed and pliable, still wrapped around the unconscious figure.

"Not as far as I know."

"And even I know pretty well what losing wings means to you people. I think he'd want to take the chance. I would."

Reekess shifted uneasily. "All right. With one other provision. I talk to Rekchellet as soon as he can talk."

"How will you know?"

"I won't unless I'm told. If I find out later that I was delayed, from Rekchellet or anyone else, there will be trouble. I'll leave it at that."

"But I don't want you to be—wait a minute. I'm going to rule this a safety matter, and if Barrar and Spreadsheet-Thinker don't agree they can give Ted my job, which they may be planning to do anyway. I'll stay with you, and help you check at the Guild, and go up to the Naxian station myself if it seems indicated. Jan, you can fly this machine back so Ged won't complain about our monopolizing it, and take S'Nash with you—"

"I have to stay and go up to the station. Rekchellet is my responsibility, too, as I told Reekess. Also, it will be pleasant to get out of armor for a while."

Hugh gave up.

"All right. I don't know how I can justify *that* as a safety problem, but you can probably take care of Administration yourself."

"I'm sure I can." Janice added the remark to her file.

"Is that all right, Reekess?" Hugh asked.

"Yes."

"Good. Let's go." Hugh pressed his faceplate briefly against his wife's, not caring what the Naxians read, and followed the Crotonite out of the flier without waiting to watch the transfer of Rekchellet to the shuttle. This must have been done quickly. The two had not reached the Guild offices, only a few minutes away even in Pwanpwan's maze, when the Naxian vessel began to lift.

The officials in the roofless Crotonite section of the offices were primly courteous to Hugh and extremely sympathetic with Reekess when they heard the story. It seemed to be true, they agreed, that some Naxians had a reputation for skill in tissue regeneration for other species as well as their own. An Erthuma at the Guild office, they said, often displayed a normal-appearing hand which, *he* said, had lost three digits in an accident only two Habranha years before. They were told of, and referred to if they cared to check with him, a Locrian chemist with a newly grown eye.

A Naxian whose function seemed to be to wipe raindrops or snow from the weather hoods of the office equipment listened with seeming interest while the visitors were told that Rekchellet was quite certainly safe and, if the crawlers in the orbiting hospital had given the assurance, almost as certain of complete cure. Even Hugh could guess at the conflict between reluctance to worry Reekess and reluctance to praise nonfliers which was bothering the speaker; his enthusiasm was plainly forced. Hugh could not tell whether Reekess observed this.

They left the office and started to discuss what should be done while they waited for word from orbit. Hugh was getting uneasy about matters at Pitville, while the Crotonite was starting to wonder aloud whether she shouldn't have insisted on going up to the station. How would Rekchellet feel when he regained his senses and found no one around him but—she did cut the last word off.

Hugh was trying to reassure her about Rekchellet's objectivity when they were interrupted. A Naxian stopped beside them and raised the forward third of its body with obvious intent to capture their attention.

"I heard your problem while you were inside," it stated without preamble. It must have been using S'Nash's language, as both personal translators handled the words. "I can offer you more than words as assurance that our laboratory can handle alien medical problems. There is a Cephallonian who suffered loss of his main swimming organ—his tail—in a recent accident, and who can show you what we did for him. Would it comfort you, Crotonite, to see our work?"

Hugh thought quickly enough to accept the offer before his companion could say anything.

"Yes. Can you tell us, or are you free to show us, where this swimmer may be found?"

"Telling would be very complex. I can show you to the Dock of Deep Study, where he is often ashore."

The trip itself was complex enough. Pwanpwan was far enough from the growing edge of the ring continent to be clearly of some age; and while Crotonites had discovered the world over a hundred Common Years before, the city predated the arrival of nonflying species. The concept of streets had not occurred to the Habras until nonflying aliens had introduced wheeled vehicles for transporting heavy loads. Roofs existed only when something particularly needed protection from weather. Walls, however, were universal, as the natives had a strong and complex territorial drive and territory was a variable on Habranha. Most of the openings in the walls were

drains rather than doors, though the latter did exist—
equipment too heavy to fly sometimes had to be
moved. The air distance from the Guild office to the
dock was something like three hundred meters; the
path followed by the Naxian was over four times
that long before they reached a real road on which a
mud transport was passing. This still left them three
hundred more to get to the dock area. Reekess was
annoyed enough to forget Rekchellet for the moment; she could have flown to their goal in a few
seconds if she had known where it was. Hugh wondered why the Naxian had not given her direction
and distance, which would have been simple
enough. He guessed later.

The dock area had probably occupied a bay in the
ice at one time; it was now completely separated
from the sea by bergs which had merged with the
continent in later years. The only access to the ocean
was downward, which did not bother the natives.
The only seagoing craft they knew were submarines.

Four of these vessels were under construction on
ways giving on the two-hundred-meter-wide open
pool which was the Dock of Deep Study itself. More
than a dozen others were moored at the edge of the
ice. Two of these were unloading mud obtained five
hundred kilometers below, to be spread on the ice
for agricultural purposes. As far as aliens could tell,
this was the Habras' principal industry.

The Naxian spoke again.

"That ship," it indicated with a straightened body,
"is the research vessel which the Cephallonian you
seek finds of greatest interest. You will recognize
him easily; his tail is not yet quite of the same color
as the rest of his body, and in any case I think he is
the only one of his kind here just now. I stupidly forgot to suggest that you obtain translator units for his
speech while you were at the Guild office. I must return there now; shall I have them sent to you?"

This time Reekess spoke first. "I'll get them," she

replied tersely, and took to the air. Hugh added thanks, realizing that the fellow probably couldn't follow his code but could presumably read the intent. It departed without even having introduced itself.

Reekess was back in two or three minutes with modules for both of them, and they approached the submarine indicated by their guide. This was of the usual open framework construction, with spherical containers for cargo, ballast, and buoyancy fluid spaced along its interior. It appeared to be old; the pods around its midsection contained simple electric motors—the natives were good enough chemists to have developed organic conductors; free metal had been almost unobtainable until the star travelers arrived—rather than the fusion thrusters the Habras had learned to construct from their alien visitors.

It also had a number of natives working around it, and Hugh asked one of these whether a Cephallonian might be found in the area. The fellow put down what appeared to be a piece of electronic gear and answered willingly.

"Yes. Shefcheeshee is working under the ship, but I'll call him up if you like."

"No, thanks. Let him finish whatever he's at. Our wish is less important than his work." This was standard Habra courtesy and the native would have ignored its literal meaning, but Hugh stopped his turn toward the water with another question.

"Is a ship of this age still in use for mining? I find this surprising."

"It would more than surprising. The *Peeker* is far underpowered for modern needs. It's a research vessel. The water dweller is helping us in a bottom study project."

"Can he get to the bottom? I hadn't heard that diving fluid had been developed for his kind."

"To his great annoyance, it has not; his depth limit is only a few kilometers. He has provided much of our equipment, however, assists with its installation and maintenance, and spends much time publicizing results among both our people and aliens, and seeking material support for further research. He has great personal interest in this project. In fact, a large number of aliens seem to share it; there are some similar operations on, and I have heard in, the Solid Ocean as well as this ordinary sea bottom search."

"Can you tell us more, or are you too busy?"

"I'm afraid I'm needed right now. When Shefcheeshee appears, I know he'll be eager to explain—perhaps more than you'll be to listen, after a while. Is there such a thing as overenthusiasm among your people?" Hugh's translator had no difficulty with the word; he wondered briefly whether there were a Crotonite equivalent. Reekess remained silent, but the Erthuma keyed an emphatic affirmative, followed by appropriate thanks. The native picked up his burden and departed.

The two waited silently; both had plenty to ponder. So there was a sea bottom project having some connection with the work on Darkside—the Solid Ocean of the natives. It was probably wishful thinking, but was somebody actually looking for fossils in the bottom mud? There was no obvious reason why they shouldn't form there, if life existed at or bodies settled to such depths and got buried. There should be a constant, though slow, deposition of silicate material—not just from the traces the Habras constantly lost on the inner side of their melting continent, but from the much greater quantities scooped from the little world's rocky core by glaciers of high-pressure ice flowing from Darkside and distributed as the ice dissolved, changed phase, and otherwise spread itself through the Liquid Ocean.

This should have been going on long before the Habras' ancestors had arrived, if indeed the creatures were the descendants of colonists. There could reasonably be organic remains below the sea bottom; quite possibly someone was trying to find them. If the Cephallonian were indeed of the enthusiastic type, there might be more to learn here than how good the Naxian doctors were. Hugh did not want to interrupt any more Habras obviously at work, but there were two or three Naxians in sight with no obvious occupation. It might be worth asking them if they could communicate.

Hugh had almost made his mind up to ask, as one of them snaked its way more or less toward the dock where he and Reekess waited, when an interruption occurred. For a moment he almost felt at home.

The alarm was on radio, of course, but there was only one Habra language and his translator handled it perfectly.

"Help below bow section three! The alien swimmer is in trouble!"

10

THE CLOSEST SEARCH MAY FURNISH BUT A HINT

The local workers seemed well trained. People scurried in many directions, but Hugh could see the underlying organization. Every native who was carrying something put it down carefully and took time to make sure it wouldn't slide, roll, or block pathways. All in diving armor headed for the edge of the water; those not so equipped took up stations at the mooring lines of the submarine, on the upper portions of the hull itself, or along the water's edge next to mooring bitts, racks of emergency floats, and other items of less obvious but presumably rescue-oriented equipment.

Hugh himself hesitated only a moment before leaping toward the water. As usual, there was a tautness in his stomach as he remembered the five hundred kilometers through which he might sink if things went wrong, but he had spent enough time on and under Habranhan seas to be able to ignore this. Also his brain, if not his lower nervous system, knew that he was equipped for bottom pressures. He could survive down there for a long time, even if—

He pulled his mind sharply away from the thought of being *lost* in those depths.

He didn't actually dive in, but sprang to the submarine's side, obtained a firm grip on its skeletal structure, and began to climb downward. Reekess said nothing. Without breathing equipment she couldn't follow him; she simply kept out of the way of scurrying natives and waited.

Once submerged, the Erthuma let go of the ship
briefly. His buoyancy should still be slightly positive
for the liquid air density of the Pits. A moment un-
supported in the slightly denser water set him drifting upward and confirmed the belief. He juggled
briefly with suit controls and began swimming
downward again before they had finished responding. The effort decreased over the next few seconds
as cylindrical tanks around his waist and hips drove
their enclosed pistons upward, admitting water below and forcing some of the buffering oxygen on the
other side back into its storage tank. Hugh could detect the change, and might even have returned to the
surface if it had not occurred, but was more concerned with finding the Cephallonian.

He could see well enough. Water was appreciably
less transparent to Grendel's redder-than-Solar light
than seemed normal to Erthumoi, but he was still
close to the surface. The whole length of the submarine could be distinguished, but he didn't have to
look that far. The being he sought was under the hull
beside one of the thruster pods, about as far back
from the bow as Hugh had entered the water. It—no,
he—did not seem to have panicked; there was no violent thrashing. The Cephallonian might have been
doing something with his small and rather inefficient
hands, but the great driving muscles of his flukes
and after body were relaxed. Two armored Habras
hung beside him, working with ropes. Hugh swam
closer to get more detail. This revealed itself in
slow-motion playback fashion.

The pod was sinking gently away from the hull
frame, snapping a final support cable as Hugh
watched. The streamlined form of the Cephallonian
settled with it, the two-body system twisting slowly
to bring the thruster underneath and conceal it from
Hugh's view. He could now see that the swimmer
was wearing a fairly complex work harness, and got
the impression that the pod had somehow become

attached to this and was dragging him away from the surface.

The Habras had closed in and were now also partly hidden beneath their fellow worker, whose body was much longer than theirs—he was far larger than the Cephallonians whom Hugh and his wife had known earlier. Whether this was an individual peculiarity or racial characteristic implying a different world of origin was unimportant at the moment; the fact itself was what had to be faced. It might either help or hinder. Hugh set his own buoyancy a little further toward negative and approached the group as quickly as he could.

"Can't they get you loose?" he keyed. The two stage code-through-Falgite-to-Cephallonian translation caused some delay in the response.

"Probably not," the answer came. "I wasn't expecting them to try very hard."

"I have a good knife. Is cutting your harness acceptable?"

"No. We don't want to lose the driver."

"What can I do?"

"How much buoyancy can you furnish?"

"Only two kilograms-water-equivalent. You could swim upward with more force than that, I'm afraid."

"Please try, anyway. More support lines are coming; the slower we sink, the easier it will be to get them to us."

The Erthuma closed the remaining distance between himself and the Cephallonian and secured a one-handed grip on the harness. With the other he twisted his buoyancy control to full positive. As he had feared, the effect on their group sinking rate was very small, though he could feel the tension on his arm.

He wondered briefly how deep they could go before pressure endangered the other, but decided not to ask yet. If that problem became urgent, he could expect to be told. He coded what he considered a more immediate question.

"Can't you swim upward yourself?"

"Not with the thruster where it is, ahead of my center of buoyancy; I can't turn upward. The Habras are trying to shift it closer to my tail without losing all hold on it. Your hands are much more dexterous than mine, and your arms longer than theirs; perhaps your best tactic would be to match buoyancies so as to free both arms, and help them with their rope work."

Hugh tried following this suggestion, but found that even at greatest negative buoyancy he still sank less rapidly than the group. He would have to use one arm for holding on, at least at first—maybe he could lash himself to the cluster if there were enough cord, or put an arm through part of the harness. He reminded himself once more that he had no depth problem himself, since both he and the Habras could face sea-bottom pressure with their equipment, and strove to match the apparent calm of the Cephallonian who was being dragged toward an unpleasant death. His kind could stand several kilometers without technological assistance as a result of their evolution, and had never had any reason to develop the diving fluid.

The big swimmer had been right; human arms could reach between him and the pod far more effectively than the Habras. The thruster was firmly entangled in harness straps, but Hugh could, he was sure, work it loose in a minute or two. He reported this to the others. The Cephallonian repeated his earlier desire not to lose the equipment.

"Let them attach lines to both sides of my gear, long enough to let the pod hang three or four meters below me and fastened far enough from my head so I can direct myself upward. Don't free the tangle, please, until you are sure they've finished this with at least four lines; I know they have that many. If you can see well enough underwater, please check their knots at both ends. They know I mean no offense by asking this."

It was getting darker as they sank, but the light which had annoyed Rekchellet was still part of Hugh's armor, and he switched it on. He was able to help with the knotting and, as a matter of tact as well as safety, asked the Habras to check his own work. There was no way for the Cephallonian to see that far back on his own body, but he seemed willing to accept the word of the others that the attachments were secure.

"All right, Erthuma, you may free the pod from my harness if you can. It will help if you are reasonably quick; I'm beginning to feel some slight need for air. I foolishly did not wear full work equipment, not expecting to go any distance from the surface, and had been working under the boat for some time when this incident occurred."

Hugh reflected that if the swimmer could spend that much air in talk things couldn't be very serious yet; then he remembered that the other's vocal equipment was a tympanic membrane not driven by an air stream from his lungs, and bent hastily to his task.

His estimate had been a little optimistic, but it was less than three minutes before the thruster fell away from the stream-lined body. None of the others had uttered a word during this time, though the water around them was growing frighteningly dark beyond the range of Hugh's light.

As he felt freed of the weight, the Cephallonian nosed upward and set his swimming muscles into action. It turned out almost at once that he could not go straight up without having his flukes encounter the lines which held the pod, but he modified his climb angle slightly and continued to swim. Hugh could see after a moment that he was actually dragging motor, thruster, and housing upward, after another moment that the climb was faster than the Erthuma's armor rose at full positive buoyancy; he had to swim. The ascent was uneventful and silent; nothing more was said even about oxygen shortage.

They were close enough to the surface to see the bright area of the port, where sunlight fell on open water, before they met a dozen descending Habras pulling lines behind them. The Cephallonian firmly refused to relinquish his burden until these were all attached to the thruster, but the moment he was assured of this he spoke to Hugh with urgency obvious even through the translator.

"All right, cut me free!" Hugh managed this in four quick slashes, and the long, streamlined body surged upward. Hugh, the Habras, and the equipment followed much more slowly. By the time they reached the surface, the Cephallonian had almost finished replenishing his personal oxygen reserve, and was awaiting them impatiently. Hugh saw no reason to help remount the thruster, but wanted to get the swimmer somewhere where Reekess could see him, and suggested that they rest out on the ice for a while.

"I can relax better afloat," the answer came. "It's much harder to breathe without water to support one's weight, even here. However, I'm sure you'll be more comfortable ashore. By all means emerge, and I will stay as close as I can. I am interested in learning how you happened to appear so conveniently."

Hugh told him frankly, while climbing a cross between a grooved ramp and a flight of stairs leading out of the water and presumably designed for armored Habras, that he and Reekess had been told about his recent accident, that they had a friend now undergoing Naxian treatment, and were interested in learning how effective this had been. He also introduced himself and the Crotonite, who had come to the edge of the water upon seeing Hugh emerge.

They quickly learned that willingness to talk about personal surgery was not confined to Erthumoi; the opportunity motivated the Cephallonian, who introduced himself as Shefcheeshee, to hurl himself onto the open ice after all and allow—actually, encourage—inspection of his personal repairs.

Since neither Hugh nor Reekess had known him before, they had to take the patient's word for the state of things prior to the accident and the damage done by the latter. All either of them could see was that the skin of Shefcheeshee's flukes and for half a meter forward of their point of attachment was visibly, though not strikingly, lighter than the blue-gray shade of his dorsal surface and the near white of the lower. The swimmer claimed that that entire part of his anatomy had been severed, that he narrowly escaped bleeding to death, that only heroic first aid measures by the natives had spared him from the latter fate, and that the Naxians who had arranged the regeneration of the lost body parts were benefactors of all galactic intelligence.

This was how Hugh summarized the account later, to Janice. The Cephallonian himself went into enormous detail, much of which he must have picked up from others since he had admittedly been unconscious almost from the moment of the accident itself. He was starting to go into factors leading up to this event when Hugh managed to change the subject. He later regretted doing this; it almost certainly cost him data which he had to seek out specifically and at some inconvenience afterward. He failed to realize this at the time, though, especially since the new discussion also proved useful.

This dealt with Shefcheeshee's work with the sea bottom project in which the submarine was being used, and found the swimmer still enthusiastic. There *had to* be fossils in the bottom sediments; they should be possible to find even by simple dredging and coring; the information they would

supply would be of enormous interest and value to
the Habras themselves, as well as to scientists from
other worlds. Shefcheeshee himself held no strong
opinions one way or the other about off-planet origin
of the Habras, inclining casually like most people to
the positive, and seemed to care even less about the
possibility that they might be descendants of the
Seventh Race. He was an enthusiast, but an unusually objective one.

"I'd like to hear as much as possible about any results you get," the Erthuma finally tried to stem the
word flow. "You're publishing them, I trust."

"Oh, yes. We're keeping careful records, which
the Guild maintains for us, and have published ten
papers so far." Hugh found that statement impressive
and somewhat annoying; he had thought himself familiar with all the significant Habranhan paleontology in progress. More honestly, he had thought his
own group was doing it all. First S'nash and Barrar
had mentioned other work on the dark hemisphere,
then whatever Ennissee was doing, and now this. He
wondered briefly how Spreadsheet-Thinker would
react to the news, and then whether she knew it already and hadn't considered it worth mentioning to
her safety chief. But the Cephallonian was talking
on.

"I give regular talks here at the port on our results, and what they mean to the natives in both
philosophical and practical ways. The next one is
not yet planned in detail, but the Guild office will
tell you a little later when it's to be given; I'll make
a point of asking them."

Hugh thanked him, suggested that he get back in
the water and rest after his near-accident, and
thanked him again more fulsomely than was really
comfortable in code. The swimmer, unhampered by
code constraints, returned even more voluminous
gratitude for Hugh's help and finally admitted that

others must be waiting for him. Erthuma and Crotonite left the port area deep in thought.

"I guess they'll do all right with Rek," the latter said as they approached the road. "Can you find your way back to the office? I can steer you from overhead if it will help."

Hugh reviewed his memory of the Naxian-guided trip and accepted the offer, so they entered the Guild structure together a quarter hour later and reopened with the first Crotonite official they could find the discussion of Rekchellet's safety.

This one, who had not been present at the time of their earlier visit, also admitted that the Naxians in the orbiting station did claim ability to do major physical repairs even on fliers, but no one had yet been willing to take them up on the offer. He knew a male named Ennissee who had lost wing membranes to freezing and was currently using prosthetics; these were less than satisfactory, but he had loudly declared that he would never be the first to subject himself to the experiments of a bunch of crawlers.

Hugh and Reekess heard this with great interest but little surprise, nor were they astonished to hear that the Guild office did not know Ennissee's present whereabouts. He was believed to be somewhere on the Solid Ocean, but his vehicle had no neutrino transmitter.

At this point, the most obvious explanation for what had happened to Rekchellet was a little hard for a civilized being to believe, in spite of the way some Crotonite societies treated their ambassadors. It tended to make Reekess think rather more kindly of nonfliers, or at least to narrow the culture gap a little. They thanked their informant and let him go his way.

Hugh took the opportunity to call Pitville, in the line of duty. Nothing serious had happened in the dig, and he had of course postponed the intended ex-

amination of the Cold Pole site until his return; the
people he had drafted had returned to their regular
tasks. He wanted to be there himself if and when
anything were found. At the moment, Pitville life
was pure routine, Janice told him with a straight face
and steady fingers. Hugh promised to return as soon
as possible to corrupt it for her, and turned his attention to an impatient and verbose Guild subordinate
who seemed to care for little except that everyone
should know he was a native of Earth itself and that
he wanted to use the transmitter. The discussion provided no useful information.

Hugh had not thought to ask about the age of the
corpse since his wife had evaded S'Nash's question
so many hours before, and for the moment nothing
was farther from his mind.

Even with the rather halfhearted enthusiasm of the
Crotonites in the office, Reekess seemed to feel a little better about Rekchellet's being under Naxian
care by the time a call came down from the orbiting
station. She listened closely, however, as the few
words came through their translators.

"Rekchellet is conscious. His mind appears undamaged. He wants to talk to friends. His wings will
need extensive regeneration, as will his hands and
feet. This will take about half a Habranhan year."

Hugh acknowledged with appropriate thanks, and
turned to his companion.

"I'll go up to see him. I assume you'll come too,
regardless of air."

"I can get a breather here. Certainly I'm coming.
You sent our flyer back with Janice; how do we get
there?"

"Our machine wouldn't have made it safely anyway; it could drive in space, but might not protect its
occupants properly. There are regular Naxian shuttle
flights, I gather. Get your mask and come on."
Reekess obeyed, and a few minutes later they were

back at the site where they had left their own craft a few hours before.

There was another Naxian shuttle waiting, and no objection was made to their boarding, though neither attempted any explanation. It did not lift immediately, however; it seemed to be a sheduled carrier, and fifteen or twenty minutes passed before its hatch closed without announcement and the craft headed skyward. Over a quarter of an hour was spent on the flight, much of it in maneuvers presumably designed to match orbits without straining passengers used to low gravity. The vessel did not attach itself to an outer lock via catwalk or tube, but entered a much larger one, and waited for the doors to close behind it and the surrounding space to fill with air. The lock chamber was only a little larger than the shuttle, however, so the latter process was brief.

They were at the station axis, in free fall. Hugh and Reekess were both reasonably experienced in this condition, and followed a Naxian guide with no trouble. Presently rotation, still by far the most reliable form of artificial "gravity," made itself felt, and in a few minutes they were progressing along a passage which had a definite floor. Weight increased until they had about a quarter Erthumoi normal, standard for Crotonites but noticeably more than either Hugh or Reekess had experienced for a long time. A few meters of travel along a corridor at this weight level brought them to a door, like all in the station capable of making an airtight seal, and this led into Rekchellet's room, if it could be called that.

It was much larger than a typical hospital chamber and contained much equipment, only a little of it obvious in function to the visitors. A number of Naxians were busy at various stations. The Crotonite's body was hanging from padded straps; all his limbs passed through sealed sleeves into opaque tanks in which, presumably, the cold-damaged tissue was being replaced by new growth.

The general setup impressed Hugh as an experimental arrangement combining biological and mechanical gear, which might not be too far from the truth.

If Rekchellet could move any limbs the fact was not evident, but his eyes were open and it became clear at once that he could speak.

"Hugh! And—Reekess, isn't it? Sorry I made such an idiot of myself."

"We don't know much of what happened," the Erthuma answered, "but the fact that we found you just as you planned suggests that you handled things pretty well. We gather you came up against another Crotonite, so you needn't feel too low."

"What have you figured out? I'll correct what's necessary and fill in the rest. It's a little hard to talk with my wings pinned this way."

"I won't say I understand that, but I can believe you. All right, you met this other Crotonite—Ennissee?—who was accompanied by several Habras while you were herding the truck westward on the long leg of its map. Somehow they got your translator away from you, and delayed you while they took over the truck from Third-Supply-Watcher. Then you came back to the truck, got or were given your translator back, and had an argument or at least a discussion with Ennissee, who seems not to speak your language.

"We don't know what was said, of course. Eventually the autodriver was set on a westward path and the truck started, the Locrian was freed and told falsely that interfering with the autodriver would shut off the general power and endanger her life. You had written a rather obscure note about not giving Ennissee date information freely, while he or she was setting up the driver. The two of you left together. We found another note from you on a food wrapper which did help us find you; we knew you couldn't have been planning to fly directly to the Cold Pole, and searched the truck's line until we found your note, and then were guided by it until we found you. I'm afraid there's a good deal you'll have to tell us, even if talking isn't easy. Make believe you're in my armor, full of diving juice and using code."

Rekchellet's rigid features, consisting largely of beak, did not permit a grimace, but a sound much like a human snort suggested the same meaning to the Erthuma.

"That was Ennissee, all right. He's a Wildwinder, a Trueliner, firmly convinced that we're descendants of the Seventh Race and entitled to everything they've left."

" 'We' meaning Crotonites in general."

"Of course. Well, ones who agree with him, anyway. He's heard of my disagreement with that idea somewhere—I've never made any secret of it, though I've never flown around making public speeches on the subject—and has a low opinion of me. My association with Naxians, Erthumoi, and similar crawlers doesn't help either, except to reinforce his opinion."

"I suppose he tried to change your opinion in the truck."

"No. I don't know whether he considered that hopeless, or considered me worthless. He talked about the Pit project, and what we must have found, like plant roots, and maybe whole bushes. What it all led up to was a query whether our people might date the frozen body in the truck."

"We have, though I don't know what answer Jan got. Why do you think Ennissee wants to know?"

"I can't even guess. I'm just suspicious because he didn't simply ask us. You Erthumoi would have done the work and given him an answer without thinking twice, and Spreadsheet-Thinker is just the same. A Crotonite wouldn't, and he was being very Crotonite, and trying to trick us out of the information, I'll bet. What do you think, Reekess?"

"It seems to fit. You've met him, though; I haven't. You have, I judge, more reason to distrust him."

"I do. Plenty. When we left the truck, he'd never given me back my tracker; his Habras got that when he first took my translator. He said we'd fly to a food cache he'd established and then go on to others until we reached his own dig—he'd said a little about that, but no details; I'm only guessing that that's where he found that frozen Habra—near the Cold Pole. I was already pretty tired and hungry, and he flew fast. Those factory-made wing membranes of his saved him a lot of heat, too—you know about them?"

"Third-Supply-Watcher told us. We heard a little more at the Guild office. Tell you later."

"Well, I was pretty well done, and had dropped a kilometer or so behind, when he finally came down. I never saw his cache. I don't know where it was or what it was, so I don't know if Habras could spot it. When I landed beside him he was just finishing a food pack, and there were no more in sight. He chuckled, 'Good-bye, Friend-of-Crawlers!' tossed me the wrapping, and took off to the west. You know the rest. He doesn't like me, and it's mutual. Please don't do him any favors."

"So it looks as though the truck was sent to Pitville just to get us to date that body. He knew he'd have no trouble getting it back; we'd be bound to use it to search the track recorded by the autodriver."

"That's how I see it," agreed Rekchellet.

"Except—does he have the truck again now? He must have known we'd find it, even if he hoped we wouldn't find you and maybe hoped we'd find it too late for Third-Supply-Watcher. He couldn't have cared much about either of you. The last I knew, it was abandoned where the Locrian stopped it and transferred to our flier. We left power and lights on, so anyone could find it again easily enough, but would he or any of his people have dared to come back after what they did to the two of you?"

"I'd think not."

"That puts me back to an earlier idea I was toying with. I wonder if he's trying to get us to visit this dig he told you about—"

"He's a liar!"

"Granted. He may still want us to go there for some reason of his own."

"A good reason for not going!"

Reekess spoke for the first time in some minutes. "You really don't want to see him again?"

"I do, very much," snapped Rekchellet, "but not until I'm out of this machine and able to fly a few hundred kilometers."

"You want me to wait ten or twelve Common Days until they've patched you up, before we go out there?" Hugh stated.

"I'd certainly appreciate it. Look—think of Ennissee, waiting to see whether you've swallowed his bait—wondering when you're going to arrive— trying to explain to his Habras why nothing has happened yet—"

"I wouldn't have supposed he could get Habras to work for him," mused Hugh. "They don't go for deceit, and certainly not for the sort of thing that was done to you."

"You're generalizing," pointed out Reekess. "There must be all sorts of Habras, just as there are all sorts of Erthumoi and Crotonites and Naxians. Besides, there were no natives around when Rekchellet was abandoned, as I understand his story. Ennissee's assistants may not have any idea of the nasty part of his actions; they may simply be helping in another research dig."

"I suppose so," agreed Hugh. "You talk like my wife. I assure you that's a compliment. But they helped take Rek's tracker—"

"We can find out from them later," Reekess countered. "We already know Ennissee's a liar, and why. He could very well have lied to them, too. Are you willing to—"

"What do you mean, you know why?" Rekchellet could move no limbs, but obviously wanted to.

"It seems that he doesn't want to be the first Crotonite to undergo Naxian regeneration. We think he arranged for you to be a preliminary test subject."

"In that case," Hugh keyed hastily, "he must have made some arrangement to have you found while there was still time to use you that way."

Several Naxians approached, and one of them uttered an admonitory "You are disturbing the patient. He should remain relaxed, and make no effort to move."

"All right. There's plenty more to do. I suppose we'd better report all this to the Guild, too, before—"

"NO!" snapped both Crotonites together. "I've lost enough self-respect from this," Rekchellet continued alone. "Asking for help from anyone but personal friends and sharers of responsibility would make it worse." His beak snapped firmly shut, and he stared hard at Hugh. Reekess was looking at Rekchellet; Hugh couldn't read any expression on her features but was fairly sure she approved his words, but asking one of the closely watching Naxians was hardly advisable.

"All right. I tell only Janice, and Reekess tells whomever she considers appropriate. She can make up the group to go out to the Pole. We'll run it pretty much as we planned before, but this time carry food for everyone on the flier. You decide, Reekess, whether we take few enough folks to cram aboard or whether it's all the flying people I can talk out of Barrar.

"And if anyone comes up with the smallest glimmering of an idea why we're wanted out there, and how we can keep from doing just what Ennissee wants when we do arrive, please tell me before we start!"

He intended to get another opinion on that point, of course, but not to confide that matter to the Crotonites.

An hour and a half later, they were back in Pwanpwan, and Hugh had made contact with Barrar. The Samian seemed unconcerned about the loss of Rekchellet's services for a time, and didn't even appear greatly bothered by the fact that the aircraft were all in use again and it would be a day or so before Hugh and Reekess could be picked up. The Erthuma was beginning to wonder what a steady job of chipping ice at the bottom of a lake of liquid air would be like when the administrator went on:

"There's something Spreadsheet-Thinker wants checked at Pwanpwan while you're there. We understand there's another fossil dig being planned," Hugh's eyebrows shot up, "and we'd like details. Apparently the entire crew is native, which is reasonable enough, but makes it awkward for Guild contact. You have Habra friends—you've been here longer than most Erthumoi, longer than most anyone except the Crotonites, and I can't see using them where tact is wanted." Hugh glanced at Reekess, but she seemed to be developing the sort of control Rekchellet had learned. She showed no sign of irritation. "Let us know when you hear something, please," Barrar continued. "Then we'll send an aircraft as soon as possible for the two of you."

He signed off before Hugh could either point out that the flight would take only minutes or ask sarcastically whether the return was conditional on his getting the information, and long before he could report what they had already heard from Shefcheeshee. After a moment of thought he decided that this might be just as well, and refrained from calling back.

He deliberately ate before doing anything else,

and then began taking steps to locate his various Habra friends. He should probably find out more than the Cephallonian had told them.

The planet's population was only in the millions, but even one million is a very large number. They had a single culture spread over the "Iris" continent. Any native might be anywhere, as work or whim dictated. This did not promise well for finding anyone.

On the other hand, the Habras were highly civilized, had a single worldwide language, communicated naturally by electromagnetic waves, and had a sophisticated search system which worked very quickly for people actually on the continent; ones on the dark hemisphere or working undersea were quite another matter.

In less than an hour, after talking to three natives on or over various parts of the Iris, he had found Bill, the first native he had come to know at all well and with whom he and Janice had shared danger under Habranha's seas. Bill knew all about the proposed fossil dig, though he was not involved himself; it was no secret, though no one had bothered to make a point of telling alien visitors about it. He had not known that a Cephallonian was involved.

It was to be on the ocean bottom in silicate sediment rather than ice. The Habras were quite used to dealing with this material; they mined it regularly to fertilize the ice of their floating continent. There were only two new developments involved. One was a technique for boring vertically into presumably hard mud instead of skimming soft stuff from the surface; this the Habras had worked out themselves.

The other was a means of sensing and identifying organic remnants in the material being searched. This involved a Big Box, an Erthumoi artificial intelligence. The Habras did not share the prejudice against such equipment held so firmly by the five non-Erthumoi star-faring species, and had not

proven very susceptible to efforts to transmit it. Bill
was enthusiastic, and wished he had gone on the
trip, but the crew—of two—had already been selected when he had heard about the project. Ship and
workers had been visiting the bottom now for over
two years. He was voluble with details about the
submarine, which he had himself handled, and displayed an interest in fossils and paleontology which
he had never shown during his earlier association
with Hugh, Janice, Rekchellet, and their other
Crotonite partner.

Remembering the question Rekchellet had attributed to Ennissee, Hugh sounded Bill out on his attitude about Habranha evolution. No strong feeling
was aroused. Bill shared an apparently general belief
that the process did occur, but that, for chemical
rather than mystical reasons, his own people could
not be part of it. Hugh wondered if he had found another reason why some Habras were working for
Ennissee.

He spent over an hour reminiscing with Bill before the native had to go his own way. Hugh headed
back toward the Guild building with another minor
problem of diplomacy on his hands.

Spreadsheet-Thinker and his group were very concerned with getting good, reliable, scientific answers
from their own Pit Project so they could regard their
administrative efforts as professional and successful.

It also seemed likely that getting answers *before
anyone else* might carry weight with them. Barrar
wanted information about the Habra project, and had
mentioned interest in others. That seemed a most
probable reason.

But now the natives were going to dig with the
aid of artificial intelligence, in a place where fossils
ought, one would expect, to be plentiful.

Locrian Spreadsheet-Thinker, Samian Ged Barrar,
and the rest of their non-Erthumoi colleagues were
about to collide with the fact that they were in direct

competition with the nasty, immoral, improper, and generally unacceptable innovation of those irresponsible, juvenile newcomers to interstellar travel. They would be challenging Erthumoi-developed artificial intelligence. Ignoring the fact would leave them completely out of control of affairs on Habranha, because the natives would simply deal with people who could get things done.

Hugh gloated. Maybe his job was being done for him.

BUT NEW LIGHT ON A SCENE MAY SHOW IT TRUE

Barrar received Hugh's additional information with surprising calm, Hugh felt, and the aircraft reached Pwanpwan with equally startling speed. It was a smaller machine, and Reekess had some trouble accommodating her wings, but they were back at Pitville before this became a major discomfort.

It took some time for personal clocks to adjust, short as Hugh's absence had been. Work on Habranha was continuous, since the "day" was a spatial rather than a temporal division. People rested, or slept if their species did this, simply according to the need of the moment, whether timed by simple fatigue or evolution-rated biological clocks.

Hugh had even gotten out of phase with Janice. Assigned duty watches in Pitville were based, of course, primarily on the need to keep a position filled; but the biological nature of the beings on duty also had to weigh heavily. This sort of scheduling formed a large part of Spreadsheet-Thinker's own job description; requests for change, such as Hugh so frequently made without consultation, ranked extremely high on her list of major nuisances. Barrar had wondered several times whether he should try to make this a little clearer to the Erthuma, but was so far still favoring natural selection.

Even with nobody actually criticizing his work, however, a safety director's job remains full. When nothing bad is happening, there is time spent won-

dering when it will; when something does, one wonders why; when the reason is obvious, there is usually no one else to blame. Hugh had accepted this
long ago and now simply tried not to take his irrita-
tions out on anyone else, especially not on Janice.

He was not sure how to react to S'Nash's presence. This was frequent enough to make him wonder
in his balanced moments whether the Naxian wanted
Hugh's job, and in his more paranoid ones to suspect
it/him of being part of the Administration net.
Knowing that the being could sense his feelings
made it superfluous and even silly to relieve them
with bad language or similar unrestrained behavior;
on the other hand, the knowledge itself was, oddly,
a sort of relief.

Hugh Cedar was a good, competent, thoughtful
explorer. He was not yet a good administrator.

His wife was a good, competent, thoughtful explorer. She was also an extremely good physical
chemist, at both theory and laboratory levels. Currently, therefore, she was much better off and happier than he. She knew it. She didn't actually worry,
but looked forward eagerly to the time when
Rekchellet would be back in the air and the real,
physical, possibly dangerous adventure over the
Solid Ocean could start and let her husband relax. In
the meantime, she tried to keep Hugh's mind on
other things, an effort sharply constrained by diving
fluid and such of its effects as the need to use code
rather than speech and the impossibility of enjoying
such simple biological pleasures as eating.

They discussed the age of the frozen Habra in private; they had decided not to reveal it even to
S'Nash, to make sure that Rekchellet's expressed
wishes weren't accidentally frustrated. The body
was, in fact, much more recent than the wing which
had been found earlier, little over twenty-two thousand Common Years—well within the carbon reliability range on this world. They wondered where

and how it had actually been found. The only source either one could guess was the putative Ennissee dig, and thinking of that made Hugh impatient again. All Janice could do was point out the obvious fact that the body could have come from anywhere on Habranha where ice existed, and that this was not even restricted to the dark hemisphere. The reminder didn't really help. A confrontation with Ennissee, with a Naxian on hand to indicate whether the Crotonite were telling the truth, was very high on Hugh's want list.

Whenever he was less self-centered, of course, the list had Rekchellet's recovery even higher. Frequent calls to the Naxian station brought only the ages-old and galaxy-wide medical response—progress was normal. Since the biologists had admittedly never before tried the current techniques on a Crotonite, Hugh was tempted to ask just what the word could mean in this case.

He restrained himself, however, with Janice's help, and tried to concentrate on his work. Occasionally a minor accident somewhere in Pitville would help, or at least relieve boredom. So did the training of Erthumoi workers in the use of diving fluid and Pit equipment, against the approaching time when Naxians would be unable to support the pressure at the bottom. Work on designing a Habra suit able to protect the natives from liquid air temperatures was making some headway, Ted reported. Erthumoi and Naxians had been helpful with information about the insulations they used. The Habra could not say what the difficulty was; he wasn't involved with the matter himself, and had merely been asked by his Erthuma chief whether he knew anything about the program. Hugh, at the time of the question, had been particularly annoyed by the carelessness of some trainees of his own species, and was made no happier by Ted's answer.

Twice he was able to talk to Rekchellet himself.

The second time the Crotonite reported that his hands and legs were done, but his wings were still immersed and restrained in growth tanks. He seemed disinclined to accept the Erthuma's congratulations; wings appeared to be all that really mattered. Neither Hugh nor Janice, who happened to be in the safety office at the time, was greatly surprised, but did their best to point out the good side. The woman asked whether the Naxians were supplying proper Crotonite food, and found that this was precisely the wrong question.

"They haven't fed me a shred!" Rekchellet snarled. "By the time my wings have grown back, my stomach will have shriveled. They insist they have to keep track of every molecule that gets into me. It's all synthesized from chemically purified minerals, they brag, and is pumped straight into the tank—just enough into my arteries to keep my brain from shriveling, too! Not a drop or a sip in my mouth!"

"Do your people have organic feeding enthusiasts?" asked Janice. The other failed to get her meaning, and the discussion at least distracted him from his troubles for a few minutes. Unfortunately, her description of the people she was trying to explain carried a suggestion of extremism, and this reminded Rekchellet of Ennissee. The patient soared into another rage and was still in it when duty forced Hugh to drop out of the conversation. Hoping his wife could smooth matters over, he left his office to inspect the Pit area. He made it a point to get all the way to the bottom and be very detailed.

"I got him thinking about Ennissee waiting for us to set out for the Cold Pole and wondering whether we really would, as Reekess did before. It seemed to work," Janice said hours later when both were back in their quarters. "Rek was almost gloating. I still hope you—we—don't walk into more trouble. I'd hate to have us in a couple of those Naxian tanks growing new extremities."

"I doubt that's what Ennissee'd want for us," answered her husband. "We were born crawlers, beneath his dignity to hate from the beginning. Rek is a renegade by his standards, worth real emotion. That's hypothesis, of course; I'm not at all sure. He may not even feel strongly about Rek, may just have wanted a Crotonite subject to go through the routine before he faced it himself. Don't worry about our trip—I mean, worry as sensibly as you can; we'll be careful."

Fafnir had just risen again in the northeast as seen from Pitville when a Naxian called to say that someone could come to collect Rekchellet. He had already been brought down to Pwanpwan, and was waiting at the Guild center, or possibly flying about the city; the speaker could not be sure. It was Barrar, not Hugh, who received the call. The Erthuma knew nothing of the matter until minutes later, when Rekchellet settled beside him outside his office. The Crotonite was in very high spirits.

"Strong as ever," he whistled, spreading his broad wings to full span—fortunately there was little wind at the moment. "You'd better take a good look, so you'll know me still. The wing-face isn't exactly the same. They said there was nothing they could do about that; the basic nature of the pattern is genetic, but the details are random." Hugh obeyed. He had become as accustomed during the last Common Year to recognizing Crotonites by their wings and Naxians by their body swirls and ripples as his own species by their faces, and felt after a few seconds that he would still know Rekchellet among any number of his fellows. He was about to ask whether Ennissee might also recognize his former victim when Rekchellet forestalled him.

"Are we ready for the trip? Who's going? I want

that (no-symbol-equivalent) to have a chance to recognize me again, too."

"Almost. We decided four other Crotonites, you, and four Habras, all of you flying yourselves, at least until a lot of the food's used up, with the big craft carrying the food. The trip will take longer than if you all could ride, but we won't be so restricted when we get there. Does that make sense to you? Can you fly that far on your new wings?"

"Of course. It's the same old muscles, just new webs, and the muscles certainly need the exercise. I *want* to fly anyway. It's been much too long. What's not ready?"

"I don't have the ship, of course. I didn't even dare ask for it until I knew when you'd be here and we could go. Also, I think I'm learning something. *I'm* not going to ask for it."

"Who is? I don't carry any weight. There isn't a flying person anywhere in Administration. I can guess why."

"There are no Cephallonians, either, and only one Erthuma, for that matter. I'm it. I don't try to guess why. It took me a long, long time to get an aircraft the other time, and I think I can shorten it now. Never mind why."

"How?" asked Rekchellet.

"I'll have S'Nash ask."

"That doesn't make sense. It/he isn't an administrator, or even a section chief."

"Not officially. Just a communication engineer and documentarian on Spreadsheet-Thinker's table. But it/he gives me a strong impression of having weight to throw around, for reasons I can't yet guess, and I'm going to encourage another throw. Wait and see. I'm a little surprised it/he's not here already, but I'll call around."

S'Nash appeared at the safety office before Hugh had made his second call, and did not ask why the Erthuma was routing an official request through it/him.

This was no surprise to the Erthuma. Rather than use Hugh's communicator, the serpentine being departed after accepting the commission, leaving Hugh and Rekchellet staring significantly at each other.

Thirty minutes later, long enough to make both wonder whether their suspicions were correct and to make Hugh suspect that the delay was for just that purpose, Barrar called the safety office and told him without elaboration that the large flier was at his disposal, parked at the warehouse. The two got there as promptly as they could, Rekchellet in thirty seconds completely relaxed, Hugh in three hundred panting heavily.

Counter-of-Supplies was again ready to load cartons of Crotonite and Habra foodstuffs into the vehicle. She neither said nor did anything about Naxian supplies, and Hugh was not in the least startled when S'Nash appeared once again in full-recycling armor. The word had already gone out to those who were to make the trip, and winged forms were settling beside the warehouse every minute or two as muscular Erthumoi trundled the containers from building to aircraft. Loading and personnel count were complete at about the same time. Hugh thanked the Locrian, who acknowledged the courtesy and withdrew.

S'Nash was already aboard, and the Erthuma lifted off with caution dictated by the presence of many living fliers and possibly other aircraft in the area.

He flew slowly to the living quarters, left the ship and awakened Janice—they were out of phase again and he had not wanted to disturb her sooner than absolutely necessary—and waited while she, too, donned recycling gear.

Moments later the craft was rising slowly straight up, surrounded by its winged satellites, and at half a kilometer's height he pointed the nose west and set the autopilot for a comfortable fifty kilometers per hour, which he knew both Habras and Crotonites could maintain for hundreds of kilometers. Janice had already gone back to sleep; there were scores of hours of travel ahead of them.

They passed only a short distance from where the truck had been abandoned; the Habras, for whom it was well within sensory range, reported that it was still there. This was not very surprising, but neither would its absence have been; there was no way to read Ennissee's mind. The vehicle was dark, and no one tried to find whether anyone was aboard. Hugh flirted briefly with a mild regret that they had not brought a Locrian, but didn't ask anyone to open the vehicle. They flew on.

From time to time one or another of the fliers would come aboard to eat and rest; there was not room for all, or even many, of them at once with the present stock of food. Plans were discussed, but had to be vague; there could only be guesses at what lay at the end of the flight. Conceivably there would be nothing; the hypothesis that Ennissee wanted them there might be wrong or irrelevant. He might not have cared whether they knew about the site, and even the location might be a deception.

They could plan on the latter assumption, and did. A wide search pattern based on the sensory powers of the Habras and the eyesight of the Crotonites was tentatively worked out. No one looked forward to implementing it, however. A search in the dark and chill for something probably not there would be purest anticlimax.

They hoped Ennissee, and the two Erthumoi for whom there was some evidence, and the Samian who had been reported as boarding the truck at the port, would all be there and all be able, willing or not, to explain the apparently senseless activities of the truck itself and at least one of its erstwhile occupants. Rekchellet, quite frankly, hoped that Ennissee would *not* be willing to cooperate; Rekchellet wanted an excuse. An on-the-spot excuse, since he had obviously suffered no permanent damage, and civilized people were above resenting mere temporary inconvenience.

Ennissee, one could hope, would be neither sneering nor uncooperative—except just at first. Rekchellet flew westward with that "at first" in his mind. Reekess, a few meters away, said little, but knew his thoughts and shared them.

Fafnir ceased rising behind them and to their right, and began to sink again very slowly; even the flight speed of living beings was greater than that of Habranha's equatorial rotation. The shadows below grew long again.

The hills still resembled dunes. No one could be sure whether they moved, since no one elevation was in sight long enough, but the winds were generally less violent at the height where they were flying. Twice there were sharp, steep escarpments angling across their path; Habranha was far too small for plate shifting, but there must be slow currents in the deep ice, accompanied presumably from time to time by phase changes and glacier quakes far below, even this far from the sunward side. Chaos still ruled this world, however snaillike the pace of its armies might be here in the chill darkness.

Presently Fafnir was left behind, and only the distant stars lighted the icy surface. They flew on. Janice woke up and relieved Hugh at the control panel, though flight was still automatic; the only breaks in its monotony were pauses to open the lock and let people in and out. It would have been possible to open at their slow cruising speed without disturbing the handling of the ship, but entry into and departure from a portal with a fifty-kilometer-per-hour wind across the opening seemed risky to Hugh. All the fliers claimed they could handle such a maneuver, some even expressing indignation that the Erthuma should regard it as dangerous; but Hugh insisted, to the extent of stopping the craft instantly

whenever he heard someone attempting to use the
outside hatch controls in flight. His translator passed
on a few Habra words not, apparently, directed at
him which sounded suspiciously like "thinks we're
children," but he reminded himself that the natives
didn't really regard this imputation as an insult and
remained firm in his policy.

Possibly as a result of this, all his personnel were
uninjured and reasonably rested and fed a hundred
kilometers from their goal, after what he thought of
as nearly four days of flight. They had agreed on an
approach tactic, and now descended to a level just
above the hills.

These were far more jagged than they had been
nearer the terminator. The wind was much weaker,
at least at the moment; and while there was still a
good deal of blown ice dust filling cracks and hollows here and there, this no longer seemed to be the
principal shaping agent of the landscape.

Hugh lowered his speed to let the fliers precede
him, and watched them spread out in fan formation,
Habras slightly ahead, as had been agreed. He kept
his eyes on them, while Janice watched the tracker
and reported distance and direction to the selected
spot. They knew this might not be a precise location;
Rekchellet had seen coordinates on the map, and
was reasonably sure he was reading the numbers
correctly even though the language was not his own,
but there was no way to be sure what sort of trust
could be placed in the map itself.

Every kilometer the aircraft's upper light blinked the
corrected distance in a simple improvised code, while
the Crotonites winged steadily forward and the faster
Habras swept back and forth in front of them, scanning
the ice below with eyes and electric senses.

They were a dozen kilometers short of the indicated point when the Crotonite at the left of the line
flashed her light back toward the others. Hugh and
Janice saw it at the same instant; S'Nash started to

speak, and fell silent. A touch on the board left the aircraft floating motionless a few meters above a barely visible ice peak, holding its position against the urge of a feeble breeze. Hugh opened the outer hatch and waited, but no one came aboard. A pair of broad Crotonite wings swept above the canopy after two or three minutes, however, and their owner's voice came through.

"Miriam felt metal several kilometers in front of her, and the others now agree. They say it's a large amount, and are sure they could not themselves be felt by another Habra at that distance. They will go no closer until they get your word, Hugh, in case you want to take the aircraft there before they themselves are sensed."

"We thought of that," agreed the Erthuma, "but couldn't see what to do afterward. No, let's follow Walt's idea. Let the Habras approach the metal in single line, one far enough behind the next so they can just sense and talk to each other. You Crotonites will follow in the same direction as best you can with your lights out, and I'll bring up the rear, well to one side, also dark. Whoever is in the lead look for signs of other living beings—Habras, of course, but any others he or she can infer from whatever they sense. If none are detected by the time the leader reaches the object, whatever it is, pass the message and any description back along the line to me as quickly as possible and we'll come forward to look it over. If anyone living is detected, or any sort of trouble or danger shows up, relay the word back and I'll be up there with all my lights going three seconds after I get it. That's why I'll be staying to one side; I don't want to run into any of you. But if any emergency message does come through, turn your own lights on again, too, so I'll be more certain to miss you. All right?"

"All right," agreed the Crotonite. "It will take several minutes to get your words up to the nearest

Habra. I'll send a double-double flash when that's done, and you can then be ready for more messages."

All three of the flier's occupants were now in the control section, the Erthumoi hunched over the panels, the Naxian behind them partly coiled but reared up enough to see through the windows. The autopilot was now cut out horizontally so that they were drifting slowly with the wind, and Hugh's fingers were ready to move them in any direction at any speed. Janice's hands were at the light controls. All three pairs of eyes were looking outside; the interior lights of the flier had been extinguished long before, though she had cut in small riding lights to let any of their companions find the vehicle.

The minutes dragged on. Hugh, realizing from a glance at the tracker that the breeze was drifting them into line behind his crew, gave a brief kick of power to send them five hundred meters to the right. He was almost ready to repeat the maneuver when the promised double flashes of light finally came and he realized that the real wait was only beginning.

He was wrong. Scarcely thirty seconds later a second, blindingly bright blaze came from beyond the crags ahead. It lasted several seconds, lighting up the sky, drowning the stars, and showing eight black spots in silhouette against the suddenly glowing background. One of these was just identifiable as a Crotonite form; the others were presumably the rest of the crew, too distant to see in detail. Hugh did not wait for any other signal.

He sent the aircraft hurtling toward the flash, grateful that the single glimpse of his people allowed him to be sure of missing them all. He had no weapons, and nothing he could have improvised as a weapon other than the craft itself; he wasn't thinking weapons or deliberate violence; but he was used to accidents, and he intended to place his hull between his people and whatever had produced the flash. It was too bad that Janice was there, it occurred to him later, but he told himself firmly that she was an adult, had come along willingly, and he might have needed her help. He hoped the Naxian would not be a nuisance; he had no idea how any of that race might be expected to face personal risk—had never been sure that S'Nash had regarded the earlier blowing-away episode as risky—and had no time to find out now. This also failed to reach his conscious mind until later.

He did not use full speed, since he had to keep some awareness of how far he was going. He passed the farthest forward of his Habras in some five seconds, seeing the being easily now that Janice had turned their search and landing lights on full. In five more he brought the vessel to a halt, and his wife swept the air around and the ice below with her beams.

The air was empty, but there was a cloud of dust or steam or both rising from the ground almost straight ahead of them and another two kilometers or so away. Hugh nosed down and headed rapidly toward it without consulting either of his companions, and brought the machine to a halt a hundred meters above the ice.

Whether what they saw was a menace or not was hard to decide at once. Steam was still rising from the extremely flat floor of a crater some thirty meters across and five deep. Beside the pit at a distance of less than twenty meters was a square metal structure about fifteen meters on a side and three high, as featureless as a food box and apparently undamaged. There was no motion in the vicinity but the rising steam—more probably fog, Hugh corrected his thought. The flat bottom of the pit was probably liquid water, at least for the moment. Whether energy was still being released to keep it that way was not yet obvious.

Something had exploded, just as his Habras had started to approach the building.

Hugh had a very low opinion of coincidence, backed by the Erthumoi tendency to recognize it when it wasn't there.

He spent no more time examining building or crater, but lifted and swung back toward his people. In a few seconds the natives became visible, no longer strung out in a line; they had either never finished that maneuver or had had time to get back together since the blast. Distant, flashing lights showed that the Crotonites were also still in the air, and Hugh hung where he was, hatch open, waiting for the group to reach him.

This took several minutes, as even the nearest Crotonite had been a dozen kilometers or more away. They still lacked room for everyone aboard, so the aircraft was landed and its riders emerged as the winged members of the party settled around them.

"Is everyone all right?"

"We're getting our sight back slowly," replied Miriam. "The flash completely blinded all of us; we were flying on electrical sense for minutes, but could see your lights by the time you came back toward us. Do you know what happened?"

"What about you others?" Hugh asked the Crotonites, putting first things first without intending discourtesy. "Do you have alternate flying senses, too, or were you far enough away to avoid being blinded?"

"It wasn't so much distance as having a hill in the way," replied Rekchellet. "I suppose that was a booby trap. I still don't like that (no-symbol-equivalent)."

"We don't know yet. There's a building, apparently undamaged, beside what looks like an explosion crater. I was going to suggest we look it over, but your idea makes me wonder if that's a good idea. I wouldn't have thought of traps, myself—at least, not really nasty ones like that."

"I've met Erthumoi who were less civilized," muttered another Crotonite voice.

"I'm sure you have. But what do we do? Ordinarily I'd have searched that building for survivors of the explosion, as normal procedure. Now I'm not so sure I want to go near it, and I certainly can't let any of you approach it until I've—"

"I can. It's my business," snapped Rekchellet.

"It's *my* business. I'm talking responsibility, not revenge, if that's what you have in mind. Reekess, is there any use in my arguing about this? Is it just Rekchellet, or am I bucking general Crotonite ethics? Shut up, Rek. I trust you, but you're excited, and just as likely to be sure you're right as I would be. Reekess?"

"He has the right, by custom."

"Even if we're not sure Ennissee had anything to do with all this?"

"The probability is good enough."

"All right. Get aboard, Rek. You and S'Nash stay here, Jan—no," as his wife was about to object, "it's quite a walk from here. I'll fly us over to within a couple of hundred meters, set down, and you take the flier back—remember the others don't have recycling gear, and all the food is in it."

Janice entered the vehicle without a word, but gestured the Naxian in after her. Hugh frowned, but decided not to make an issue of it; after all, there was no way S'Nash could manage the aircraft. The handlers on its/his armor were far too clumsy, and if it/he chose to shed the armor—possible, in Habranhan environment even in this temperature, though not for very long—the prehensile fringes on the serpentine body were even less facile.

Besides, Janice probably wanted to keep the Naxian in sight. Theories need observational testing.

Hugh and Rekchellet boarded together, the rest of the group waiting silently, and Hugh brought the aircraft back toward the scene of the explosion.

Neither he nor the Crotonite was in any great hurry to commit suicide. They flew low over the crater, confirming that there was liquid water, with needles of ice now growing across its surface, at its bottom. They circled the building a hundred meters away and ten or fifteen off the ice, finding a door on the side away from the crater but no other visible opening. They made one more circle at half the distance, drew back again to a hundred meters, and landed. Hugh and the Crotonite emerged, while Janice silently took the controls. Not until she had lifted off and the flier was dwindling in the distance did the others realize that S'Nash had emerged with them.

There was certainly nothing to be done. There seemed nothing to say. The three approached the door, not at all hastily.

Ten meters away, Hugh remarked, "It would have been handy if one of us were a Locrian. Why didn't I bring Plant-Biologist along?" There seemed no answer to this, either, and neither of his companions attempted one. They stopped some five meters from the building, and examined the door as carefully as they could from that distance. It showed no peculiarities, and they started forward again.

They failed to reach it.

They were still three or four meters away when the portal opened and three beings emerged.

Two were Erthumoi, neither of whom Hugh had ever to his knowledge seen before, one apparently female, the other a male a head taller than Hugh himself.

The remaining person looked like a slab of leather, supported by a mechanism resembling a headless human skeleton, with the Samian body ensconced in the rib cage. Hugh thought of the report about the truck users which he had received from the seaport what seemed like months ago, rather than ten or twelve Common Days. He tried some spreadsheet thinking of his own, without marked success. He rather expected to see a fourth figure emerge from the still open door, but none had appeared by the time the three were confronting the newcomers from less than two meters away.

Rekchellet, too, had his expectations.

"Where's Ennissee?" he hissed. "I need words with him."

"Not here," came the answer in Samian tones. "We are very glad of your arrival, Hugh. Our communication equipment was in the mole, which for some reason developed power plant trouble, and we have no way of calling for transportation. You must have been close enough to see the explosion. We were greatly worried; we don't expect Ennissee back for nearly a year, and while the resources of this site should keep us alive, we would all be most uncomfortable. We would be grateful if you could transport us to Pitville."

"You expect Ennissee back in a year?" Rekchellet asked the question; Hugh was still filling spaces in his mental chart.

"About that. He departed recently, leaving me in charge."

"Where did he go?"

"To the Naxian biological station. He learned very recently, we understand, that they can provide treatment for injuries he suffered some time ago, and for which he had been using rather unsatisfactory prosthetic equipment."

Hugh forestalled a second explosion.

It was less difficult than he expected; Rekchellet's rage subsided almost at once to a cold, controlled fury which held S'Nash's full and possibly admiring attention. All Hugh really had to say was, "He'll have a hard time getting away from those growth tanks, won't he?"

The Crotonite gave the wing-flip equivalent of a nod.

"And when he does, it will be nice that he has no more handicaps. I can meet him in the air." He relaxed visibly, and Hugh was about to resume courtesies with the Samian who had been speaking, when S'Nash joined the conversation.

"It's a little surprising to find you this far from Pitville, Ged." The Erthuma looked down at the Naxian, then up again at the occupant of the skeletonlike walker. The other human figures remained silent, giving no sign they were following the conversation; Hugh recalled the unfamiliar tech translator modules which had been found in the truck, and wondered which if either of them was indeed from the home planet he himself had never seen. There was nothing about either person to attract special attention.

His curiosity was brief, as S'Nash's words got through to his consciousness. Ged? Barrar couldn't be out here. The walker looked like his, of course, though Hugh could never have sworn to all the details of the machine, and one Samian looked as much like an excessively thick steak as another. But Ged Barrar must be back at Pitville, making sure that the various details envisioned by Spreadsheet-Thinker were actually occurring as the Locrian decided they should. He was the administrator's main connection with reality, or had presented that image. But this one had addressed him by name, he suddenly realized, and its next words removed any doubt.

"The various contingency plans feed back very nicely into the main program, and it has been some time since I have had to devote much attention to Pitville—even with Hugh's conscience and curiosity operating," the Samian answered calmly.

"It is you!" Hugh muttered.

"Oh, yes. I'm sorry if it surprises you, but I did mention that I had other interests."

"Not that you were working on them. How does

this connect? More important, did you know what was happening to Rekchellet?"

"Not until almost too late. I'm very sorry about that. Ennissee has been useful, but I'm afraid I didn't fully understand what his injury had done to him. I certainly never supposed that he would only submit himself to Naxian treatment, tempting as it was, until after a—uh—test. It was foolish of me, because I do have some idea of what flying means to your people, Rekchellet. Since he could fly, however, I underestimated his—well, general bitterness."

Beside Hugh S'Nash stirred briefly. There was no way for the Erthuma to tell whether Barrar perceived this or not. After a moment, the Naxian spoke up.

"I told you myself."

"So you did. I still underestimated. Perhaps no one but another Crotonite, or perhaps a Habra, and now that I think of it, a Naxian, can really appreciate what a threat or injury to its wings would mean to someone who flies naturally. If you recall, I had already deduced that you have been playing that addictive Naxian game which involves what I can only describe in language as 'composing emotional tunes' out of the readings you obtain from non-Naxians, and therefore I had reason to doubt your objectivity. If you had actually told Hugh and Janice what you do for amusement when they asked you a year or so ago, I might have felt otherwise."

Hugh wondered how the Samian had known about that bit of conversation, but failed to pursue the thought as S'Nash gave its/his answer.

"It's not exactly a game; it's normal behavior. And it's not just with aliens, though you're a lot less boring than my own people, I admit," his tones flowed calmly from Hugh's translator.

Several frames in the Erthuma's mental spreadsheet filled themselves simultaneously.

12

AND WORD UNKNOWN GUIDE STRAIGHTER THAN A PRINT

Barrar resolved the Erthuma's unuttered wonder.

"S'Nash told me about that question, Hugh, for reasons of its/his own which I understand fairly well. I assure you I wasn't eavesdropping. Please come inside, now; I have a request. Mahere, Jayree, and I do need transportation, but not just for ourselves. There are things I very much want you to take to Janice so that she can examine and date them. I'd stay here myself rather than have them left."

The Samian turned back to the building. He said nothing to his Erthumoi companions, but they followed him. Hugh, Rekchellet, and S'Nash, after a brief hesitation on the Naxian's part, trailed them inside.

There was no air lock; the whole interior was under Habranhan conditions. Its only furnishings were benches and tables, nearly all carrying instruments and tools and specimens. The largest work surface bore a block of ice, and both Hugh and Rekchellet had an inkling of what they were about to see. They were almost right.

It was not a complete Habra body this time, just a portion of thorax, with much of the head and two right wings attached. Even the Erthuma and Crotonite could see that there were differences between this body and the natives they knew; the head was narrower, the remaining eyes much larger. The wings were much shorter than was usual on the natives they had seen, leading to the speculation that this being might have been smaller or at least lighter than they. Hugh could understand Ged's interest; this had to be a key find in Habranhan prehistory, and a proper description of it would ensure anyone a reputation.

"Where did you find it? How deep?" he asked. "Let me call Jan; she'll want to see it."

"Then you'll carry it back and do the measuring for me? Wonderful! But I didn't find it myself. Ennissee did."

Rekchellet stiffened, and his wings spread slightly.

"Where?" repeated the Erthuma. "And I suppose he found the other one, that was left in the truck, too?"

"Yes. We wanted that dated without having Spreadsheet-Thinker bothered. Has that been done, by the way?"

"Jan has figures," Hugh evaded. "What about this one? Can we see the site?"

"I'm afraid not. Our means of reaching it is gone." Barrar paused, possibly for effect. "It was under the ice at a depth of two hundred sixteen point four one kilometers."

Hugh and Rekchellet were not just startled. They were more dumbfounded; perhaps reasonably, S'Nash seemed more interested in watching them than in pondering Ged's statement. Hugh glanced at the other Erthumoi to see how the words affected them, and judged that they were not even listening. They had found seats across the single room and were waiting with apparent indifference. It would hardly be news to them.

"How did you get a shaft that deep? It can't be anywhere near here; there are no pump buildings or waste piles or—"

"There was no shaft. Ennissee had financed the development of a digging *vehicle* which could carry explorers, usually him and one of his Erthuma helpers. It had seismic and other sensing equipment to tell of fossils or other objects nearby, and such details as its depth below the surface. He collected a great deal of material at various depths from this area, mostly root fragments, but there are a few entire bushes, too. Everything is in this building. Janice must examine it all. This specimen, however, is the prize.

"It was the mole—the digging machine—which destroyed itself just before your arrival. I do not look forward to telling Ennissee."

"You don't know what caused it to blow? Was anyone in it, or using it, at the time?"

"No one was aboard, and its power was off except for minor things like maintenance heaters."

"Did it have any sort of automatic control, like the truck?"

"Oh, yes. Ennissee sometimes sent it down on test trips unoccupied. It also had remote control, and could be operated from here." The Samian stepped over to another worktable bearing an obvious directing console and several vision screens.

"Did you ever go down in it yourself? And did you ever pilot it yourself?"

"Yes to both, though not on really deep journeys."

"I suppose it had a standard fusion unit for its basic power."

"So I always assumed. I don't really know, but it seems likely. What else could there be?"

"Those aren't supposed to be dangerous. I wonder what could have happened." Hugh was frowning, and it did not require a Naxian to perceive his mystification. He thought for several seconds while his fingers rested. Then, "Did Ennissee have a training simulator to go with these controls, or did he teach you on actual trips?" It was a last-hope question.

"I learned by driving the real machine, under his

supervision. It was not difficult." There was another pause.

"Did he teach you any emergency procedures?"

"No. I have no idea what emergencies he had envisioned, nor what he would have done about them."

The last hope seemed to be gone. Hugh could not believe that any rational being would design a machine without backup equipment for the more predictable sorts of failure, but he had no specimen of the machine to examine in the hope of guessing what was predictable. Equipment, even fusers, did sometimes malfunction. The trouble was that the mechanisms which used the fusion-produced energy were more usually at fault, and the fact that the building he now occupied was still intact suggested strongly that the explosion had not been nuclear. However, no further look at the explosion crater seemed likely to furnish informative remains.

"All right," said Hugh. "Get your specimens and their documentation together. We'll get the flier back and load them aboard. I'm afraid it will be pretty crowded; we still have a lot of food. What would you have done, Ged, if we hadn't shown up? Wouldn't Spreadsheet-Thinker be missing you fairly soon?"

"There was a transmitter in the mole. There are several people at Pitville who could have come for me in a flier when I called. Without communication, as I said when you arrived, I was in trouble."

"Are you going to let Spreadsheet-Thinker add this project to her picture, now that it seems to be finished?"

"I've been thinking about that. Eventually, yes, but I'd prefer to wait until I get detailed measurements from Janice—"

"And have written your own report, crediting her and Ennissee, of course."

"Naturally." Not for the first time, Hugh wished he had the Naxian power. He hated himself for it, but was beginning to feel that he couldn't trust anyone, and wishing that he had more of his wife's built-in civilization. He said no more, but went outside and gestured to the aircraft waiting a few hundred meters away and forty or fifty above the ice. It approached immediately; Janice had been watching.

He boarded, and as quickly as possible summed up what had just happened. His wife, who should have been delighted, frowned thoughtfully.

"It sounds exciting, but you don't like coincidences any better than I do. I take it you want me to be very, very critical of all this material."

"I do. A plausible motive isn't enough for a conviction, of course. I never cared any more for Ennissee, from what I heard of him, than Rek does; but Ged and S'Nash I've always thought were pretty sound people. I don't like suddenly having to wonder which one is less reliable."

Janice nodded silently, and rearranged her features to show proper interest for this Samian's benefit as they entered the building. This was presumably a waste of time with S'Nash, but within moments of her seeing the fragmentary Habra body the Erthuma no longer had to pretend. Her full attention and interest went into examining it for many minutes.

"I'm not a biologist," she said, looking up at last, "and Plant-Biologist will have to get his eye into this; but as far as I'm concerned, the sooner we're back at Pitville the better. Tell you what—maybe we could send for another flier? This one has to stay with the Habras and Crotonites, of course. Maybe you should stay out here with them anyway, Honey. You came to look around, and haven't spent much time at it."

"Getting rid of me?"

"Oh, no. Come back whenever you're ready. I just didn't want you to feel you'd wasted the flight and food and time. You haven't as far as I'm concerned, but I didn't think you'd be satisfied." She kept a perfectly straight face. Hugh glanced at the Naxian, but it/he chose not to be helpful.

"All right." Hugh could play any games his wife could, he felt sure. "Ennissee is presumably tied down for a while, so Rekchellet's in no hurry. The others expected to stay a while anyway. We'd better ask, though—Ged, did your borer start any holes at other places around here? Ones we could check? It would be nice to know what disturbance it made of the ice it went through, and that sort of thing. Maybe we should get some ice specimens from the inside of its holes for Jan to test. Maybe she should stay and get them herself."

"Oh, no. You can do that perfectly well." Janice looked again at the icebound material still on the benches. "I'll wait until you've called for another transport before I move this—"

"It might be better to have Ged call," Hugh keyed. The Samian showed no Erthuma-detectable reaction to the implication even he must have perceived, but set his walker in motion toward the flier. Hugh, embarrassed, found himself following close behind, hoping that his motive was not obvious. They went aboard, and within five minutes Ged announced that another machine, large enough to hold Janice and the specimens, would be with them shortly. How the administrative head had reacted to the new information, which Ged had sent along with the request, was not mentioned.

"I'll have to go back to Pitville with your wife," he added. "I can't stay out of touch with Spreadsheet-Thinker for the days it will take you to get back. There's no use my talking to your wife, though, until she has the information and I can start writing. She may want to give some guidance in the wording, too, I expect; I suppose it will really be her article, too. We won't have to wait for Ennissee, though; I'll simply give him support credit for developing the mole."

"And operating it."

"Well, of course."

"Mightn't he want to describe some of the under-ice search activities and problems?"

"Well, yes. We'd better consult him, at that. Do you suppose he can talk while his wing treatment's going on?"

"Rekchellet could," Hugh assured him, and rejoined his wife, shaking his head gently. He had encountered jealousy in the exploring field, but it had always seemed to him that there were enough worlds to go around. Greed for publishing credit was not exactly arcana to him, but he had never before met it face on.

The other craft appeared overhead, flashed past trailing its sonic shock wave, slowed, and settled beside the building. The loading took a surprisingly long time, as Janice took extreme precautions to make sure that all Ennissee's notes remained with the right specimens, or as nearly with them as they already were. Her initial examination had left some doubt about some of them, which the Samian was sometimes but not always able to resolve. Neither of the Erthumoi seemed able to help, though it was hard to be sure with no appropriate translator modules available. They had made trips in the mole, Barrar had said; but they seemed to be mainly muscle and hand labor in Ennissee's project.

Eventually, however, Janice and Barrar entered the new flier, whose Locrian pilot had never left it, and moments later it had vanished in the east.

Hugh, rather deflated, set up the search arrangements which had been planned earlier in case nothing had been found, and waited for dreary hours while the activities neared and reached their anticlimax. He spent some of the time exploring two or three tunnels made by the mole, whose location had been provided by Barrar, but obtained little information. For one thing, they were extremely steep and

smooth-walled; descending them on foot was hazardous, not so much because falls might be dangerous as because return might be impossible. Foresight
worked.

The scouring of the area by his flying personnel
provided nothing except basic science information;
the patterns of the ice surface itself offered fascinating clues to what might be going on below, and
Hugh thought a little wistfully about the seismic
studies S'Nash had proposed earlier. Maybe, with
Barrar revealing himself more widely as a would-be
Respected Opinion candidate, something might be
done about that without anyone's having to be un-
derhanded.

But right now, nothing having any imaginable
bearing on the Truck Problem was appearing. Actually, it looked as though the problem itself were
pretty well solved in all but minor details. Had
Barrar, for example, actually been responsible in
some subtle way for finding the lost Crotonite? Or
was he merely trying to give that impression?

Once again, Hugh felt the acute discomfort of realizing that he could no longer completely trust
someone.

Perhaps. The "perhaps" was the worst part.

The trip back to Pitville was a little less boring.
There was room for more people on board now, with
Janice and much of the food gone; this was fortunate, because the two Erthuma had to be carried.
There was no adequate way to talk with them; their
translators seemed to work only between Ennissee's
speech, which none of Hugh's Crotonite group
knew, and their own Erthumoi languages—different
ones; they could talk to each other readily enough,
but had to use translators. They had kept to themselves during the stay at the explosion site, eating
their own supplies—their environment armor was
not full-recycling—and sleeping on air cots which
were set up in one corner of the building; but when

Hugh gathered his flying group and sent them in close formation on an eastward course, with the once again rising Fafnir ahead and to their left, the pair had no trouble interpreting the situation. They pointed to themselves and to Hugh's aircraft; when Hugh nodded assent, they salvaged some cartons of food from the building and went aboard.

Their lack of appropriate translator modules helped ease the boredom of the flight; Hugh made a serious effort to learn the language of one of them, something he had never really attempted before and had no real idea how to do.

The one who had offered her help in the exercise answered to the name of Mahare Chen. She had a slightly different skin shade and facial shape, especially around the eyes, than the Falgan norm, but Hugh had seen Erthumoi displaying far wider appearance variations and was conscious of this only as a recognition feature. Before they had been exchanging noises and sketches for very long it was clear that she claimed to be from the original home world of the Erthumoi. Hugh had learned a little Swahili as part of required Human History during his basic education, but this proved not to be the right tongue, and progress remained slow.

Rekchellet's drawing skills proved useful occasionally, but the Crotonite could not remain aboard for long at a time. He left his pad and stylus with Hugh, somewhat reluctantly the latter felt sure, and the equipment did resolve an occasional impasse in hand signs. Mahare was a better artist than Hugh, but far below Rekchellet's level. Once or twice even S'Nash was of some help by explaining that a particular sketch had produced more humor, or concealed anger, than enlightenment, though it/he could never give a reason for the reaction.

Personal names and most of the immediately appropriate nouns came across fairly quickly. Hugh could name Naxian and Crotonite and human being

and Habra in the Erthuma language without making
his listener laugh at his accent; he could name the
planet and speak of flying and walking and crawling
and a few other activities, since the others were not
wearing recycling armor and the flier lacked equivalent facilities and had to land occasionally. The
world's name sounded like "I-Bawl;" a Crotonite
was a "Snutibat," and a Naxian an "Eednite." Sometimes there was more than one word, not surprisingly; when Rekchellet drew the specimen which
Janice had taken back to Pitville ahead of them,
Mahare called it a "Palaksee" or a "Pilldahn,"
though she had called the living Habras "Needulz."
She had also glanced at her companion and laughed
for no obvious reason. Hugh had no success relating
any of these sounds to his own language; apparently
even the comparatively few centuries separating
Falga's population from Earth had allowed, or possibly caused, too much linguistic evolution to permit
easy tracing.

The whole flight time was not, by any means,
spent at language lessons; Mahare sometimes slept,
sometimes chattered at length to her tall male companion through their translators, sometimes sat and
thought or simply watched the Habranhan icescape
below or sky above as they flew. If there was any
connection between the two other than their common employment by Ennissee, it never became obvious.

Both passengers knew the word "Pwanpwan," and
used it often enough to make Hugh realize that they
hoped to get there eventually. He assumed that there
would be no great difficulty about this, but tried not
to make any signs likely to be taken as a promise
that he would carry them there either himself or at
once.

As it turned out, this was no problem. Hugh reported arrival to Ged as they slanted down toward
the lights of Pitville, mentioning his passengers, and

did not even have to arrange quarters for them after he landed. The small flier which had brought him and Reekess back from Pwanpwan was waiting beside the warehouse, as was Ged Barrar himself. The Samian shepherded the two Erthumoi aboard with almost discourteous haste, and they were gone before Hugh had a chance to more than wave a farewell.

"You'll be less surprised later," S'Nash remarked. The Naxian's words were surprising enough right then. Clearly it/he knew more about everything going on than had been made clear so far, but this sounded almost as though the devious character intended to provide answers it/himself. Hugh refused to worry about it; he had not seen Janice for several Common Days. He left the unloading of what was left of the supplies to the warehouse people.

As far as his wife could tell, the specimens from Ennissee's dig were very old. This merely meant older than the carbon dating limit; there was no reliable way to go farther with organic specimens. Habranhan "Fossils" were entire frozen remains, not mineralized. The only radionuclide in them with a respectable half life was potassium-forty, and there was very little of that; Habranhan life made do with an extremely low mineral content, not too surprisingly. The argon-forty which was one of its decay products could diffuse fairly rapidly, on the geological time scale, from the immediate area of its production; cross-checking with calcium-forty, the other product, pointless on other worlds because it was ubiquitous, might help a little here, but still all one could hope for was a minimum age. Actually, Janice had found only a little of the potassium and too little of its decay products to measure. The main specimen was certainly older than one hundred sixty thousand Common Years, with another faint probability that it was older than five hundred fifty thousand; but she had no faith whatever in the latter figure.

Such of Ennissee's plant material as she had had time for was all much younger, safely inside the carbon limits. This, surprisingly, included that which seemed to be associated with the Habra remains. She had no explanation for this. She was still correlating her various results with Ennissee's collection notes.

"What do our biological friends say?" asked Hugh.

"Just what you'd expect. Irritated because this or that part is missing, so they can't check this or that theory of Habra evolution."

"But they are sure it *is* a Habra ancestor?"

"They seem to be taking it for granted. I may be doing them an injustice, of course."

"It's a pretty key point. If there is this much evidence that the Habras did evolve here, that undersea project gets very important indeed." Janice had not heard about this; Hugh had been too occupied otherwise to remember to tell her what he had learned from Bill and Shefcheeshee on his earlier return from Pwanpwan. He clarified the story now, and she nodded.

"Have you told Ged about your dates yet?" her husband asked.

"Yes. There seemed no reason not to."

Hugh was less sure of this, but reflected that it would take the Samian time to get his article written, if it were to be of degree caliber. If Ged didn't realize that, which he might not, then perhaps it would be just as well if Janice's name didn't appear on the work. In any case, it was a safe bet that the author would be back with more questions, since Janice was still at work. No need to worry.

In fact, there suddenly seemed no need to worry about anything. The original frozen body, beyond serious doubt, had been brought back in the truck and foisted on them more or less as a dress rehearsal. It would be nice to know where it had actually come from—Ennissee's mole? From how deep under the ice—but that information could be worked out of Ennissee. It would be a little surprising if both specimens had been found near the Cold Pole.

And Hugh suddenly realized how surprising it was. His own native assistants could never have reached that point without the supplies in the aircraft, or some complex arrangement of food caches such as he had set up earlier for the Crotonites. That was something to be checked immediately through Ted; there might be historical records of such an expedition, or even several, though it was surprising that nothing of the sort had been mentioned in earlier discussion of the truck specimen.

If the other find represented a remote ancestor of the present natives there would of course be no historical record for it—but *how had it flown that far?* It had smaller wings than the present species, and at least superficially a smaller brain. How could the Habra equivalent of a Lucy have made such a journey? Where had the specimen actually been found? Granted the general Habranhan chaos, which presumably extended to the surface and subsurface glaciers of the night hemisphere, what were the chances of a primitive flier from the ring continent being carried by a storm to or shortly past the terminator and then borne by ice currents all the way to the Cold Pole?

The first chance was probably respectable, granting Habranha's storms. The second seemed remarkably close to zero. The seismic study of the Solid Ocean discussed a year or so ago by S'Nash suddenly seemed urgent.

Ennissee would have to be questioned in such a way as to establish the truth or falsehood of his answers beyond reasonable doubt, no argument about it. Rekchellet could be trusted to help with that, since it would make the other Crotonite look subser-

vient to an Erthuma. There could hardly be a better
revenge in Crotonite eyes.

The truck might bear further study; it could have
been used to transport the second specimen as well.
In any case it ought to be either returned to the Port,
or have its location reported to the owners. That was
not really Pitville responsibility, but Hugh's people
had been involved, and it would be a courtesy. No
further excuse should be needed.

Maybe Jan and I should fly out, Hugh thought,
with someone to take the aircraft back, and drive the
truck back here ourselves. That could be fun; not
even a Locrian within dozens of kilometers. We
need a vacation from the diving juice. I'll have Rek
give me a quick lesson on that autodriver—no, he
doesn't know how to make it avoid elevation data—
wait, that's all right, if we're just setting a new route
and not back-tracing—

Janice thought it a great idea, though there were
many small specimens yet to be dated. Barrar made
no fuss this time about a few minutes of flier use;
both had rather expected this after recent events.
Most unfortunately there was no chance to dejuice
themselves; inspection of the Pits was still important, and no one else could yet do it. Hugh, exasper-
ated, had a long conversation with Ted, who seemed
to know the people working on the Habra cold protection problem. He got some encouragement, but
no assurance of any immediate solution. The
Erthumoi decided to take the break anyway.

Third-Supply-Watcher flew them out to the truck,
which was still where they had abandoned it, let
them off, and waited until they had powered it up
and signaled that everything was in working order.
The Locrian promptly departed, and the couple began setting up the controls.

It was some time later, with the vehicle well on its
way back to Pitville, that an object in the living
quarters caught Hugh's eye.

"That's the tech supplementary translator we found before, when we hoped to figure who the Erthuma on board might be. Remember that one I told you about, who claims to be from Earth? She probably is. One of the modules seemed to be an Old Planet language."

"Is it still there?" asked his wife, not greatly interested.

"I suppose so. The unit is. We took the modules out to examine, and then—Hmph. I don't remember. Let's see."

Hugh opened the device. Apparently whoever had been holding the modules when the line of activity had swerved had felt that the best place to put them down was back in their own sockets; they were indeed there. Hugh extracted them, one by one, checking the symbols and nodding slowly, putting each back before extracting the next.

"This is it," he said at last. "Do you know what it is?"

"No. Like you, I'd guess it's Mother Planet. Shall we take them with us when we get back, and try to find out?"

"Strictly speaking, we have no business doing anything of the sort. They're not our property."

"They're probably Ennissee's," the woman pointed out.

"If either of us were Rekchellet, that would probably be an excuse. Tell you what. We'll write down the ident code, and call the Guild office when we get back. We might even want a copy of that module; couldn't you use some information from that Erthuma on collection details? Ged said that one of them usually went with Ennissee in the mole, and you were worried about some of the sample labels. They weren't helpful out at the site, but maybe talking to them *without* Ged around would be different."

"We could ask Ennissee himself."

"We could, but I'd rather not, for several reasons.

The way he treated Rek is only one, though it's the basis of the others, I suppose. I know Rek plans to find him and settle matters—"

"You mean a duel or something like that?"

"I don't think so. Crotonites are civilized. He wants revenge, but not violence; he wants to embarrass the fellow. It will complicate things for Rek if he finds us dealing on friendly terms with his enemy, and maybe complicate his feelings for us."

"I think he's safely our friend now, regardless. He's known us a long time, and makes allowances of all sorts for our being crawlers and Erthumoi."

"You may be right, but let's not strain it. We'll try those Erthumoi assistants first, until Rek finishes his business; after all, *he* may get the knowledge we want. Making Ennissee come crawling to us with information would be a very satisfactory revenge, I suspect."

"So you said before. All right, let's get in touch with this Chen person."

Nothing further relevant to the problem occurred on the way back to Pitville, and with the truck parked by the still undisturbed Habra corpse they went to Hugh's office.

The Guild was able to help them. Mahare Chen was indeed, according to their records, a native of Earth, and the office had translator modules of her language. If Explorer Cedar would load his communicator appropriately, a duplicate would be transmitted for his own unit at once. A Falgite module would be provided for Engineer Chen, and the office would attempt to locate her, deliver the module, and request that she make contact with Explorer or Chemist Cedar at Pitville. No trouble.

Janice went back to her lab. Hugh called Ged and tactfully tried to find out what progress had been made on his article, especially in the matter of getting information from Ennissee. The Samian replied ruefully that he had had no time for either the article

or Ennissee, that some of Spreadsheet-Thinker's
chart sections needed serious modification, and that
he hoped Hugh would not need fliers or large numbers of people for the next few Common Days.
Hugh promised to do his best but mentioned the in-
trinsic nature of his job. It sometimes called for—

"I had noticed that," interrupted Barrar, and ended
the conversation. Again, Hugh found himself wondering unhappily how much of what he had been
told could be believed, and intensely disliking the
sensation.

S'Nash came in, and Hugh wondered whether the
Naxian had sensed his emotions from outside.
Janice's theory, which she had not yet explained in
detail, implied that the beings had to see the subject
of their analysis. She was not, however, sure of this
and Hugh was even less so. S'Nash seemed to turn
up very often when it/he could be of help; maybe
people broadcast something more subtle than a visual image.

It was nearly two more hours, and the Naxian was
still in the office being useful, before Mahare Chen
returned his call. It was five minutes after he had
started talking to her, just after Janice had also come
in, that he discovered with shock what the words
"Palaksee" and "Pill-dahn" meant, and decided with
relief that he could probably trust the Samian after
all.

Ennissee, however was another problem. Hugh
could only hope that he was safely immobilized.

And S'Nash was still another, but he tried to put
this out of his mind for the moment.

Hugh asked several more questions, which Chen
answered, but sometimes rather hesitantly.

"Are Jayree and I in trouble?" she asked bluntly,
after one of them. Hugh shrugged.

"Not with the Guild, as far as I'm concerned.
Most of your work for Ennissee was legitimate. All
anyone could object to is this joke, if that's what it

was. If your consciences bother you, tell the story to
Rekchellet. He should be very much on your side."

"We thought it would affect only a few Crotonites
who didn't seem to be flying with both wings and
were about ready for a correspondence course in as-
trology anyway. And the pay was good," she added.

"If you mean extra pay for the joke, that should
have warned you of something. Never mind, though;
we'll try to calm down the rest of the population. I
suggest you stay around Pwanpwan, or leave a very
specific forwarding address if work takes you elsewhere. It will make a much nicer picture with the
Guild than disappearing, and I'm sure Rek will be
delighted to take your side if any Trueliners get indignant about your telling me the story. I don't suppose there are many of them on Habranha anyway,
and you could make Ennissee look pretty foolish
among the ordinary Crotonites if he tried to make
trouble for you."

The woman still looked slightly uneasy, but admitted that Hugh was probably right. He hoped her
trouble was conscience, but couldn't be sure under
the circumstances that she had one.

He was about to break the connection when another thought struck him.

"You might get a lot more people on your side,"
he pointed out, "if you and your friend helped re-
construct that mole. You must know a good deal
about it, and I know at least one person who is already very upset about what happened to it, and is
going to be a lot more so when he finds out about
the faking. You know him, too; it's the Samian who
was out there with you."

"Didn't he know about the trick?" The question
startled Hugh; it was a possibility which hadn't occurred to him.

"I don't think so, but I can find out pretty reliably,
I think. Keep in touch with the Guild, anyway."

Janice and he took brief counsel, but there seemed

only one decent thing to do, and that at once. They asked S'Nash whether he could and would tell them whether Barrar was hearing something new when Hugh told him about the fossil, as he proposed to do immediately.

"From here, even if I can watch him on the screen, I doubt it," was the answer, "but if you'll give me time to get over to his office so I can watch him first hand, probably yes. Samians are something of a challenge, but it will be fun to try. Give me time to get over there before you call him." The Naxian left the safety office without waiting for an answer.

The Erthumoi allowed what seemed a reasonable time to pass, and called the administration center. They thought at first they had gotten Barrar directly but realized almost at once that they were talking to another Samian wearing a similar walker. Ged, they were informed, had left firm orders that he was not to be interrupted; perhaps his recent complaint about his work load had been based on fact. Hugh wrestled briefly with his own conscience, won, and stated that the call was an emergency one from the safety office, glad that the being on the other end was not a Naxian and rather happy that S'Nash had left. Of course, it/he would presumably not have betrayed him, but Hugh was embarrassed at lying before anyone but his wife. She would understand.

An image of Barrar, wearing a dome-shaped body with a dozen arms ensconced on a platform in the center of what he probably thought of as a desk and surrounded by numerous data-handling and communicating devices, appeared in a few seconds. Hugh gave him no time to complain.

"Ged, did you ever have much talk with the Erthumoi working for Ennissee?"

"No. Practically none, and that little was all through him. Neither they nor I had appropriate translator mods. Why?"

"Did you ever hear them talking between themselves? And if you do, do you remember the words 'Pill-Dahn' or 'Palaksee?' "

"Thanks for the flattery. I have a brain, not a mechanical recorder. I heard them talk often enough, but don't remember a syllable. Why? Get to the point, if any. Spreadsheet-Thinker is screaming about empty cells."

"I'd like to hear a Locrian scream, but you'll have to do. The words both mean the same, in the language of one of the Erthumoi—the female, if you care."

"I don't. Get to the point. What do they mean?"

"*Faked fossil.* I don't know why that should rate a single word, let alone two, in any language but I suppose it's a historical—"

"Shut up!" Barrar's speech mechanism was not designed to produce a scream, but it had a more than adequate volume control. Hugh and his wife decided it might not be necessary to ask S'Nash how the Samian was feeling.

13

EVERY IDEA HAS TO FACE ITS TEST

"Why, how, and how do you know?" The questions came with surprising speed, considering the usual pace of Samian thought, and at a much more moderate volume than the initial reaction. Hugh answered them together, describing his conversation with Mahare Chen in detail though not verbatim.

"Ennissee is from Wildwind, where a lot of Seventh Race material has been found. Crotonites like to assume that it was a flying species, though if you really corner one he'll usually admit there's no real proof. It's generally taken for granted, though, on Wildwind, and often carried to feeling that Crotonites are the natural heirs to any relics left by the Seventh Race."

"I've heard of that idea, but never took it seriously."

"I don't see why anyone should, but people do. Anyway, when Habranha was discovered by Crotonites a few decades ago—Common time, not Habra; they've been here longer than any of us—it turned out likely for chemical reasons that the Habras hadn't evolved here but are descendants of some colonizing race. Since there is only one other star-faring species we've ever had a trace of, and the Habras certainly aren't related to any of the Six, the natural implication sent the wilder Wildwinders out of control.

"To boil things down, Ennissee came here to 'prove' that the Habras had evolved here. Like a lot of true believers, he didn't much care how he did it;

he was spreading the truth, and if he had to juggle mere facts a bit to convince the unbelievers that was all right. Personally I don't think much of that attitude, but I can't say all Erthumoi are above it. How many other Wildwinders were in it with him, or even how many would go that far, I have no idea, but I'm afraid we'll have to publicize this affair in the interests of ordinary historical honesty and protection of the naive."

"But—well, yes, of course. I see that. But what evidence other than the word of this Erthuma do you have that the fossils are false? How were they made? Was the first body—"

"The first body was genuine enough, and fairly modern. Jan has it well inside carbon range in age, and of course it's a perfectly ordinary native. It's a real accident or storm victim, apparently, found by Ennissee on Darkside. Chen says there were several more at the same site, but that Ennissee had said one was enough."

"He told me it had come from just a few meters down," said Barrar, "and he was sure it was recent, too, but he said he found it with his mole instruments while he was testing it and deciding where to start boring. Now I wonder how good the mole was, really. I never went very far down in it."

"Oh, it seems to have been all he told you, according to Chen. Janice has found quite a bit of the plant stuff from Ennissee's base to be beyond carbon range in age. It could have done good work. I hope it can be rebuilt. He destroyed it to keep anyone from checking the spot where he claimed to have found the second specimen."

"*Destroyed it!*" How could he? It was—it was *useful*! How could anyone destroy such a thing? A mass-produced truck, or aircraft, or communicator, something easy to replace, one could understand; but this was specially designed equipment! And how could he have taken such a chance with the Erthumoi and me?"

"The explosion was thermite, set off under the ice where he'd parked it. Of course the steam made it impressive, and he must have been planning the whole thing well in advance to have so much thermite at the site. He would certainly never have used it for fossil digging. I'm a little surprised that the building you and the Erthumoi were in survived. I know the stuff isn't really an explosive, but that much of it under ice would have to make a lot of steam. He probably cared a little more about you and his workers than he did for Rekchellet, but not too much. He also knew about when we would be coming—didn't he? You were out there, after all."

"Yes," admitted the Samian after a pause. "He left in the aircraft I had used to get there, shortly before you arrived. I still can't believe he would have risked us."

"I've always been unhappy with coincidences," answered Hugh, feeling a trace of smugness which presumably didn't show in his key work. "After all, he must have had a flyer from somewhere. I'm sure you didn't deliberately send him to Pwanpwan on one of the Pitville machines, but you might ask whoever piloted you out there last time just where he or she dropped the Crotonite off." Ged made no answer.

"And you didn't know what happened to Rekchellet until afterward," Janice remarked. The Samian seemed, if anything, grateful for the change of subject; Hugh felt he would have a lot to ask S'Nash at their next meeting.

"Yes. I am friendly with many of the local Habras, just as you are, and had asked them to help me keep in touch with Ennissee whenever he was in the neighborhood. Some of them helped when we brought the frozen body back by air. The truck has never been very far from Pitville; Ennissee set up the autodriver and its record after he decided we were ready to get you people out to his dig and display the first body."

"You got it that long ago?"

"Oh, yes. Several years. He was going to show you the mole, and all the other specimens he had collected, and his records—everything, he told me. That was why I was so upset when the mole was destroyed, and begged so hard for the material to be taken here for Janice to examine. How did he actually get the specimen? You say it's faked somehow?"

"Yes. You've wandered off the question of how you found out about Rekchellet."

"Oh. Sorry. When Ennissee asked them to help him take Rek's translator and tracker, they complied because it seemed to fit my request but weren't really happy about it. They decided to watch Rek, too. Unfortunately, only one of them at a time did this while the others reported back to me. She saw the two Crotonites leave the truck, followed them, saw them land together, and then start to fly once more with Ennissee drawing ahead. My instructions had been to watch Ennissee, so she lost track of Rekchellet fairly soon. However, she had a very good idea of his actual path. She also knew just what he was wearing and carrying, so that she knew what he—well, about the only word is 'looked' like to Habra electrical senses. She was in your search group, not by chance I assure you; I had managed to get instructions to my people by then. She was responsible for the change in search pattern which bothered you, I gather, but which resulted in Rekchellet's being found."

"Why didn't she just tell the story? We could have concentrated on the right area much sooner."

"She wanted to, and was bothered by the conflicting requests. She didn't have a clear idea of what was going on, and did not want to upset either your plans or mine."

"She's one of my people, too?"

"Yes. Holly. A very capable person. You should tell your assistants more of the background when you have them out on missions. She could have decided much more quickly and easily."

"But if Ennissee wanted Rek found while he was still alive to serve as a test subject for the Naxians, he must have made some such arrangement, too. Didn't you know about that?"

"Of course not. I knew nothing about his plans then, or about what happened to Rekchellet after he and Ennissee separated until you told me you were looking for him. Then I got word to Holly through other Habras. Now let's get back to *my* question, please. How was that primitive specimen made, if it wasn't real?"

"It's an experimental tissue culture from the Naxian bio lab, part of their early work toward repairing Habras. Chen didn't know how Ennissee got hold of it, but he'd been up there finding out about their repair methods, remember. Maybe seeing that thing scared him enough to make him unwilling to take a chance on being the first Crotonite to go through the line."

"Maybe. If that's so, maybe he did want Rek found, too, after he'd been fairly well frozen, as you say, and would have made sure it happened even if I hadn't. We'll really have to talk to that (no-symbol-equivalent). But you should have told Holly and the others—"

"*You* should. She knew we were looking for Rek, and that he might be in danger. Your secrecy was unimportant compared—"

"Save it, please, Cultured Beings," Janice cut in. "We have most of the picture now, and blame doesn't seem useful. It's happened, and at the moment Ged seems to be suffering most. He no longer has a subject for his paper, which means quite a lot to him, I gather."

"It shouldn't take a Naxian to tell you that," admitted Barrar.

"It didn't. S'Nash isn't here, for once," answered Hugh.

"I know. It/he is here, to help me compare earlier duty arrangements with the ones I'm trying to set up. I thought some time ago it was time to put his communication and recording specialties to work, instead of using him mostly on safety watch, but he couldn't get to me until now. I'll have to pin its/his schedule down more firmly."

"Leaving, I hope, some spaces in your own," keyed Hugh. "I did suggest to Chen that she and her friend might recover grace by helping you rebuild the mole. And who *is* on watch? My own job screen, which I thought I'd made out myself, shows blank for the next sixty hours."

"That's one of the things I've been rearranging. Get some sleep. You start sentry in two and a half hours. Janice, I'm not scheduling you; I assume you're planning lab work around your own need for sleep, and I don't have you posted for anything else. If the two of you will let me get back to work, we can talk later." The communication panel went blank, and Hugh's schedule screen suddenly filled.

"For once, I hope watch stays boring," Hugh said slowly. "There's too much here for me to get straight all at once. I wish I didn't have to fill my mental chart one box at a time."

"Don't change. At least, don't turn Locrian. I prefer mammals. And don't let it keep you awake," replied his wife. "Get that sleep Ged advised. I'm going back to the lab."

She turned toward the door, but lingered while Hugh thought for a moment, then recorded a message to Barrar, to be taken at the latter's convenience. She listened with interest.

"Remember the submarine fossil hunt. I have contacts, if you want." Janice grinned and left.

No one was surprised that Ged did want, or that he scheduled Hugh for contact with the submarine group a very small fraction of a year later. For once, the latter spent no time wondering whether he should get rid of the diving juice. There had been some sort of breakthrough in Habra armor design, and he would, he hoped, have to be back in Pitville fairly soon to train native Pit workers. Janice, the Cold Pole material all dated and her regular work back at routine level, went with him.

Bill was not at sea, though about to be under it, according to the word Hugh and Janice received in Pwanpwan. There was little difficulty in confirming that the submarine he commanded was in its usual port, and with a small flyer at their complete discretion—they wondered whether Spreadsheet-Thinker knew about it—the fact that the port was a thousand kilometers farther north meant nothing. There was no such thing as a large city on the planet. Even streetless Pwanpwan could be crossed by an Erthuma on foot in an hour or two, since the winged natives had no particular reason to assemble large aggregates of dwellings. Their principal industry was agriculture. Such devices as electric or fusion powered submarines with open framework hulls made of wood or plastic were merely an adjunct to farming, and the fact that Erthumoi science historians had trouble feeling right about this made it no less true.

The Cedars decided to update initially from someone other than Shefcheeshee; it seemed a good idea to face the Cephallonian with ammunition which could provide leading questions.

Bill would not be leaving port for another twenty hours or so, and responded happily within a few minutes to Hugh's paging. Habranha's social amenities did not include bars or anything very similar;

few intelligent flying species went far in personal use of chemicals which interfered with either sensory acuity, motor coordination, or breathing efficiency. The Erthumoi, however, had foresightedly brought snacks for themselves, and the three ate on the ice beside Bill's ship while talking.

The sea bottom fossil hunt was still going on, but its personnel remained in touch with the Iris and were reporting positive results. Very positive. Organic remains, it seemed, occupied practically every cubic meter of the sediments. They were seldom well preserved, and so far had consisted almost entirely of species known to use ATP rather than azide. As deeply as had been probed so far, they were not truly fossilized; the material was mostly original tissue, though of course more decomposed than that found in Darkside ice. Mineralized remains might, of course, be found in deeper strata.

This lent hope that Habra relics might turn up some time, but no one expected that it would be soon. The current hypothesis was that azide remains were destroyed by microorganisms of their own sort before or shortly after reaching the bottom; this was considered to lend some support to the idea that the Habras had come from elsewhere, too recently for really effective ATP scavengers to have evolved from the microorganisms they had presumably brought with them. Not even the sternest critic of Wildwind logic would call it proof, however.

The philosophical implications were fascinating, but Bill lacked time to go into them deeply; he had to start pre-castoff checks for his submarine's next trip. His farewells included best wishes for their planned interview with Shefcheeshee.

"That alien's not really a student," the Habra remarked. "He's helpful, knows a lot of the appropriate technology, but he's extremely emotional, it seems to me. He gets very excited about things. He usually has several Naxian Snoop-players in tow."

"What's a Snoop-player? That's new to me," said Janice.

"You find them where people are doing dangerous or otherwise exciting or surprising things. You know Naxians read emotions."

"Of course."

"Some of the less usefully employed, to put it kindly, make a sport of finding excited or stressed beings and trying to read them in as much detail as possible. I gather they try to describe the emotions competitively, later, and I've heard that some of them try to recreate the feelings for themselves; but it's hard to get a Naxian to talk about that. I only heard that much when I finally got very annoyed with one who wouldn't get out of the way when I was preparing to launch. Apparently I *frightened* it/him, thereby arousing gratitude in several others."

Hugh was very thoughtful as they left their winged friend, Janice even more so. Neither felt sure how closely the Habra version of Naxian amusement matched that mentioned by Barrar, but there could easily be a connection.

After walking for a while through the maze of the port—in spite of the minimal Habras use for streets, their most recent settlements on the cold side of the Iris had made some concession to the presence of wingless aliens—Hugh asked slowly, with his translator off, "How do you feel about being used?"

Janice looked surprised, but followed his example with her own instrument before answering. "I don't suppose I'd like it, except when it's mutual, of course."

Her husband shrugged impatiently. "I don't mean that. Do you remember when S'Nash confessed to Rek about 'using' him, at that meeting it/he'd called with us and the robot?"

"Of course. I wondered then why it/he admitted it in front of us. Some of the things said during the apology I thought must be aimed at us, but I couldn't see any way to make sure."

"Neither could I. When S'Nash first asked us to that meeting it/he said something about making it look normal. I pointed out that we ski for fun, and Rekchellet flies for fun, but I didn't know what Naxians did which would make good cover—well, I didn't say it just that way, but you don't always pick your words carefully talking with Naxians; they know what you mean most of the time anyway, from the feelings that go along with the words. Right?"

"Supposedly," Janice answered carefully. "I've wondered for years—and I don't mean Habra years—how that sense of theirs works, and I'm sure it must have limits."

"They're not supposed to be able to read *thoughts*."

"No. On the other hand, no rational beings would want it generally known if they could." The woman was still coding slowly, as though her ideas were far ahead of her words and only a fraction of her mind were back keeping her sentences coherent.

"You think they can?"

"No. I'm almost sure they can't. I've been trying to figure out how they do it for a long, long time, and I've set up situations where a Naxian would be put in an awkward position *unless* it could get my real thoughts, and they've always fallen into the trap."

"Have you ever set one of your traps so the Naxian would be badly hurt or killed?"

"No. Of course not."

"Then you can't be sure. They'd certainly go a long way to keep a secret like that. Risking ridicule or even pain would mean nothing. You or I could put up with it as long as we thought it was important. We have to credit them with as much guts as we have. As far as ridicule goes their own people

would know the truth, and they wouldn't care about
our ridicule."

"True." Janice thought for a moment. "I still don't
think they're really mind readers, but I admit my
reason's a bit circular. I've been incubating a theory,
and it doesn't lead that way, and good deal has happened lately to support it, including what Bill said a
few minutes ago."

"What's your idea?"

"I suspect that they sort of muscle read. That they
perceive the tiniest motions and twitches and physical reactions in the people they see, and that some
aspect of their nervous systems—some built-in wiring we'll be a very long time understanding because
we don't have it—gives them a special facility in associating those reactions with fear or anger or libido
or the feeling that goes with knowing you've just
told a lie. Remember S'Nash's pattern-spotting out
on the road?"

"But the reactions would be different for different
species, and the Naxians can—"

"I know they can. I'd bet they have to learn. I'm
postulating something we can't imagine in detail for
the same reason we can't imagine a dog's universe
of odor, except that I think the difference with the
Naxians is more in processing than in perception. It
fits with S'Nash's remark that Samians were a particular challenge—remember?" Hugh nodded.

"Look, you can learn fantastic, detailed things if
you start early enough," she went on. "You know
your own language, which is complex enough. You
can distinguish my voice from my sister's, which is
fantastic. The average human being can identify
hundreds of people by face; with the right cultural
start they apply the same ability to identifying tracks
of people or animals they're following—without
conscious analysis, they dismiss the part of the landscape which is undisturbed and notice what has been

upset in some way practically invisible to others. I'm not saying it very well, but—"

"But you're using extremely good analogies. All right, it's at least testable. You think what Bill said about Snoop-players fits in?"

"Yes, especially with the idea that it's something they can learn, and improve with practice."

"I like it. It fits my thoughts, too."

"What part of them?"

"My question of a few minutes ago: How do you like being used?"

"But you wouldn't say a Naxian was *using* you as long as it/he just read your emotions! That wouldn't be any worse than," she smiled, rather impishly, "girl-watching, would it?"

Hugh let only a flicker of her smile cross his own face.

"No," he said slowly, "I wouldn't mind, as long as it stays a—well, a spectator sport. If I ever had reason to suppose I were being manipulated to cause me to have special emotions, or if I got the idea that I had even the most remote resemblance to a gladiator in an arena, I would certainly feel differently."

"Of course you would. So would I. But no one's pushing us around. Who could?"

"I don't know, and hate to sound paranoid. I just can't help wondering whether everyone associated with us who has caused us anxiety, worry, fear, or their opposites in the last few Habra years, let's say, has been acting with complete, comprehensible common sense? That *they're* not being pushed around?"

"But we can't expect them to! They're not all Erthumoi—"

"And only we have common sense?"

"Don't be silly. You know what I mean. Each race has different ideas of what makes for common sense."

"Or ethics? Down at the life-risking level?"

Janice was silent. So was her husband, for a time,

but before they reached the aircraft he keyed out one more notion, or part of one.

"I was wondering how Shefcheeshee got his harness tangled in that thruster. I wish I'd examined it more closely, and not just worked them apart." Janice said nothing.

Finding the Cephallonian through the Guild office was not too difficult, but starting a conversation once he was found was another matter. The Cedars had worked with Cephallonians before and liked them—Janice, of course, liked everybody. It is, however, awkward to talk to someone from even a very low flying aircraft when the party is swimming, and apparently totally absorbed in doing gymnastics with the wave patterns of a singularly chaotic ocean dotted with ice floes. It is worse when the floes are punctuated by city-sized bergs and a conscientious autopilot insists on moving the aircraft tens of meters with very little warning.

It is not, however, impossible, if one is patient. The porpoiselike swimmer eventually ceased his violent antics and slid out on top of a half-hectare floe, and began to check his environment suit and oxygen supply; the ammonia in Habranha's sea was a strong irritant to Cephallonian skins, while the one third atmosphere oxygen partial pressure, high enough to be risky to human beings if breathed for too long, was inadequate for the sea folk when they were being really active. The Erthumoi were now able to get his attention. He had not been rude—they knew his kind well enough to be sure of that; he simply hadn't noticed them. Hugh introduced his wife.

Shefcheeshee was as willing as before to talk at great length about anything connected with the deep-sea fossil project. This time he seemed more upset that no one had yet perfected a diving fluid for his race, so he could not reach the ocean bottom himself. Instead of happy reports, he complained extensively. Hugh wondered whether nothing had been learned from the sea bottom since their last conversation, or Shefcheeshee were simply in a different mood this time. The latter seemed more probable; the mere fact that the Cephallonian remembered everything he had said earlier to one Erthumoi appeared unlikely to stop him from going through it all over again for another.

Neither Janice nor Hugh tried to make suggestions; Habranha's gravity was feeble, but under five hundred kilometers of water it still produced a hydrostatic pressure of about ten thousand bars. Vessels could be built to resist this, but not so far to let people work through their walls to dig rocks. The Cedars simply listened sympathetically, and eventually the subject matter became more interesting.

Shefcheeshee was as sure as anyone that the Habras were descendants of colonists, not indigenous to the planet, though he lacked strong feeling about the matter. In response to a question slipped in edgewise, he had heard of the Trueliners, but none of them had ever approached him with an attempt to change his mind on that subject. If any of them knew anything relevant, naturally, he'd be glad to hear it; could the Cedars put him in touch with such a person?

Hugh, carefully not looking at his wife, said that they knew an enthusiast on the subject who might be available in a few Common Days and would be, Hugh felt sure, most willing to expound his views. Shefcheeshee, shifting position to keep from melting his way too far into the floe, responded as they had hoped, with wild excitement.

"Wonderful! The Box at the digging site reports by sounder every thirty hours, and as soon as I can make a summary of its information I incorporate it in my next public presentation at the Port of Deep Study. I told you about the one after we first met; I'm sorry you couldn't be there, but you are both welcome to the next, in about thirty hours. I intend it for the Habras mostly, of course, since the knowledge concerns their planet, but there are always many listeners."

"Naxians, largely, I expect," Hugh couldn't resist suggesting.

"Oh, yes. It was a Naxian group which contributed heavily to the project originally. I was rather surprised, since an Erthumoi artificial brain was involved in the actual work, but they admitted that probably nothing else could be used at such depths since Habras would take a long time to train in the instrumentation and coring equipment, and there are too few Erthumoi free, competent, and interested. It's a great pity that we have not yet produced a pressure fluid for my race, especially since we are, after all, the natural ones for undersea research."

Janice started to key words at once sympathetic and discouraging to a return to that subject, but this proved unnecessary. The Cephallonian was wavering only slightly in his course.

"I have, of course, been tactful about the wordage of my explanations—if you were not Erthumoi I would say I had kept it clean where mention of the artificial mind is concerned; but you know what I mean."

This time it was Hugh who agreed, but both filed the same thought. Naxians were probably the most likely of the Races to accept artificial intelligence eventually on pragmatic grounds, in spite of the Cephallonian philosophical bent. Since there were many more Naxians on Habranha anyway, this was probably convenient. The principal remaining uncertainty was the one newly raised by Bill's information.

Were the supporters interested, pragmatic Naxians who would carry weight with the rest of their kind, or were they just the Snoop-players? And were Snoop-players more nearly the Naxian equivalent of artists, sport fans, or chemical dependents?

This didn't seem to be anything which could be learned either from Shefcheeshee or by casual inquiry at the Guild office.

The talk with—more accurately, by—Shefcheeshee went on for nearly another hour, since there seemed no courteous way to terminate it, but both Erthumoi were guilty of allowing their thoughts to wander much of the time. Fortunately, the Cephallonian was quite content to talk, and asked few questions of his audience.

They both agreed, when he asked, to attend his next presentation, since they had already decided to do so; they wanted to observe any Naxian attendees themselves. The fact that their own feelings would be plain to the serpentine listeners could not be helped, and might possibly be made useful.

Shefcheeshee eventually decided that he was straining his oxygen budget, since he had fifty or sixty kilometers to swim. He once again made sure they would attend his talk, and slid into the water. The Erthumoi reentered their flier, which Hugh had parked on the floe after careful testing of the latter's buoyancy, and decided to return to Pitville for sleep. There was after all ordinary work to be done, especially by Janice. They reported to Administration before going "home."

They had forgotten to check on Ennissee at the Naxian medical station, and Ged claimed to be annoyed. He only forgave them, he said, because Rekchellet had been really responsible for the matter. It was too much trouble to point out that he could call the Naxians just as well himself; the couple simply listened. The Samian said nothing about S'Nash, and neither Erthuma caught sight of it/him between flier and office or office and home. They didn't even think of individual Naxians.

Just of the species in general, and even more generally, the subject of Entertainment.

Neither Hugh nor his wife was surprised when

Ged Barrar stated his intention of attending the Cephallonian talk. They were even less so when S'Nash appeared unannounced at the aircraft. The man gestured to Janice to take the controls, but the only one to speak was the Samian.

"It's lucky I hadn't started actually putting that article together," he remarked. "But now that I think of it, maybe something could be made of it after all. Janice, did you find anything about the specimen itself to prove it was not genuine? Is there anything to go on except that Erthuma's word?"

Hugh had given his wife the controls in the hope of sparing her this predictable inquisition, and did his best to answer for her.

"It was a good job, unless you want to call Ennissee just lucky. Remember, the Naxians do their culturing from chemically purified solutions and synthesized compounds, and start their synthesis from minerals—I think I mentioned Rekchellet's complaining about that. Naturally, that meant there was no carbon-fourteen present in the specimen, since the carbon would have come from carbonate rock somewhere off Habranha, and it registered maximum age on that count. Of course, there was no argon-forty either and no way to tell whether there was too much calcium-forty; but the first was explainable enough. It was frozen in ice I, which has a very open structure, and you could argue that the argon had leaked out as fast as it formed."

"How about the biological structure itself? Was it a reasonable one for an ancestral Habra?"

"I couldn't say, except to point out that one dot on a graph—or two, if you count the present species— don't go for much. McEachern didn't seem very startled by anything, but of course he hasn't had much time with it yet. The mere fact that it was an early attempt to grow a Habra body would have given something reasonable along that line, I'd guess."

"Then we have only the Erthuma's story?" Barrar was plainly disappointed. Hugh smiled rather grimly.

"No. There's one other fact. According to the claim, the item was found at a depth of—I forget just how many kilometers, but it was far below the depth at which Ice I would change to the distinctly denser Ice III. I don't know how the collection was done, but I don't see how the body could have been brought down to normal pressure without a lot of cell damage as the ice changed back, or for that matter during the original compression. There's no evidence of such damage. Its ice had never changed phase."

"But wouldn't there have been damage anyway as it froze originally? Liquid water expands as it forms Ice I. That's why freezing is so bad for most life forms."

"Habras, like Crotonites, have alcohols in their blood which inhibit crystallization, Jan says. You'll really have to have a talk with McEachern, though, if you want enough details for a meaningful paper."

"But Respected Opinion McEachern would expect—"

"Academic credit. So does Janice. We're landing. We'll have to show you the way. Shefcheeshee has a setup down at the port, here—a tank with microphones."

Barrar showed no sign of being disgruntled either by Hugh's last statement about his wife, or by the rather pointed change of subject, but of course the Erthuma couldn't tell. S'Nash might be getting a real kick from the reaction, he suspected. *Which is to be found out.* He exchanged glances with Janice, who gave a half smile and nodded. It didn't matter that S'Nash must know their feelings; it shouldn't even matter, in a few minutes, if it/he could actually read their minds.

The Habras were not very real estate conscious

except when they had to relocate people from the melting side of the Iris, and Shefcheeshee had apparently met with no objection when he turned the top of a local hill into a lecture hall, though "hall" was hardly an appropriate term; the Cephallonian had never seriously considered putting a roof over his winged audience, the Erthumoi were sure. The ice was bare, smooth, and by nature or art shaped like half a stadium bowl focusing on a level area originally at the edge of the sea. New icebergs had changed this last fact, but the Habras maintained the open water of their port behind his lecture platform. The Cephallonian had arranged to place meter-square patches of roughened polymer sheeting, separated by narrower lanes of bare ice, over most of the sloping surface to provide traction.

There were a few enclosed cubicles, also of clear polymer, around the upper edge of the bowl, for attendees who were uncomfortable in Habranhan atmosphere or temperature and preferred not to wear armor too long at a time. Hugh and Janice had learned about these earlier, and made them part of their plan; what they wanted to do would be discourteous if the general audience could hear them. They guided Barrar to one of the cubicles and entered, watching with interest while S'Nash decided, after visible hesitation, to remain outside.

There was a bench, not specifically designed for Erthumoi but usable, and the two sat down. Barrar remained standing in his mechanical walker.

There was already a large crowd, mostly natives, and it was possible to turn up translator receivers again without hearing only a hopeless blur of incomprehensible overload noise. The Habras, Janice noticed, were quite willing to press side by side, wings folded, with far too little space around most of them to allow takeoff; the few Crotonites, predictably, remained near the upper edges of the bowl and made sure they could spread their wings. Erthumoi, Locrians, and Naxians were scattered through the area, indifferent to flight opportunity. Janice nudged Hugh without speaking; her hypothesis had made another correct prediction. One might have thought that the snakelike part of the audience would have wanted to gather at the front, where they could hear and especially see the speaker more easily, since there were no facilities for them to elevate themselves above the floor anywhere in the bowl. They did not seem to be doing this.

Janice now strongly suspected that it was not just the speaker they would want to watch. Both Erthumoi looked around more closely, but couldn't be certain that there was any real concentration of serpentine bodies around Crotonites. The Naxians were too hard to see in the crowd.

The Erthumoi tensed as Shefcheeshee leaped far out of the water into the huge, transparent tank which formed the speaker's rostrum, and began his talk without preamble.

14

AND STILL BE "ONLY THEORY"
AT ITS BEST

It was as though he were addressing a class rather than delivering an oration. A speaker in the booth transmitted his sounds faithfully enough for the translators. He spoke for some time of general Habran prehistory, and Barrar began to grow impatient, judging by the uneasy motions of his walker and its handlers. This was nothing new—Hugh felt he could almost read the Samian's mind—and nothing he could use.

Then Shefcheeshee began an explanation of the artificial intelligence which was guiding the bottom search and identifying, selecting, and analyzing the finds, and the Samian froze. Shocked? Revolted? If the speaker could stomach the subject, why couldn't a would-be scholar? This time Hugh was more amused, familiar as he was with the attitudes of the Other Five.

Janice nudged her husband again. There were four—no, five snakelike forms within a meter or two of their booth, every one staring at Ged Barrar. As she started to form a triumphant grin, one of them shifted its gaze to her; as the implication of that change in attention struck both Erthumoi, the other Naxians also turned their eyes on the pair.

Hugh expected them to turn away again after a moment, to avoid betraying themselves, but Janice had a different picture. A clearer one, she thought. Yes, they had sensed her feeling of triumph; no, they didn't—they couldn't, surely—realize its cause. She

basked happily in the glow that any scientist feels
when an infant hypothesis, nurtured lovingly for
weeks and fed carefully with observations, speaks
its first words—makes one of its earliest predictions.
She knew, of course, that the feeling couldn't last
long; theories this young were usually far too tender.
It would be hurt by something very soon, and need
help. Still, the gold-brown Naxian optics remained
fixed on her, and she could enjoy that while it lasted.

That wasn't long. The glow vanished as it occurred to her to wonder what they might do to convince her they had *only* emotion sensing powers, and
were not mind readers. . . .

It had been wonderful while it lasted, but she was
back on the ground. She glanced once more at the
watchers. Their eyes were still on *her*. Maybe they
were reading her thoughts—no. She brought herself
up sharply. That may not be impossible, but don't
worry about it; just file it as something to devise a
test for at some handier time.

Shefcheeshee was still speaking. Ged Barrar was
still listening. The subject was now more specula-
tive, on why no fossils recognizable as azide-
chemistry organisms had been found at the sea
bottom. Hugh muttered his own notion, expressed
earlier by Bill and, apparently, already widely held.

"Because the ocean is loaded with azide-using
scavengers who evolved here, and can take care of
the remains before they get to the bottom!"

Barrar heard, and thought for a moment.

"But why wouldn't there be other scavengers,
too?"

"I'd guess its non-azide life is all descended from
things the Habras' ancestors brought with them, deliberately or otherwise, when they arrived, and that
there hasn't been time since then for evolution to fill
very many niches. You ought to consult McEachern
or an educated Habra on that."

"All the Habras seem to be able to talk about that

sort of thing, whether they're farmers or submarine operators or chemists or—"

"I know. It's interesting. Maybe you should do your article on Habra sociology."

"You're laughing at me." Hugh glanced outside without answering. Naxian attention seemed to be fading. There were now only three of them near the booth, and these seemed to be concerned with a nearby Crotonite as Shefcheeshee casually dismissed the idea that Habranhans might be descended from the mysterious Seventh Race.

"But don't let that keep you from star travel," he went on. "You can be a Seventh Race yourselves, or an Eighth if you consider that number taken. There are wonders beyond your atmosphere rivaling those under your sea. You have the knowledge, or most of it; what you lack, we who already enjoy the sights and adventures both of worlds like your own and worlds marvelously different can gladly supply. You can—"

Hugh looked outside again; the question of Habras joining the star-faring races was one on which many Crotonites felt strongly, some on one side and some on the other. Maybe this one was reacting, and the Naxians were enjoying the display.

But the Crotonite unceremoniously spread his wings and departed before either of the Erthumoi could decide whether the Naxians were watching him especially or not. Also, there was no way Hugh could infer either from their own motions or those of the watching Naxians that the Habras were responding at all intensely to the Cephallonian's appeal. Shefcheeshee finished a few minutes later with a summary which told the Erthumoi nothing that they hadn't heard from him before and must have left Barrar deeply disappointed. Hugh and Janice rose and started to leave the booth.

Two things delayed them, one sight and one sound.

Hugh's eye for the first time really caught the ice which formed the floor of the small chamber, and perceived that it was covered with a pattern of cup-like dents like those S'Nash had pointed out on the road east of Pitville. They did not form any sort of regular trail, however, and this time the reason was obvious enough. They had been made by Barrar's walker, and his motions in the booth had been irregular. Even Hugh could see them without trouble, since there were no interfering marks.

Before he could comment or explain to Janice, much less confront the Samian, a sound took his attention. Barrar had opened the door, and auditory patterns from outside were reaching his translator again. Some of the loudest were far enough above background to let the equipment separate and interpret them.

"Where have you been, master? Did you hope to find inspiration here? This swimmer doesn't even rouse Crotonites any more."

The tone was Naxian. The words had certainly not been addressed to Hugh. Suddenly, however, as one of the nearby serpentlike forms moved and left the one beyond it recognizable as S'Nash, another pattern flowed together in his mind. The words combined with memories to make sense, and the sense was promptly supported.

S'Nash had turned toward the newcomer who had plainly been addressing it/him; now it/he swerved to face Hugh again, hesitated, then finished the turn, with a simultaneous gesture of one of his handlers apparently intended for the other Naxian. The words to Hugh were the same as long before, but this time no effort was made to cut off the sentence.

"Good for you!" That was all; the two wriggled away together. It was for once enough, at least for Janice.

Barrar admitted the details on their way back to the aircraft. He had been tied much more closely with Ennissee's project than he had admitted earlier. He had helped convey the frozen Habra body from flyer to truck, since the Crotonite had not been strong enough to do the job alone and his Erthumoi were at the "dig." He had then been carried back by the Crotonite in the Pitville aircraft Ged had been regularly and surreptitiously providing, but only to the outskirts of Pitville, to minimize the time he would have to account for; Spreadsheet-Thinker was not as casual an administrator as Ged had implied when claiming to have all routines worked out. The truck had come to Pitville on its own autodriver, starting enough later to hide any obvious connections, while Ennissee had taken his borrowed flier back to the Cold Pole dig to work out, presumably, the rest of his plans. Ged still disclaimed any closer involvement in these than he had admitted already. The Erthumoi kept their remaining doubts tactfully to themselves.

They still felt quite uncertain. The picture was fuzzy, but there seemed no way to clarify it without interviewing Ennissee, and neither one particularly wanted to do that. Rekchellet would, no doubt, come through in that direction, and neither wanted to spoil either his fun or his results.

More of the picture, however, came from S'Nash after they were back in Pitville, the Samian safely occupied in his office, and the Naxian verbally cornered in Hugh's office.

"Emotions are fun," it/he said quite directly. "I almost told you about that long ago when you asked what we do for amusement. A little later I thought you'd about figured it out, but then decided you'd simply spotted the trick Rek and I were playing.

"A lot of people enjoy watching fear or surprise or similar excitement—the obvious stuff. More cultured and artistic ones try to read and grasp really subtle emotions such as those accompanying—oh, the realization that one's reasoning or inspiration has been correct, or the glow of perceiving how *both* parties have profited from a deal."

"And you're one of the latter, of course?" Janice asked.

"I sense irony. I like to think I am, of course, but there are many other challenges to the art. Some beings are much more difficult to read than others. Erthumoi collectively are the easiest, Samians by far the hardest of the Six, though there are of course exceptions like you two in both groups. I like to think I'm an expert with Samians." Janice had drawn her brows together; her husband was sure what she was thinking about, whether S'Nash knew or not. In fact, both must have been wrong, for her next words rolled out almost without planning or thought on her own part.

"You'd get quite a reading if we told Ged that you've known all along what Ennissee was doing, wouldn't you? That the people at your medical station had enjoyed his feelings as he stole that specimen? I wonder whether they merely gave tacit assistance, or actively tricked him into doing it. That they passed the information on to you and maybe other Naxians here at Pitville so he could be kept under observation as a source of—of amusement?"

"How did you—?" once again the Naxian cut off his speaker too late; as if realizing this, he turned it back on almost as though making a gesture of surrender. "You're surprised—but you didn't know until I spoke—you're triumphant now—I told you myself, then—but you must have had some suspicion, or you could never have said such a thing! Where did the suspicion come from?"

"Like me, Jan is uneasy about coincidence," her husband answered. "I know as well as you do we Erthumoi often have an unrealistic idea of what makes an improbable coincidence, but you should have allowed for that. As I'm sure you can see, it was all her idea, not mine. We just aren't as conscious of what goes on in our heads as you people are, I guess. At least, I don't know why I can recognize Jan's face or voice. Anyway, you've certainly told us now. I wonder what Ged will say, and do? It's a pity Jan and I can only infer his feelings from his words and actions, isn't it? They should form a real work of art."

"But you won't really—but you will! Why? You don't feel any strong emotion that I can find. Neither of you does, most of the time. You've been very disappointing that way, though you've been very helpful in—why do you intend so firmly to tell Barrar what I just confessed."

"Call it an experiment," Janice replied, as expressionlessly as she could. She wondered whether the Naxian were telling the truth about her and Hugh's being hard to read, but for the moment didn't care much, since she *had* made up her mind. "Come along, S'Nash. You wouldn't want to miss it, would you?"

The Naxian watched as the Erthumoi couple turned toward the central office. It/he started to follow them, hesitated and turned away, shivered the length of its/his serpentine body, reached a decision, and followed once more. The Erthuma was right; this would be something no one had ever read from a Samian—though what the Samian would do next—

He was civilized, of course. There would be no risk of violence. But he *was* in charge of work assignments.

It would certainly—almost certainly—be worth it.

It wasn't, S'Nash insisted later to Hugh and Janice. It was, in fact, very disappointing. Ged Barrar was far too objective, and his internal simmerings were just barely readable. They had been a real challenge, to look at the bright side. The Naxian's eyes had remained fixed on his unwaveringly and the snakelike body might have been cast as a tight coil of metal. The Erthumoi had watched with equal intensity.

"I can't decently complain," Barrar said after some moments of silence. "I was doing very much the same thing for my own plans. Still, we can't have this sort of thing going on *too* freely among people who need to trust each other, can we?" He paused thoughtfully, and might have been examining the charts on his walls, though not even S'Nash could tell where he was actually looking.

"The Pits are getting pretty deep," he said at length. "Spreadsheet-Thinker feels we need a communication center at the bottom of each. It will, of course, have to be manned by an Erthuma or a Habra eventually, but until the pressure becomes excessive a real communication specialist would probably be best to set things up. Don't you agree?"

"Well—" began S'Nash.

"There's really no one but a Naxian I can assign, anyway. Please spread the word. I'd prefer volunteers, of course. You will have to tell me just what equipment will be needed—remember it will have to stand liquid air temperatures. I know you Naxians already have good armor for that. I'll need a listing in, oh, six hours or so. I can tell you in two more when the gear will be available, and set up a watch schedule. I'm sure I won't have to draft someone who just happens to be handy; there will be plenty of volunteers, won't there? Let me know."

The Naxian maintained its/his tension for another half minute, though the Erthumoi could only guess why. *Something* was holding its/his attention, and did so until Barrar finally said rather loudly, "That's it, S'Nash. Any questions?"

It/he shivered, relaxed, intimated understanding, and accompanied Hugh and Janice out of the office.

"You're still alive," the woman remarked.

"Oh, yes. It was interesting, but not inspiring.

What are you folks going to do for the next few hours?"

"Do you care?"

"Not for the reason you suspect. I've already said you two are rather disappointing as subjects; you don't seem to have very intense emotions. Janice now was just cold-bloodedly trying to observe the results of the 'experiment' she was performing. There was none of the nice anger or satisfaction of revenge feeling which some of my less artistic acquaintances would have expected."

"And maybe even wanted?" cut in Hugh.

"Conceivably. But that would call for a rather— well—crude observer. What *are* you planning?"

"Work, of course," keyed Hugh. "We've been letting that slide for much too long. I'm surprised Ged didn't have something to say about it. Maybe he's too bothered by what happened to his own hopes. At the rate the Pits are going, digging and emplacement routines are going to have to be changed pretty quickly now, and we're not ready for it. I wasn't really expecting to get enough Erthumoi able to do the job; there aren't enough of us on the planet, and most of them can't seem to learn enough personal control to work safely with diving juice. I was hoping we could solve the Habra armor problem before we had to go recruiting on other Erthumoi worlds."

"Just what's the difficulty?" the Naxian asked.

"Thermal insulation. They never bothered with it for their wings, which aren't living tissue. In their undersea equipment they just make sure their diving fluid doesn't leak around the wing roots, and flap at their pleasure—an experienced Habra submariner talks casually of 'flying' under water. If they tried that in the Pits, their wings would shatter almost at once at liquid air temperatures. Ted said something about a breakthrough not long ago; I'm calling him again as soon as we get to the office."

"I thought he was just one of your safety people."

"He is, but he really wants to do Pit work himself, and has been keeping in touch with the Habras who are doing the armor development. Stay with us; you may get a kick out of watching me get good news—or bad."

"Even second hand, I would prefer the former."

Some hours later, he expanded on that remark.

"Hugh, I'm still refining my skills with Habras, but right now they seem even happier than you. I've watched six of them now in the Pits, and while the analogy may not be good, I'd say they were *dancing*. Even you must be getting some sort of impression—if your own glee isn't drowning it out."

"I am. I knew they'd like it; Ted's frustration at being able to watch the work there only from above was clear long ago even to me. I expect the excitement will die down a bit when they settle into routine, but they have a good, solid interest in the work over and above its novelty. That's part of the reason you're sensing so much happiness from me."

"And Jan, I notice. She is less directly affected; I can't understand why her feelings should match yours so closely."

"You probably will. Ten hours from now we'll be rid of this diving fluid for at least two years, Ged promises. We'll be able to eat. We'll be able to talk. We'll—"

"Is it that uncomfortable? And why would he have made such a change in his charts—oh. You persuaded him; your self-satisfied triumph is blatant. How?"

"It's not so much uncomfortable as inconvenient." Hugh went back to the first question. "You should have listened to my words instead of trying to read my feelings. You should have stayed here for the last few hours instead of going off to watch Habras, too. You missed a lot.

"Just after you left, I had an idea, and got back in touch with Ennissee's Erthumoi helpers. I knew they'd been present when the body in the truck was originally found, because the female mentioned the circumstances. It was one of a group of natives who seemed to have died at the same time and place. I asked if either of the two could find the actual site again, and after some back-and-forth between them that I couldn't follow because they cut the sound off, they decided they could, within two or three kilometers, and maybe closer when they got another look at the locale. Ennissee, they assured me, could get us there more precisely, but I didn't want to get in touch with him before Rek's had his chance.

"To make it brief, Ged now plans to make a study of the mass-kill site, and try to work out just what happened to the group, and why apparently none escaped to get their adventure into Habra history. With his original fossil disqualified—you know what that did to his feelings—he jumped at the chance for another paper, and will be with us on the search trip. I don't know or care what he said to Spreadsheet-Thinker."

"I wish I'd been with him when you made the suggestion."

"I'm sure you'd have enjoyed yourself. I suggest you visit Ged and see whether he'll include you in the group. It's a pity you can't *influence* feelings." The Naxian's answer was slightly hesitant.

"You have a procedure called *tact* which I've been watching you use with Crotonites. I am not sure of my own expertise in it, of course, but trying it on a Samian will at least be interesting. Thank you very much, Hugh." The Naxian left, apparently deep in thought.

S'Nash was lucky, luckier than either Erthuma felt that it/he had a right to be, on two counts. It/he arrived at Barrar's office just as the Samian, in his slow way, finally got around to calling the Naxian hospital. He was hoping, without regard for Rekchellet's desires, to get from Ennissee where the

frozen bodies had been found; and S'Nash was able
to enjoy his reaction when the Naxians assured him
they had no Crotonite under treatment. Ged's next
call was to the Guild office, which informed him casually that Ennissee, still with his prosthesis, had
left Habranha long before on a Crotonite hyperjump
vessel. For once, even a Samian was easy to read,
S'Nash said later.

It/he then practiced tact by offering to tell Rekchellet this news so as to spare Barrar the touchy
task, and Samian gratitude got the Naxian a place in
the forthcoming expedition, after only a little argument.

Whereupon S'Nash went in search of Rekchellet
and broke the news of Ennisee's departure. The results were all it/he could have hoped, even to a mo-
mentary thrill of fear for its/his own safety. The
Erthumoi admitted they would like to have watched.

In spite of their low speed, two trucks were used
for the search; they would want to bring the bodies
back if they found them. Hugh and Janice took turns
driving one. Rekchellet taught them what he knew
of the autodriver, but they seldom bothered to engage it, merely allowing it to record their path. It
had been decided not to bring Ennissee's former
helpers along, and the other truck was handled by
Barrar, with S'Nash, and two of Counter-of-Supplies
Erthumoi stock handlers to furnish muscle.
Rekchellet and one Habra, Miriam—Ted was enjoying Pit work too much to come along—accompanied
the vehicles but seldom entered them. Plant-
Biologist rode with Hugh and Janice since it was
fairly likely that the bodies would once more have
been covered by drifting ice dust. The Locrian liked
to discuss his subject, but got little chance, since his
Erthumoi companions were reveling in the new freedom of their vocal cords.

The area described was about three hundred kilometers north and a little east of Pitville, not too far

from open ocean. The notion that the victims they
were seeking had perished in a more or less ordinary
Habranhan storm seemed reasonable. The Erthumoi
had learned from their native friends that this was
not very unusual; the disappearance of even a large
party near the terminator would probably not have
gotten into history.

Chen and Spear had given detailed descriptions of
the landscape where the discovery had been made,
and it seemed unusual enough to offer little trouble.
The spot was at the foot of a nearly vertical cliff,
some three hundred meters high and several kilometers long, extending northeast-southwest.

Faulting had not, as far as anyone had seen,
played a large part in forming the topography of the
Solid Ocean. This was what had attracted Ennissee's
attention in the first place; much of his early searching had consisted of examining the cliff face, and
much of the testing of his mole had been at its base.

Finding what seemed to be the right neighborhood
proved easy enough. Narrowing the search down
from that point turned out to be more awkward,
however.

About half the five kilometer length of the cliff
had—not exactly collapsed, but seemed to have been
partly melted. Rekchellet's immediate conclusion
was that Ennissee had come back with a heavy duty
heat beam to destroy traces of his work. This appeared much less likely to the others, but argument
seemed pointless. Habranha's chaotic weather might
very well have brought a mass of warm air, or even
a heavy rainstorm, even this far beyond the terminator. The Crotonite asked sarcastically why a cliff
which must have stood for hundreds of Common
Years—even he did not claim thousands, on this
world—should pick the present moment to get itself
destroyed. He was not impressed by Hugh's answer
that one time on Habranha was as likely as any
other, and that he was showing a rather Erthumoi at-

titude toward coincidence. This silenced, but did not convince, him.

After some hours at the still undisturbed part of the cliff face, one of the mole's test tunnels was found, and a little later another. The separation of the two could be matched with the detailed instructions given by Chen and Spear, and led the party to the edge of what would have been called a talus slope on a silicate world. The upper part of the cliff had been partly melted, but much had simply broken away; jagged ice boulders extended a hundred meters from the cliff's foot and formed a heap lying against the vertical face.

Half an hour of careful searching by the Locrian, who was in turn being carefully watched by Janice, revealed a suspicious object at approximately ground level under the heap only a short distance from the escarpment's foot. Even Plant-Biologist could not see distinctly through that much broken and tumbled ice, to the Erthuma's intense interest, and a difficult and dangerous job of digging had to be started. There were no heat projectors with the group. There were no picks, either, to Hugh's disgust; it should have been obvious, he growled loudly, that something besides shovels would be required. Not all the ice on Habranha was fine dust. The shovels were strong enough to be used for chipping, but progress was slow until Rekchellet flew back to Pitville and had two picks improvised in the shop there. No one was willing to wait until a sweeper with a heat beam could be driven to the site, and none of the sweepers would fit through the lock of an aircraft.

Since Hugh had provided careful specifications, the tools brought back had two disadvantages. They were light enough for Rekchellet to carry in flight, which meant that they were too light to make full use of Erthumoi muscles; and they were too heavy as well as having poorly shaped handles for anyone but the Erthumoi.

They took turns digging. S'Nash and Barrar watched, Plant-Biologist climbed about and over the heap in search of a spot from which he could see into it more clearly, and the fliers scoured the area from above in the faint hope of learning that tunneling would not be needed after all.

Three or four hours of chipping and prying brought the diggers close enough to allow the Locrian to state with certainty that a number of Habra forms were indeed embedded in the ice ahead, so that the party was either at the right place or one equally worth examining.

Rekchellet promptly pointed out that Ennissee was obviously responsible for the melting and general cliff damage, just as he had claimed earlier; this time even Barrar wondered whether he might be right. The nondiggers now congregated around the mouth of the tunnel and as far inside as they could get. Barrar and Miriam could now make themselves useful carrying ice fragments away from the digging face, and strained their various senses to determine details of what still lay some meters ahead.

Plant-Biologist informed them happily that the Habra forms were surrounded and more or less intermingled with tumbleweeds and other local vegetation, and thereafter focussed most of his attention on this material. Miriam was beginning to get some details of the Habra bodies through her electrical senses.

A meter or so short of the nearest body the work had to slow down. The Locrian reported that the ice a little beyond the corpses contained a large, tightly packed bundle of plant remains of the azide variety, so that a pick blow might cause an explosion of possibly inconvenient magnitude. No one, they agreed, wanted to risk destruction of the specimens after all their work, and also Plant-Biologist wanted to study the tangle itself; the vegetation did not resemble at all closely any solid Ocean forms he had seen, he claimed.

Janice was fascinated; the biologist must have been able to observe near-microscopic details of tissue to identify the chemical nature of the things. Or could he sense the chemistry itself?

Conceivably the Habras ahead had accumulated the growths for some reason—perhaps to blast a shelter for themselves into the face of the cliff, Rekchellet suggested. It seemed to Janice a little early for hypothesizing, but she agreed that the idea had possibilities. S'Nash absorbed another lesson in tact.

Work became slow and cautious, the small metal spikes which were carried on the truck to work ice out of its tracks replacing the heavier tools. There were enough of these to let everyone work, and the tunnel end began to widen in both directions. In spite of the danger, most of the crew stayed as close as they could to the inner end of the tunnel. Plant-Biologist's desire to examine the plants as closely as possible in case they did explode before he reached them overrode any fear he may have felt; S'Nash watched the Locrian for reasons Hugh and his wife could now easily guess; Janice's attention was divided between the two while she mulled over developing theories. Even Barrar, anxious to miss nothing, crowded among the others and distracted the Locrian with questions about the Habra bodies which even the others could now see fairly clearly through the ice. He was not visibly taking notes, but Hugh felt sure his "body" incorporated recording equipment.

The bodies, all with wings folded back, were grouped next to the mass of vegetation as though they had died together while pushing it toward the cliff. They were not, as far as even the Locrian could see, wearing any protective equipment—certainly

nothing like that now employed by Ted, Miriam, and
their fellows. They might indeed have been a group
blown long ago away from the sun and over the
Solid Ocean in one of Habranha's storms, dying
while seeking shelter against or inside the cliff.

But what had killed them all at once? The bodies
were not crushed or visibly injured, any more than
the one Janice had already examined; they had certainly not been under an avalanche or anything like
one. They were not, for the most part, in physical
contact, so an electrical jolt from the plants could
hardly have caught them all at once.

Barrar suggested that a sudden gust of ultrachilled
air, not strong enough to blow them away but cold
enough to kill or paralyze them until they were
buried in an ordinary drift was conceivable. The
bodies would have to be examined in detail to test
this, and native help would be needed; no one else,
except possibly the Naxians in the orbiting station,
knew just what effects freezing might have on
Habras. Since the plan was to secure all the corpses
anyway, this hypothesis had no effect on procedure.
The work went on slowly.

Digging around and over the bodies was tedious
but not too difficult. Digging *under* to free them for
transport was another matter. S'Nash was drafted, in
spite of the clumsiness of its/his handlers, since
work space could be excavated much more easily for
its/his slender form.

Once his head was out of sight under the body,
Janice tried another experiment. She was reasonably
sure by now that a Naxian had to see its subject to
read emotions. S'Nash could not see them now, and
it was easy, snuggling next to Hugh even in armor,
to assure a burst of emotion. As she had hoped, there
was no obvious reaction from under the ice block.

Of course, S'Nash might have guessed what she
was up to; no one ever performs the final
experiment—the one which removes all possible

doubt. This, the Erthuma reflected ruefully, is why science never gets past theory. But she could be *pretty* sure, now, about Naxians. The Locrians, though—

She let her own incidental flutter of emotion die down—she had been depending mostly on Hugh's for the experiment—and turned her attention back to Plant-Biologist. Hugh enjoyed his own until S'Nash reported that it/he had removed all the ice below the corpse except for supporting pillars at each corner of the block. These should remain until it/he emerged.

Two or three minutes later the first specimen was moving slowly back down the tunnel. In due time it was followed by a second, and a third, and a fourth. There were ten more bodies, but Plant-Biologist now wanted to take out the much larger and less tractable block containing the mass of plants. Ged disagreed, pointing out the risk to the other specimens. The Naxian's eyes were swiveling around the group as though it/he wanted to keep them all in view at once, and Janice felt once more the glow of another fact supporting her ideas. She felt morally sure of her Naxian theory, and didn't care whether S'Nash fully grasped the source of her feeling; she simply enjoyed it while the argument finally climaxed.

The Locrian won. It was obvious that the whole tunnel would have to be widened to accommodate this specimen, and the two Erthumoi from the supply station cheerfully volunteered to take the picks to this job. The rest, with reputations for scientific interest more or less at stake, began to work their way around the tangle of frozen vegetation with the smaller tools. They were very, very cautious, wary of projecting blades and stems which might actually be in the way of their strokes, and had not completed the job by the time the heavy labor on the tunnel was finished.

No one suggested that the picks be brought back, and their wielders did not volunteer; with no com-

ment but a simple "All done," they went back to
their truck to eat and rest. It was another hour before
the botany specimen was ready to move.

Hugh and Janice provided most of the motive
power, though Barrar's mechanical body helped. The
Locrian's physical strength would have made practically no difference and it would have been sensible
for him to get outside first, but he walked slowly beside the moving mass, examining it and making frequent comments which Hugh hoped the Samian was
recording since he himself understood less than half
of what was being said.

Outside, it was quickly decided that the material
already collected should go back to the Pitville laboratories as quickly as safety allowed, while most of
the party should resume digging around the other
specimens.

Barrar, of course, wanted to stay; everything
about the digging itself should be recorded, since
there was no way of guessing what aspect of position and orientation of the specimens might turn out
to be important. The Samian did, Hugh realized,
have some scientific competence; maybe there was
hope for his paper after all.

The Locrian, just as obviously, would be returning
with his plants. Neither flier had any wish to ride;
they would stay to do what they could.

Hugh and Janice offered to drive, enthusiastically
enough to attract S'Nash's attention, since the other
two Erthumoi were enough to do the heavy digging
which was now presumably safe. S'Nash, after eye-
ing them for several seconds as they were entering
the truck after Plant-Biologist, suddenly decided that
he would return to Pitville, too.

Janice blocked its/his way politely but firmly.

"You'll be needed to undercut those blocks. Getting them out will take much longer without you,
and you know it."

The golden eyes fixed themselves on the Erthuma.

"That's not your reason for wanting me to stay. Your feelings are—"

"Are our own business. We like you, S'Nash, but would rather you weren't along this trip."

The Naxian became almost outspoken, in spite of its/his increasing grasp of tact.

"But why should you mind *me*? You have a *Locrian* with you. You can keep me up in the control room if you—"

Janice interrupted. "You miss the point, friend, and thanks for letting me know you have to see us to read our feelings. You understand our basic Erthumoi attitudes quite well, but I want Plant-Biologist with us. I don't care what *he* sees; *I'm* observing *him*."

15

EPILOGUE

More than a hundred kilometers below the nearest sunlight, a river of ice worked its way slowly toward the Liquid Ocean. Where it met the water its fate differed from year to year and from hour to hour; sometimes its face simply melted smoothly away; sometime a tongue of glassy solid projected a kilometer or two into the liquid before cracking gently off; sometimes stranger things happened.

For some Common Years now the river had borne more than its usual load of sediment blown from the warm hemisphere. The ice was denser than usual and the river was not only traveling sunward but trying to sink a little deeper into its surroundings. This had several results.

Some of the sediment was fairly soluble, and dropped the melting point of the ice. Just a little. As the river sank, the pressure increased. Just a little. However, the river was flowing along the pressure/temperature boundary between two of ice's solid phases, and that little was enough.

As the mass of ice and impurities groped into the Liquid Ocean, one of the much faster random currents sweeping along the nearly vertical face between Solid and Liquid chanced to be just a trifle colder than the solid. and began to absorb heat from it.

For perhaps a year or two, this merely cooled the ice and moved it more definitely across the phase boundary. Nothing impressive occurred until, with no warning, the shift started at a point just where the tongue of river emerged from the Solid. Perhaps some living creature exploded against it; perhaps some still colder jet of water played briefly at it; many things could have been the cause.

A crack started in the river, and a second later the several cubic kilometers of ice were drifting free. The part of the river still surrounded by solid was shrinking, yielding to the pressure of ice around it.

Growing smaller.

A shock wave spread from the interface as the two kinds of solid hunted for a new equilibrium. The speed of waves in ice is slow by seismic standards, but not by humans ones. It was less than a minute before Hugh Cedar felt the wave.

An Erthuma-high pile of ice shavings a hundred meters from the cliff face marked where the *Ice Badger V* had clawed its way out of sight. Barrar was learning, Hugh reflected; this tunnel went down at a very modest slope, and spikes on one's soles made it easy to follow without much danger.

The *Badger,* of course, traveled much faster than a walk, even here. He could make a running slide every minute or two and probably keep it in sight, but had no intention of taking such chances with his armor. Besides, there was too much to check along the walls of the tunnel. This mole, at least, was leaving walls smooth enough to see through, though there was nothing in the ice so far to attract attention. Even the Samian was losing some of his fossil hunting hopes; *Five* and her predecessors had collectively bored over twenty kilometers of tunnel without sighting a specimen worth keeping.

Ged was not giving up, of course. To the amusement of the Erthumoi and fascination of S'Nash, he had developed a deep interest in the mechanical problems which had afflicted each of the present machine's predecessors, and contributed more and better ideas for modification as each model developed. Unfortunately, in spite of several frightening experiences, he remained casual by Hugh's standards about safety procedures.

"I don't really take chances," the Samian insisted after being melted out of the cliff face with *Badger II.* "Exploration and research have certain built-in dangers, which I recognize, of course; but if one postpones action until these are all evaluated and countered, how will anything ever be done?"

"I'm not suggesting we foresee them all," Hugh had answered with some annoyance, "but carrying spare parts for a few of the mechanical items under really heavy strain, like your scraper blades, isn't being overcautious."

"I had the spare blades. I thought of that possibility. There was no way, though, to get outside to install them; the port could not be opened against the ice. Obviously we will have to move the entrance to the rear of the mole, so we can escape into the tunnel if necessary." Hugh had agreed, and forborne to ask why this had only now become obvious.

Five, however, seemed to be doing well. Barrar had promised not to descend more than fifty meters until he had bored an untroubled hundred kilometers with the same mole, and Hugh consoled himself with the reflection that he could be rescued from that depth by conventional equipment.

All the testing had so far been done near the mass-kill site they had examined earlier. The cause of this prehistoric disaster was not yet clear, but the terrain was unusual enough to encourage the hope that it might have shared some of the responsibility; and even that small chance had kept in the Samian's mind the hope that what had happened once might happen again.

The mole was out of sight ahead, now; its driver was testing the steering equipment, the main purpose of the present run. Hugh rounded a fairly tight lefthand bend in the tunnel, but failed to see the machine; another turn, this time to the right, started only a dozen meters further on. He followed, without considering particularly in which direction he and the mole were now heading.

An hour later, after a dozen more turns both horizontal and vertical—once the Erthuma had had to use the radio to warn Ged's copilot about descending too far—he finally caught sight of the polymer shell. Barrar and his crew had stopped. There had been no call by the Habra on board, so presumably there was nothing wrong; Hugh did not increase his pace. It took him a minute or so to reach the machine, but rather than open the hatch leading inside he brought the microphone to his face. There was no reason to go in; the place was cramped enough already. A meter from the white hull, he started to speak.

Before a word emerged, the tunnel floor suddenly struck his feet. Then the ceiling two meters above struck his head—no, he decided moments later when his head cleared, the ceiling simply hadn't moved fast enough to get out of his way. Something had hurled him violently upward, and even through his helmet his skull must have come close to major damage. His head hurt, but after a moment that claimed very little of his attention.

Where the *Badger* had been, a meter from where he stood, there was a smooth wall of ice. Like that surrounding the tunnel, this was very clear, and it took Hugh only a few seconds to see the mole, now some ten meters to his right and six below. At almost the same moment Miriam's voice came from his translator.

"Hugh, can you hear me? Do you know what happened?"

"I hear you, all right. I can *guess* what happened. The cliff just got a bit higher, or maybe lower. I hope higher."

"Why does it make any difference?"

"If the *Badger* is all right, it won't. If the shock crippled you, maybe a lot. If the cliff went up, I went with it, and the fault will have cut the tunnel somewhere behind me. I wasn't keeping track of where we went, and I don't know which way I'm facing, but I hope very much it's northwest. That puts *you* inside the cliff, but leaves me a way to walk out—unless there were more twists and turns in your path than I remember. Is the mole working?"

"Ged's testing it. Power is on." Hugh felt a steady vibration, hoped that it wasn't an aftershock, and relaxed as the mole moved slowly away from him through the ice.

"We'll come around and pick you up, Ged says," came the Habra's voice. "You needn't worry about which way we're facing."

Hugh was not completely reassured, but watched as the vehicle drew away from him and became progressively harder to see. It was managing to turn, slowly, so steering as well as drive seemed to be working.

For several minutes it was almost out of sight and changing direction; its radius of turn was at least fifty meters. At last it seemed to be heading back toward him, and he called Miriam. She acknowledged, and the mole grew clearer until he could see the motion of its diggers.

"Up a bit. Either you went down or I went up." He held his breath until he could see that vertical steering was also still working.

"You're coming right at me now. Stand by a moment—I'll have to back down my tunnel a bit. I don't want you to go through me. You should have put a hatch on the front of that thing, too."

"Ged says he doesn't see how that's possible. We'll go on past, and you can get to the hatch all right."

Cedar watched the moving blades slash free in emptiness as the mole cut back into its earlier path, and rode on across with the aid of the track-mounted spikes. Hugh had never seen an earthworm, but Falga had creatures which used their setae in the same fashion. The stern of the machine appeared and crossed the tunnel, and the vibrations ceased. A moment later the hatch opened.

"Going to ride, or try the tunnel?" came Barrar's voice.

"I'll come with you, if you're sure there's room."

"But the whole idea of your following was for safety," Miriam objected. "It was so you *wouldn't* be trapped in here if anything went wrong."

"You're right," admitted the Erthuma. "And don't say anything about lightning not striking twice; I know it does. Start on out, if you know which way is out; I'll come along behind. Ged, have you an emergency procedure to use if that fault plane had cut through your machine instead of a few centimeters behind it?"

"I'm afraid not. Can you think of anything?"

"Sure. Have two moles traveling together. What are the chances of the same plane slicing both of them?"

Barrar made no answer, and the trip was resumed. An hour later the machine emerged, within ten meters of the cliff's foot, and crawled forward to clear the tunnel opening. Hugh Cedar emerged after it, and moments later Erthuma, Samian, and Habra were looking consideringly at the cliff.

"Do you really think we should have a second, just on the chance of something like that's happening again?" Barrar asked at length. "After all, what are the chances?"

"What were the chances of the plane's cutting between your machine and my face?" asked Hugh. "The reason I was tempted to ride with you afterward was that I wasn't sure my knees would hold me up even in this gravity. I wonder how Rek would have reacted?"

"He'll never go underground. The thought's too much for him," replied Miriam. "I know how he feels, of course, and I'm a bit the same way, but I've had practice. I've spent a lot of time with Liquid Ocean around me; Solid isn't that different."

"You could still get him to try it," Hugh assured her. "He has a brain, and it would override his emotions if he thought the job were important enough."

"What would make it important for him, as long as there were crawlers to do it?"

Cedar grinned. "You might use his feelings, too. If he won't admit to the possibility of such a wild coincidence, tell him he's thinking like an Erthuma."

The logic backfired, but not from Rekchellet. Hugh found himself using it on his wife after she heard of the test, and Janice *was* an Erthuma.